I, Antigone

I, Antigone

Carlo Gébler

NEW ISLAND

I, ANTIGONE
First published in 2021 by
New Island Books
Glenshesk House
10 Richview Office Park
Clonskeagh
Dublin D14 V8C4
Republic of Ireland
www.newisland.ie

Print ISBN: 978-1-84840-814-2
eBook ISBN: 978-1-84840-815-9

British Library Cataloguing in Publication Data. A CIP catalogue record for this book is available from the British Library.

Typeset by JVR Creative India
Edited by Djinn von Noorden
Cover design by Anna Morrison, annamorrison.com
Printed by FINIDR, s.r.o., Czech Republic, finidr.com

Gratefully supported by the Arts Council of Northern Ireland

New Island Books is a member of Publishing Ireland.

10 9 8 7 6 5 4 3 2 1

ANTIGONE: Sirs, sirs, you are just and reverent men;
Though you refuse to hear my poor blind father,
Because of the things he is known to have done –
Though they were none of his own devising –
Yet have some pity for me, I beseech you!
Only for my father's sake I am pleading.

Oedipus at Colonus, Sophocles

THE FAMILY TREE OF ANTIGONE

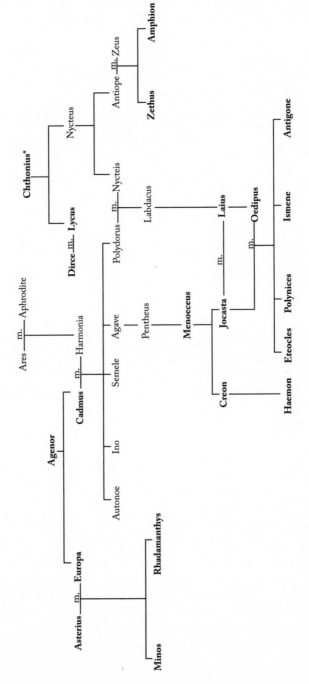

*One of the Sown Men

Prologue

I, Antigone, have closed my eyes.

I hear the stylus scoring the wax tablet as the scribe inscribes my words.

I, Antigone, have closed my eyes.

Every word is to be written down. The scribe and I agreed that before we began. He writes down every word, and that includes *I, Antigone, have closed my eyes.*

In my head I hear the sounds of Colonus, the faraway clanging of the sheep bells, the rustling of the dry leaves of the olive trees, the chirruping of the sparrows as they bathe in the dry bitter dust of the red earth.

My voice is deep and quiet, dark and slow, like a river moving over rocks, never stopping, never ceasing, endless.

After we fled Thebes and went to Colonus together, Oedipus, my father, was miserable. I should not have done such and such, he wailed, and I should have done such and such. He felt such guilt, such shame. At the end of our time in Colonus, Hermes came to my father in his dreams and talked to him. Straight afterwards, my father told me everything Hermes had said to him, and now I shall tell you.

Like a sailor going hand over hand down a rope, I shall trace the thread of my father, the late king of Thebes. I shall show that he never intended to cause the harm he was warned he would cause, but as he struggled not to cause it, he did cause it.

He was to blame for the father-murdering and the mother-marrying and the rest of it and, at the same time, he wasn't to blame.

He was wholly at fault and he was entirely innocent.

This is true of us all if we only knew it. His fate is everyone's.

In the dark making place deep within me, the sound of the sheep bells and of the fluttering leaves of the olive trees and the twittering of the sparrows bathing in the red dust is slowly quietening and, in their place, gradually growing louder, I hear waves rolling up the beach at Tyre and standing on the sand I see a shape gradually sharpening into a girl, young and lovely, smiling, gentle, supple-limbed ...

All I need to do now is speak what I see and hear. The scribe will write everything down and what would otherwise be erased by time will become permanent.

BOOK ONE

Europa, brown-skinned and brown-eyed, wore a long, loose white shift and a chaplet of red and yellow flowers on her head. She was squinting out to sea, watching a dark spot moving towards her. Originally, she'd thought it was a seal but now, what was this? Instead of a long snout, round eyes and a smooth domed head, she saw a blunt mouth, a broad face and blade-like horns sticking up at the sky. It was not a seal. It was a bull swimming in.

The animal reached the shallows and began to wade. When he got onto dry sand he stopped and shook himself. The heavy fold of skin under his neck was flung now this way, now that, like a heavy, wet piece of leather, and tiny water droplets flew out in every direction from his body. For a moment these hung in the air and caught the light – they were like little silver beads, Europa thought – and then they vanished.

The bull stopped shaking himself and ambled off. With each step his hooves sank straight down, like a pestle into grains in a mortar, and in the sand behind him two lines of hoof-shaped holes appeared. His direction, Europa noticed, wasn't towards her but slantwise along the beach.

The bull stopped, lifted his head and gazed at Europa. His look seemed – what? – surprised. Yes, surprised, she decided. Then he pivoted slowly round until he was facing out to sea, bent his back legs and sank down onto the sand.

Europa heard the sea and, coming from the bull, low moans. His pelt looked beautifully smooth. She wanted to stroke him, as she might a horse or a ferret.

She began to take small steps forward. Her tread was light. Unlike the bull, she left no marks on the sand. Closer, closer, closer she went, until she was right by the bull. She smelt his odour, like a cow's, but stronger, meatier. She saw how thick his legs were, and how substantial his tail was. It was like a ship's cable and she imagined it would be hard to lift. She saw his chest rising and falling and she heard the air going in and out, in and out.

The bull lifted his huge head and looked at her and, if she wasn't mistaken ... No, she wasn't ... He was looking at the chaplet of flowers on her head.

She knelt down near his head, took off her chaplet, separated a few flowers and offered these on her palm. The bull sniffed her offering and opened his mouth, revealing his flat, square teeth and his red, wet tongue. She laid the flowers along his dark, thick bottom lip, stems inwards, blooms outwards, all the way round, from one side of the mouth to the other. When she finished the bull closed his mouth gently and she stretched the chaplet over his horns and worked it down to his forehead.

She stroked his neck. The pelt was smooth and warm. The bull shrugged and put his face to her stroking hand and from his two moist, black nostrils, warm air furled out and ran backward and forwards like water over her knuckles and around her fingers. Then, slowly, the bull moved his nostrils up the length of left forearm to her elbow and then on to her shoulder and then to the side of her neck, her chin, and finally her cheek. His breath smelt of warm grass. She felt calm and still. She could put her head down, she thought and sleep. Well, why not? What a perfect thing to do.

She put her right hand on the neck and her cheek on her palm, her own little pillow of bone and skin. The smell of animal and salt and the bull's ribcage going up, going down, and the heart beating away behind ... She closed her eyes and began to slide ...

When he heard Europa's breathing, slow and quiet and gentle, the bull – who was in fact the great god Zeus – gently shook the sleeping Europa onto his back, stretched out full length, her head on his neck and her feet by his tail. Then he walked back out into the sea, spat out the flowers Europa had put in his mouth and launched himself forward.

At the end of the afternoon when Europa did not return home, as she had done every day of her life up until then, Cadmus, the youngest, stood with his brothers in the court-yard of his father Agenor's palace.

'Find your sister,' Agenor shouted at his sons.

The brothers, with the exception of Cadmus, hurried off in different directions to search for their sister. Cadmus, who was the most attached to her, thought he'd be better asking his father's cowherd, who by chance was just in front of the palace driving some cows.

'Did you see my sister today?' Cadmus asked.

'I did,' said the cowherd. 'I saw her this morning.'

'Where?'

'Heading for the beach.'

'Alone?'

'Yes, alone.'

'Were you on the beach yourself?'

Cadmus knew that sometimes the cowherd brought his animals down to the sea.

'Not today,' said the cowherd. 'I had all the animals inland.'

Cadmus set off along the track that went down to the sea. On the way he passed some trees where doves were roosting. Their cooing sounded to him like a deep and reassuring purr, like a lion might be heard to make, a lion that was content and at peace and was stretched, half-asleep, in the shade. Was it a good omen, he wondered, to hear this? He hoped so.

He passed beyond the trees and there, ahead of him, stretched the beach. In the bright day the sand was yellow but now the light was fading it was a light grey. He went on and underfoot earth gave way to sand. He'd arrived, right at the beach's edge. A great swarm of small black birds, disturbed by his sudden appearance, jumped into the air, flitted about and settled again a little way off.

He moved over the sand. It still held heat from the sun. He could feel the warmth off it. He looked around. The beach was empty. There was nobody in any direction. Nor were there any footprints. He did notice, however, that in one spot the sand appeared disturbed. He went to look and saw some sort of creature had been sitting there, and there were holes in the sand nearby. They were like the hoof marks made by cows, which he'd noticed before when his father's cows were on the beach. He put his hand into one. It was deep enough to take his whole hand, right up to his wrist. No cow could have made a mark that deep. The animal who made this was bigger and heavier. A bull, perhaps?

He stood up and followed the hoof marks. They led out of the sea to where the sand was flattened and then back to the sea. A bull, if he was right that it was a bull, had come out of the sea and then gone back into it. That didn't make sense.

He walked down to the foam, which marked the line between dry and wet, and looked out. The sky was purple and the sea was very still. He saw nothing of his sister. He saw just sea and sky.

Far out at sea and well out of Cadmus's sight, the bull swept his legs backwards and forwards. His strokes were unhurried but powerful and they moved him on, back the way he had come. Europa, lying asleep on his back well above the water line, was oblivious of where she was and what was happening until a splash fell on her cheek and roused her. Then, though she was still half-asleep, she heard a lapping sound, like a boat's bow might make curving through water, and simultaneously she felt movement beneath her. This made no sense. She opened her eyes and saw, just below her head, the grey, green, wine-coloured sea, the way it ran into the horizon for as far as she could see. She shouldn't be seeing the sea unfurling in front of her like this. She should be looking out to sea.

She panicked. She sat up and saw they were heading towards the sinking sun. She looked behind. She saw no beach. She saw no shore. All she saw was sea.

'Turn around,' she shouted. 'Take me back!'

She felt the bull's legs moving and his shoulders seesawing below. She stared down through the clear water at the sandy seabed far below. If she jumped now she would find nothing firm to hold her up. If she jumped now she would go down to the bottom, like a stone. She could not swim.

'Turn back,' Europa shouted. 'Turn back!'

She pounded the bull's shoulders with her right hand but he ignored her and swam on, his legs under water moving fiercely, his head jerking backwards and forwards as he pulled himself onwards, his eye fixed on the dark line far ahead, where the sea met the sky.

Cadmus returned to his father's palace at dusk and found the cowherd he'd spoken to before. He was sitting on a stool outside the stables, whittling a piece of wood.

'Did you have a bull on the beach today?' Cadmus asked.

'I had no animal on the beach today,' said the cowherd. 'I told you.'

Cadmus went on to the palace and into the hall. It was dark by now. The lamps had been lit. Their flickering lights were pale and small in the darkness. His father and his brothers were standing, waiting.

'I know she was on the beach today,' said Cadmus, 'because the cowherd told me he saw her heading for the beach this morning, but when I went to look just now there was no sign she'd been there. But something had been there. In one place the sand was flattened and I think that's where it sat down. And there were hoof marks, which led to and from there to the sea. I'd like to say these were a bull's, except when has a bull ever swum ashore, sat for a while, then got back into the sea and swum away again?'

Agenor questioned his son. It was his belief his daughter had been seized by passing sailors and all his questions flowed from this assumption. Were there really no footprints in the sand? he demanded. No sign a boat had beached? No signs of a struggle? No discarded weapons? No lost sandals? Nothing?

'No, nothing,' said Cadmus.

More questions followed but neither Cadmus nor his brothers had any answers to give.

'My daughter was here this morning and she is not here now,' said Agenor. He spoke quietly but his sons all felt the pressure under his words, a mix of grief and anger and rage.

'She is gone but she would never have left of her own accord,' said Agenor. 'She would never do something like that. It isn't in her nature. This leaves only one explanation. She was taken. My sons, you will scatter in all directions. You will find her and bring her home. None of you will return unless it is to bring her back to me. That is my final word. Now, go and prepare to search for her.'

In the morning, bobbing in the sea around her, Europa saw bits of trees, bushes, plants. There were birds overhead and fragments of their cries drifted down and, in the distance, she saw a smudge where the sea met the sky. As the bull swam this thickened and darkened, and eventually she made out a sandy beach like the one she had been abducted from, with trees and rocks and hills behind.

As they approached, she planned. As soon as they were in the shallows she would jump. The sea's floor would be under her feet and she would sprint a little bit sideways and mostly forwards. She would lift her knees high, just as she did when she ran in the surf at Tyre. She would be fast and the advantage would be hers. She'd be on two legs. The bull would be on four. She was fresh. He was tired.

In a few paces she'd reach the shore. Then she'd really start to sprint. She'd speed up the shelving beach, all the way to the pine trees. She'd find a good one, with low branches.

She'd scramble up. It would be like going up a ladder. And once she'd reached a safe perch, she would be able to gaze down on the bull circling below, huffing and bellowing, perhaps banging his head on the trunk but unable to reach her. How could he? He was a hoofed creature, while she had hands and feet.

The bulk below shuddered. The broad back shrank. The pelt melted and feathers showed instead. The thick neck elongated, becoming long and sinuous. The heavy head collapsed into a small domed form with oval-shaped eyes at the side, each with a yellow iris and a heavy black pupil. A beak, yellow, hooked, vicious, showed ahead. Europa knew exactly what kind of a creature this was. She had often watched them wheeling in the skies over Tyre. It was an eagle and she was on his back.

The bird sprung out of the water and into the air, spread his wings and rose upwards. She gripped the neck feathers. She must not slip. The fall would kill her.

She looked down. The earth was far from her and the eagle was climbing, heading over the very trees she had been intending to run for, swooping inland and carrying her away …

BOOK TWO

Cadmus and his companions sailed west to Crete, made landfall and searched the island on foot for Europa. They didn't find her. They went on to Greece where they continued their search, again on foot, and again with no success. Eventually, though it had never been Cadmus's intention to come here, the party found themselves at the Temple of Apollo and the Oracle of Delphi.

'Well,' said Cadmus, 'having looked for my sister and failed to find her, I might as well ask the Pythia what I should do next, seeing as I am here ...'

Cadmus offered himself as a supplicant. He paid his fee. He was interrogated by the priests. He gave them his question. His question was judged worthy. He paid a further fee. He offered sacred cake at the altar. He entered the temple's grounds, taking a fat sheep. He sacrificed the animal in the proper way by cutting its throat. He captured the sheep's blood in a ceremonial bowl. He hung the carcass up by its back legs from a tripod, then skinned it, cleaned it out and dismembered it. He wrapped its thighs in folds of fat, laid these on the ceremonial fire with raw meat on top and burnt them. He sprinkled the animal's blood on the flames and the blood hissed. He cut what remained of the carcass into small pieces, pierced these with skewers and roasted them. He distributed the cooked meat amongst temple staff and Delphians who lived entirely on the food they received from supplicants like himself. He drew a lot to determine his place in the line. His turn would not be for a while. He found a seat in the forecourt in front of the temple. He sat and smelt the strong smell of mutton that hung in the air.

A supplicant, fresh from his interview with the Pythia, came out of the temple and passed in front of Cadmus. He was weeping and making loud little gasps.

The next supplicant was led in. A little later this supplicant emerged and passed Cadmus. He was laughing.

This in and out process repeated as supplicants were led in and out. Cadmus saw nobody weeping or laughing again. The subsequent supplicants Cadmus saw all had still, silent faces when they came out and it struck Cadmus that they all had a strange way of walking too, as if they were carrying something precious, which they didn't want to drop.

At last his turn came. A priest led him into the temple. The interior was dark. There was another smell along with that of mutton, something sweet but also putrid. He'd never smelt anything like it. As the priest led him forward he began to feel odd. He was in a dream, but awake.

The priest took his hand and together, step by step, they descended steps. As they descended the sweet, putrid odour grew stronger and he sensed his body had lost its bulk and had become so light it would blow away if a breeze blew. At the same time, he felt his head and his feet were drifting apart, like two floating objects borne out to sea on the tide in different directions. His tongue was dry. He couldn't stop swallowing. He saw the darkness through which he was gliding was full of silver flashes and he heard strange whispers.

They reached the bottom. He was now twice as tall as he had been. He wondered about his head. Would it strike the ceiling? He looked up. He saw nothing. There was nothing. His head was safe. They were in a space that was dark and windowless. There was something in the middle of the space and the priest led him forward towards it. He couldn't see at first what they were approaching because it was dark but when they got close, he saw that it was a drape, one of several that hung down, screening something. On the far side was the adytum, the inner sanctum of the temple. The Pythia was in there. He felt frightened at the thought of meeting her. He also felt joyful.

The priest tugged the edge of one of the hanging drapes and ushered him forward. He stepped through. The priest followed and let the drape fall behind. The space was dark and smelt of hot pitch as well as the strange, sweet, putrid odour. There were two burning brands and that was all. Their light was wavering.

The priest gestured. The Pythia was there, right in the middle, dimly visible. He stepped up and peered. His eyes adjusted. She was an old, heavy woman in a young girl's short white dress, with a scarf over her head covering most of her hair. She sat on a broad bronze seat supported by a gilded tripod. In her left hand she held a libation vessel, a flat open bowl with Kassotis spring water in it, and in her right hand she held a stem of laurel with its unmistakable dark green leaves. Her knuckles were huge, her face was lined, her mouth was open and he saw that a tooth at the top and on the left was missing. Her earrings were heavy and her lobes drooped with the weight of them. Her eyes were dark and impenetrable.

The Pythia closed her eyes and dropped her head and shuddered. The god was entering into her, Cadmus thought. Then she went still. The god was in her. The god was waiting. The god was ready.

The priest stepped up to the Pythia and whispered into her ear. She opened her eyes but kept her face down, staring into the water. The priest touched his arm.

'Go on,' said the priest.

He told his story: His sister, Europa, had vanished from the beach at Tyre. He had been searching for her but he had failed to find her. What was he to do? Where was he to look?

'You will not look anymore,' said the Pythia. 'You are done with searching.' This was the Pythia's voice, thought Cadmus, but the words were the god's words. He was hearing the god speaking in a woman's voice.

'Here is what you now do,' the Pythia continued. 'Leave here and buy a cow immediately. March the animal away and don't let her stop or rest until she flops down with exhaustion. And where that is, build a city. On that spot.'

'Where is my sister?' said Cadmus.

The priest jogged his arm. That wasn't the agreed question.

The Pythia looked up at him, stared for a moment, then closed her eyes and shuddered. The god was leaving her, Cadmus thought. What Cadmus didn't know was this. The Pythia had lost two husbands and three children before she came to be the Oracle, but the anguish caused by the loss of her loved ones was nothing compared to what she felt every time the god withdrew. This was a desolating experience, and moreover one that she had to endure many times over every day.

The Pythia opened her eyes. The god was gone. She was herself again. He felt the priest touch his wrist. 'Come,' said the priest. 'We leave now.'

Cadmus rejoined his companions. He told them what the Pythia had said he must do. They left the temple's grounds together and set off along the road that went south to Phocis. After a while they spotted a herd of cows ahead and they heard the clanking noise of the bells hung around the animals' necks, and the raucous cries of the cowherds watching over the beasts.

Cadmus and his companions moved closer. They heard the clip-clop of hooves on the ground and the occasional sound of horn striking stone. They smelt the cows' muck, their milky breath and their dusty pelts. They came closer again. They heard the extraordinary sound of hundreds of sets of teeth grinding the grass, reducing it to wet, green cud.

Cadmus went up to a cowherd. The fellow had a long brown face and an egg-shaped lump right in the middle of his forehead. 'Will you sell me a cow?' Cadmus asked.

'I can't,' said the cowherd. 'My master, King Pelagon, wouldn't like it if I sold an animal without his agreement.'

Cadmus stared at the man's face and imagined a god pinching the cowherd's brow with finger and thumb to make the swelling.

'He won't be displeased when he learns what I've paid,' said Cadmus. He named a figure that was far bigger than had ever been paid for a cow since cows and men had come together.

'Wait,' said the cowherd.

The cowherd went and gathered the other cowherds around him. Cadmus and his companions heard them all muttering quietly but it was impossible to follow what was being said.

The cowherd returned.

'You like my offer, don't you?' Cadmus said.

The cowherd nodded. Cadmus wondered if the lump on the cowherd's forehead might be soft not hard and whether, if he touched it, it would pop back into his head.

'She's the one I want.' Cadmus indicated a small, sturdy, solid, hornless cow. She had a short grey coat and, on each flank, a full moon, white and perfect.

The cowherd nodded as if this were not a surprise. He turned to the other cowherds. 'He wants the one with the moons on her flanks,' he said.

His fellow cowherds nodded and shrugged and one shouted, 'Of course he does. What other cow would he want but her?'

The price was paid. A halter was fetched and fitted.

Cadmus and his companions set off with the cow with the two moons. They walked for the rest of the day. They took it in turns to hold the halter and haul the cow onwards. The cow grew gradually more and more sullen, yet still she kept going, or let herself be kept going.

The sun left the sky. Dusk came on and the nightjars came out and their trilling cries filled the cooling air. Then it was night. No moon. Everything black. Bats swooping. Stars bright above. Still they went on, the cow holding back, Cadmus and his companions pulling her on. Dawn came. The edge of the sky lightened. They passed out of Phocis and entered Boeotia.

'She's tired but not yet tired enough,' one of Cadmus's companions said, and the others laughed.

'She'll tire in the end,' said Cadmus. 'She must.'

The sun rose. The air grew warmer.

'It can't be long now,' said someone.

'If she doesn't sit down soon, I'm going to sit down myself,' said someone else. More laughter.

'Come on, moon beast,' said a third, 'put us out of our misery. Just sit down.'

The cow bellowed, the noise low and plaintive. Chirping lightly, two sparrows rolled in the dust at the side of the road.

They went on. Time after time it seemed the cow might sit down, but then she didn't. She kept going or she let herself be kept going.

In the sky the sun reached its zenith and then started to decline. The shadows on the ground, which had been at their shortest, began to lengthen. It was very hot. An eagle circled in the sky and every man below felt a pang of envy. Every man wished he could be that eagle, circling in the sky instead of being on the earth with his sore hands and his dusty lips, his tired arms and his bruised feet.

The cow made a sound. It was not a bellow but a wail. She put her head down and raised her shoulders.

'She's going,' said one of Cadmus's companions. This man had been a cowherd in his youth. He knew what the movement of the head and shoulders meant.

The cow folded her front fetlocks and settled her pasterns flat on the ground. She collapsed her back legs and sank down onto her right hip. She tucked her front legs under and stuck her back legs out. She was finally down.

There was a round of applause, a couple of whistles. 'She won't be going anywhere, I believe,' one of Cadmus's companions shouted. The halter's end was dropped. The cow snorted and sighed.

'A good spot indeed,' said Cadmus. 'And now, having found our place, the goddess must have her due.'

He meant Athene, helper of all involved in heroic endeav-
our, without whose aid they would never have reached where
they were, and without whose aid Cadmus would never be
able to do what he had to do next. A sacrifice must be made
in her honour. The cow with the two moons must be killed,
her blood collected, her body skinned, her carcass butchered,
her flesh roasted and the choicest parts offered in the right
and fitting way to the goddess. But first, lustral water must
be found so the animal might be cleansed in the ritual of
purification before her sacrifice.

Cadmus glanced around him. Off on one side of the
road, beyond a stretch of ragged ground strewn with rocks
and bushes, he saw a forest, its trees heavy and old and
thick. 'There should be water in there,' he said. 'Go and see.'

His companions picked their way across the ground and
disappeared into the trees.

The sun was hot in the sky. The air was dense and
motionless. The only sound was that of cicadas, the noise
they made like hundreds of wooden sticks beating on hundreds of sheets of bronze. Cadmus was covered with a slick
of sweat. He tugged his sodden smock away from his chest
and blew on his bony collarbone. He thought of the pool his
companions might find, and imagined splashing water onto
his face, and the shocking coldness of it.

In the distance he heard cries. It was his companions.
They were shouting. He ran through the light and the heat
and slipped into the forest where the light was dappled and
the air was cold. It was like diving underwater.

Over on his left, a cry came from a tumble of green rocks,
after which, nothing. He began to tread through the murky light
towards where the sound had come from. Faintly to begin with

but getting louder, he heard the plashing of water. His companions must be somewhere nearby, he thought, yet it didn't make sense that he couldn't hear anything. If lions had attacked them the lions would still be roaring. If boars were to blame he'd be hearing squealing and screeching. And if bandits had waylaid his companions, he'd be hearing them laughing and cursing. But he heard nothing except the sound of water and, very far away, a kite, which had started screeching.

He stopped. Ahead of him there was something sticking out from the end of a fallen tree. It could be a foot with a brown leather sandal lashed onto it with leather ties, but he couldn't be quite sure because of the shadows and the murk.

His heart began beating. He would change direction. He would go around the top end of the fallen tree and approach the foot from the far side. The sound of plashing. The sound of the kite. The sound of the dry stuff of the forest underfoot as it gave way when he trod it down. The kite stopped. Now just plashing and his footsteps. The silence was worrying. Nowhere should be so quiet.

He rounded the top of the tree and stopped. He was looking at a body without its head. It ended at the neck. He saw cartilage and muscle. He saw windpipe and tubing. The head was lying on the ground a few feet away. The cheeks and nose were smeared with blood. The eyes were open. The mouth was open. Some of the teeth were broken. An ear was missing. He knew who this was despite the blood and the injuries. It was the companion who'd said, 'She's tired but not yet tired enough,' and made the others laugh.

'Cadmus!' he heard someone shout.

He turned to where the cry came from and saw another of his companions jump from a tree. He landed badly. He tumbled forward and sprawled on the ground. This was the man who'd said, 'If she doesn't sit down soon, I'm going to sit down myself.' The man struggled back to his feet and started to lurch towards Cadmus. He was hurt. There was something behind him. It was dark and quick. It was the thickness of a man and the length of several men. It reared up behind his companion, then lunged forward and punched the man hard between his shoulder blades, a walloping blow.

The man toppled over. The vast shape became something like a serpent, heavy and black. It wrapped itself about the man's body with incredible speed. The man opened his mouth. But the serpent had him squeezed so hard in his coils that the man had no air in him, and so he couldn't speak. He gasped. His face went red, like he'd caught fire.

The serpent opened its jaws revealing sharp, gold teeth. Then it fitted its mouth over the man's head and snapped its jaws shut around the man's neck. Cadmus's companion writhed and struggled. The serpent made a little twist of its own head, turning the head inside its mouth one way; then it wrenched its head the other way, twisting the head inside its mouth that way too. It reminded Cadmus – later, when he reflected on what he had seen – of a farmer killing a chicken, the bird between his knees, turning the head in his rough hands one way and then twisting it the other to snap the neck.

The man went limp. The serpent tore at the neck with his gold teeth, making a sound of cutting and slicing and wrenching. The serpent opened its mouth and pushed the severed head out with its forked tongue. The head plopped onto the forest floor, rolled and stopped, its left cheek lying on the earth and its other cheek pointing to the sky, and the face between the cheeks looking straight towards Cadmus.

The head had its eyes open and, in the eyes, Cadmus saw that his companion had known that his head was about to be torn off before it was torn off. He had known how he would die and it had been terrible for him to know this.

The serpent let the body fall. Cadmus saw the gaping neck and the dangling windpipe where his companion's head was once attached to his body. The serpent began to slither slowly forward, gazing at him with its round black eyes. If he was to live, Cadmus knew he must act immediately. He saw a stone on the ground. He bent down, lifted it, sprinted up to the serpent and brought the stone down onto the flat space between the serpent's eyes, shattering the filigree bones of its face. It was a savage blow. The serpent's skin tore. Tubing and muscle were laid bare. Cadmus raised the stone again, all wet and bloody, and brought it down once more. The creature jolted. He brought the stone up again and brought it down a third time and the jolting stopped. The head tilted sideways. The jaw went slack and fell open. It took Cadmus a moment to catch up and understand what he had done.

He contemplated the serpent lying on the ground before him. He saw the teeth, golden, vicious, terrifying. He saw the body, stretching away like a ship's great mast. He stared around. He thought perhaps he could see another companion on the ground. Yes, he was right: here was another and there was another. They also had their heads torn away. That was four so far; two more and that would be everyone accounted for. Perhaps they were nearer the water. Cadmus picked his way forward. He passed a fifth body and a sixth, heads torn off also and lying where they'd fallen when the serpent spat them out. The last was the companion who'd said, 'Come on moon beast, put us out of our misery. Just sit down.'

He got to the rocks and scrambled up onto one. He saw a great basin of black water fed from a fissure in a little cliff above. The plashing he had heard was the sound the water made, having fallen about the height of a man, hitting the pool's surface. The pool was deep, he thought. He might bathe later.

Cadmus looked one way and then the other. He saw a huge nest made of twigs, dry leaves, pine needles, sheep's wool and other soft materials, with dry bones and flecks of shell lying in and around it. A great heap of heads, some with hair and skin attached, others just bare bone, were piled at the side. Here was the serpent's lair, Cadmus realised. Here it had lived and slept and whenever it needed to drink, it had just lapped the lovely water with its forked tongue.

Cadmus gathered his dead companions, their bodies and their heads. He dug a pit and buried them. That done, he could now give the goddess Athene her due.

He fetched the cow to the pool. He scrubbed her. He built an altar and lit a huge fire. He threw lustral water and barley corns on the ground. He cut a lock from the cow's head and threw it on the flames and offered prayers to Athene. He raised the sacrificial axe and brought the head down on the cow's neck, slicing though her spinal cord. The cow was paralysed. He chanted prayers. He hoisted the cow up on a tripod by her back legs and cut her throat. Black blood poured out, which he collected. He butchered the animal with a long knife. He severed her thighs in the proper fashion, covered these with fat, put raw flesh on top and burnt these, and as he did he sprinkled her blood onto the fire. Then he cut the rest of the meat off, fixed it on skewers and roasted this meat in the fire and once it was cooked through, he ate as much of it as he was able.

When he could eat no more he heard a whooshing, slithering sound.

He jumped up from the rock and stared around. What was it? Another serpent? A relative of the one he had killed, come to take revenge? He strained his ears. It didn't sound like a serpent. It sounded more like wind, gusting along.

In the distance Cadmus saw a wind moving through the trees towards him and, as it did, he saw the wind lift up small bits of stuff lying about on the ground and whirl these around.

The wind came to within a spear's length of him and stopped. The pine needles and twigs and dry leaves that had been whirling in the air tumbled to the ground and a woman was revealed. It was the goddess Athene, though she had come as a woman, with long hair and dark eyes. She was dressed in a shift belted at the waist, and wore sandals laced to her ankles. She was surprisingly small, Cadmus thought to himself, but this was not how she actually was. This was just how she had chosen to appear. Had she chosen to show herself as she really was, he would have been blinded by the sight of her.

'That great serpent who killed your men,' said the goddess, 'was the guardian of this pool.'

Cadmus nodded. He had guessed as much.

'He belonged to Ares.'

Cadmus shook his head. That he hadn't known.

She went on. When his companions had appeared earlier, tramping noisily through the trees in search of water, they hadn't known this place was the serpent's pool, nor that the serpent allowed no one to drink from its pool, or to take water away from it. Anyone who did, it attacked and killed by biting off their heads, as had happened to his companions.

In time, the serpent would have eaten their bodies but kept their heads. The serpent never ate the heads. It had guarded the spring for a long time and the skulls Cadmus had seen earlier belonged to his very oldest victims. He had killed them a long time ago and over the years their skin had fallen away until only bare bone was left. The heads, which still retained their skin and hair, were his more recent victims.

The goddess glanced around and then stamped on the ground.

'You'll build your city here?'

Cadmus nodded.

'You'll hardly do it alone,' said Athena. 'You're going to need help.'

Cadmus nodded again.

'Knock out the serpent's teeth,' said Athena, 'taking care not to break them as you do. Then sow them in the ground like seeds and stand well back. That'll give you the help you need.'

The sound of wind again. The cloud rose and vanished with a roar. The goddess was gone.

Cadmus cut off the serpent's head with the axe and lifted it onto a rock. The flat of the snout was a mess of bone and cartilage and congealing blood. He laid the head on its right cheek and propped its jaws open with a stick. The mouth was a dark red space. The gold teeth sticking out of the gums were long and sharp and smeared with a yellow glop. There were bits of skin packed between the teeth as well as an ear, which he presumed must be from that first head he had seen, the one behind the fallen tree. He set the ear to the side for burial later. The serpent's tongue, which was hanging out, was like a rope and the same deep brown as a piece of old, stewed meat. The smell from the serpent's mouth was part cloacal, part urinous.

He inserted the point of his knife under the gum above one of the serpent's front teeth and drove the point upwards. The gum split slowly, laying bare the part of the tooth hidden by the gum. Once this was revealed Cadmus worked the knife's point backwards and forwards until the tooth was loose and he could get it out, the nerve coming after it like a tail. To get all the serpent's teeth out was a long, slow, finicky business and it was not until the next day that he had all the teeth out, by which time he had also buried the ear. Then he carried the teeth to a level spot in the forest and, as the goddess had instructed, he planted them in the ground at regular intervals as if they were seeds and heeled them well in.

He stepped away. From under the ground came sounds, far away and incoherent at first but gradually growing clearer and louder. Down in the earth there were men shouting and their calls were furious. The earth began to shudder. Whatever was loose on the surface skittered and jumped. The shouts underground grew angrier. From below, wild punches pushed the earth up. A slit opened and Cadmus knew something was about to force its way out of the earth's womb and into the world.

Through the fissure a lethal leaf-shaped spearhead and then the spear shaft to which the leaf-shaped spearhead was attached and then the horse-hair ridge of a warrior's helmet emerged. On and on what was below went on thrusting into the world above until standing there, in front of Cadmus, armed and armoured, shouting belligerently, casting around for his foe, stood a warrior, heavy and powerful and terrible.

Now, all about this first warrior other fissures opened in the forest floor and from out of these came other men, similarly armed and armoured, equally heavy and powerful as the first, and all also shouting and casting around for foes.

In a moment Cadmus knew these warriors would see him and then they would chase after him. One would thrust a spear between his shoulder blades and down he'd tumble. The short swords would come out then. Hack, hack, hack ... He must do something, otherwise he was done for. And what would that be? He must turn them, somehow, against each other.

He picked up a stone and flung it – hard – at the head of a warrior. It hit his helmet right where his ear was. The warrior, startled, shocked, jumped and turned, enraged, towards the warrior beside him.

'You hit me without warning like that,' he shouted, 'don't be surprised if I pay you back.'

'Don't be a fool,' shouted the other. 'I haven't moved. I didn't touch you.'

'Liar,' shouted the first. He raised his spear and stabbed. The defender swung his shield wildly, batting the attacker's spearhead sideways and hitting a third warrior in the process.

'Who hit me without provocation,' shouted the third. He turned and saw the shield-swinger.

'I shall pay you back for that,' shouted the third.

The third warrior went to stab with his spear and in the process antagonised a fourth warrior by banging him with his spear shaft and the fourth as he went to stab the third provoked a fifth and before long all the warriors who had sprung out of the earth were at war, lunging and feinting, parrying and chopping.

A first warrior fell. A second stepped forward and slashed the fallen one's throat, which released a sheet of blood that coated his face and clogged his eyes. A third, seeing his opportunity, stabbed the blood-blinded slasher from behind, causing him to topple forward onto the man whose throat he'd cut. Then the warrior who'd felled the blood-blinded warrior had his stabbing arm lopped off with a vicious sword swipe by a fourth who saw his chance and took it. The arm fell to the ground, followed by a great gush of red, disgorged from the terrible wound at the shoulder, and the warrior who had lost his arm let out a cry, staggered, fell sideways and toppled earthwards. A fifth stepped forwards and drove his spear into the belly of the man whose arm was off. A sixth appeared behind him, drew his dagger across the spearman's throat baring his windpipe and then himself was struck on the head with an axe from behind. His skull split and brain spewed everywhere …

The warriors killed without compunction. There were no sides in the struggle; it was every man for himself; all every warrior wanted was to be the last left standing. And slowly, slowly, the numbers of dead grew and the numbers of fighting warriors shrank until finally only five were left standing: Chthonius, Echion, Hyperenor, Pelorus and Udaeus.

'Friends,' Cadmus shouted at the five survivors. 'Stop!' The five warriors stopped fighting and turned to the man who had shouted at them. 'I intend to build a city,' continued Cadmus, 'here, where you were born. Help me, and you and your descendants will form the principal families of this city.'

Leaf by leaf – a forest; stone by stone – a house; stitch by stitch – a blanket. In that way Thebes was built and then it was filled with people. Cadmus was king and the five warriors, who were known as the Spartoi or Sown Men and their descendants, were the city's nobility.

*

Meanwhile, what of Europa? The great god had raped her and two sons were the result of this, Minos and Rhadamanthys. Then Europa married Asterius, a king, and Asterius adopted Europa's two sons, Minos and Rhadamanthys, as he and Europa had no children of their own.

And Cadmus? He never forgot the sister he failed to find yet he never went to the Pythia to ask what had happened to her. He didn't go because he didn't want find out that she was dead; he preferred not knowing one way or the other and leaving the matter open. Thus, he died believing his sister might be alive, which of course she was.

BOOK THREE

I, Antigone, am a descendent of Cadmus. The lineage goes like this. After Cadmus died, his son became king. Then Cadmus's son died and Cadmus's grandson became king. Cadmus's grandson had a queen. This queen fell pregnant, gave birth and died. Her newborn was a boy, named Laius. Here, at last, the sun falls on the mountainside and the mists begin to clear and we arrive at the point where the unknown slides into the known. Laius was Jocasta, my mother's first husband; Laius was long dead by the time I was born, but growing up I heard a good deal about him; later, I heard more of his history from my father, who had his knowledge from Hermes. And now I will give you the two, plaited together; what I heard growing up concerning Laius, first husband of Jocasta, and what I was told by my father, Oedipus, Jocasta's second husband.

When Laius was only a few months old, his father died. And because Laius was an infant, a regent was needed to take charge until he reached his majority. Laius's great-great-uncle, Lycus, was considered the right choice but he was opposed by two ambitious men, Amphion and Zethus, descendants of the Sown Man Chthonius.

The parties struggled and jostled against each other, each hoping to be appointed, but as Lycus had the support of four of the five families of the Sown Men, while his opponents had the support of only one, he triumphed. He was made regent and Amphion and Zethus were obliged to flee Thebes. They went to a distant country. Here they found allies who liked their plan, which was to raise an army, return to Thebes, kill the regent and the heir, and rule the city themselves. Indeed, the allies liked the plan so much they gave Amphion and Zethus an army and the disgruntled pair set off for Thebes with their force intent on replacing the house of Cadmus with that of Chthonius.

An army on the move goes slowly. It must stop often. One evening Amphion and Zethus's troops camped by a river. An associate of Lycus saw the soldiers clustered round their fires and smelt the meat they were cooking and even heard, very faintly, the susurrus of their talk. This man hurried back to Thebes and went straight to the palace to inform Lycus and his wife, Dirce. He told them what he had seen. A day's march away, he said, there sat an army and before very long, as early as the next day, he thought, it would arrive outside the city. Lycus and Dirce knew the rest. A siege would follow and, if the seven gates were breached, catastrophe!

'Laius must be sent away immediately,' said Dirce, 'before they get here.' She suggested King Pelops, in the kingdom of Elis in the north. King Pelops would take the infant in and keep him safe.

Dirce summoned the royal midwife. She gave her a donkey to ride on and another to carry provisions, a wet nurse to feed baby Laius, and six spearmen. Dirce told the midwife she was to go north, to the kingdom of Elis, where she was to hand Laius to King Pelops and his wife Hippodamia to hold and to keep until such time as it was safe for him to return home to Thebes.

The midwife, with Laius sleeping in her arms, left Thebes in the middle of the night and began to trek north with the wet nurse and the spearmen. When morning came all the party went into a cave to wait out the day.

And at the very time they were waiting in the cave, just as the associate of Lycus had predicted, Amphion and Zethus's troops arrived outside Thebes. They demanded Lycus surrender the city. He refused. The troops began their offensive. For the next five days they attacked the city, and for the next five nights Laius was carried further and further north.

From the drop of water through the roof and death through the door there is no escape. On the morning of the seventh day, the troops breached the gates. Amphion and Zethus took a crack detachment and ran straight to the palace where they cornered Lycus and killed him in front of Dirce.

'Where's Laius?' Amphion and Zethus asked Dirce.

She would not say.

They ordered their troops to search the palace for Laius, whom they intended to kill so he couldn't father any children later on who would skewer their plans for their descendants to rule. The troops returned empty-handed. Laius was nowhere to be found.

Amphion and Zethus asked Dirce again where Laius was and again she would not say. They found a couple of palace attendants and asked them the same question. They didn't know where Laius was gone but they were clear that wherever he was, he was there at Dirce's direction. They found Dirce's principal maid and beat her savagely. The maid told them that Dirce had sent Laius to King Pelops and Queen Hippodamia, so he would be beyond their reach.

'You'll pay for this,' Amphion and Zethus said to Dirce.

They tied her with ropes to the horns of a bull and drove the bull up and down every street in the city. They did this so that every Theban would see Dirce bumping and dragging behind and understand what would happen to any Theban who defied or angered them.

Once Dirce was dead, her bones broken and her skin torn, Amphion and Zethus caught the bull and cut the ropes with which Dirce had been attached. They left the corpse and walked away. This they should not have done.

Blood poured from the body. It splattered onto the street and dribbled into the gap between two pavers and passed into the earth on which the city stood. The earth, once wet, replied with water. It shot out between the pavers and went up into the air then fell back and began to pool in the street.

In the houses all around people were watching through their windows. One or two, seeing the water, ran out with cups, caught some water and tried it. They pronounced that what flowed from Dirce's spring, as they immediately named it, was colder, purer and sweeter than any other water in the world. Dirce's body was taken off and buried.

Word of the spring spread through Thebes. People came to taste the water and they all agreed. It was incomparable, wonderful. A party of wealthy merchants announced they would pay for a well to be built to hold the water, and for benches to be erected for drinkers to sit on. Workmen were secured and the work was started on the very day the spring had started to flow. All of Thebes was delighted by this act of resistance.

Amphion and Zethus, when they got wind of the well, were incensed. But they stayed their hand. They knew they could pull down the well and they could throw over the benches, but they could never stop the water. It would always flow; and as long as there was water flowing, Thebans would drink it. A lion will not always have his way.

During the night that followed the day when Dirce's spring appeared, the midwife and the wet nurse and the six spearman and baby Laius reached the court of King Pelops and Queen Hippodamia. The king and queen were woken and came to greet the arrivals. The midwife asked the royal couple to take in Laius. The royal couple said they would and the next day the news was proclaimed; they would raise Laius with their children as if he were their own son. They would put him in their children's quarters and they would provide him with everything they provided their own children with. And they did. The midwife, the wet nurse and the spearmen returned to Thebes and slipped back into the city unnoticed.

And now we pass to people I actually know, people I actually met and talked with. These are my grandfather, Menoeceus, a descendant of the Sown Man Echion; his wife, my maternal grandmother, Iphimedia; their firstborn and only son, my uncle Creon; and their only daughter, Jocasta, my mother.

In the early days of Amphion and Zethus's rule, Menoeceus and Iphimedia and their son Creon (Jocasta was not born yet) lived in their beautiful house in Thebes. They were safe and comfortable and the city's new rulers, Amphion and Zethus, never bothered them any more than they bothered any other powerful Thebans descended from the Sown Men.

Menoeceus and Iphimedia owned many slaves and around this time Menoeceus acquired a new slave, a young girl called Callidice. Callidice, when she arrived in the house of Menoeceus and Iphimedia, was a small, sturdy, round-shouldered girl with wrists and ankles made for work. Her first job was to deal with the night soil. Every morning she would carry the stinking earthenware and wooden vessels that had been filled during the night out into the countryside and bury their foul contents. Then she would clean the vessels with sand and water and carry them back, sparkling and dry, for use the following night. Callidice was cheerful and hardworking and gave everyone the impression she was happy to do her designated and unfortunate job.

After a period spent emptying the night soil, Callidice was promoted. She was put in the laundry and made responsible for washing the cloth scraps and rags Iphimedia used each month when she bled. These things Callidice laundered in the traditional manner: in winter she steeped the red rags in water and wood ash and then pounded them with wooden paddles; in summer she took them to the river, flogged them on the rocks, scraped them with stones, then dried them in the sun. Callidice's laundering was impeccable. Iphimedia, charmed and delighted, increased Callidice's responsibilities to include her dresses and bed clothes. Callidice had done very well. As a laundry maid, she had gone as far as she could.

One night Callidice fell in with a soldier, a fellow with black hair and a mouth of good teeth. They drank together. Callidice was interested in love. She asked the soldier to kiss her and he did. She liked it. She had never lain with a man before but she decided she would start with this one. She slipped away to fetch a blanket and returned. Then she and the soldier went to an empty stable. She spread the blanket on the old straw on the floor so that her bare back would not be prickled when the soldier ground into her, as he did several times during the night that followed.

Nine months later Callidice delivered her child, a boy. She named him Antimedes.

Three days after the birth Callidice asked to see Iphimedia. Her request was granted. Callidice found Iphimedia, who was pregnant and whose belly she could see sticking out through her dress, lying on a couch with her feet up and her eyes closed. Her head was on the arm rest and her hair, which hung down in a sheet behind, was being carefully combed by a woman. The sensation of the tines tugging through her hair had put Iphimedia into a mild trance and she floated between waking and sleeping, detached from the present even as she was able to hear the sounds of her house, far away and muffled. It was a stroke of luck that Callidice had come at this moment. At the same time it wasn't, because things happen the way they are meant to happen. But neither cancels the other out. It's not one or the other. They're both true.

'Mistress,' Callidice said.

Iphimedia half-opened an eye.

'I have a child,' said Callidice. 'He is called Antimedes.'

Iphimedia opened her eye a bit further.

'Oh yes,' she said slowly, 'so I see.'

Callidice now spoke the words she had prepared in advance. Would she be allowed continue to work in the laundry and to keep him with her, she asked. She swore she would maintain the standards Iphimedia had come to enjoy if she were allowed to do this.

Iphimedia closed her eye and sank back into the glorious feeling that came when her hair was combed.

'Of course, you will stay,' she said dreamily. 'I'll speak to Menoeceus. Nothing will change. Why would it? I promise we'll keep you and Antimedes together.'

Callidice knelt and kissed the hem of Iphimedia's robe. She promised her she would not be found wanting. Every article she washed would go back to her mistress looking like new, she said. Iphimedia heard everything and didn't doubt it.

Not long after this interview, Iphimedia gave birth to Creon's younger sister, Jocasta, and Callidice, besides what she did for Iphimedia, now also took care of Jocasta's apparel. Callidice laundered the things she soiled as a baby. Callidice laundered the clothes she dirtied when she was growing up. Callidice laundered her sheets, her blankets, her cloaks. This was important, because out of proximity and closeness something like affection developed between young Jocasta and the slave.

In the kingdom of Elis, but far from the court at Pisa, King Pelops lay with a woman called Astyoche and she gave birth to a son, Chrysippus. Pelops took the newborn Chrysippus back to Pisa and introduced him to his court as Hippodamia's newest child – his queen went along with this, she had no choice – and then he placed the new arrival with his children and Laius, so he could be raised with them. Laius was four years old when Chrysippus arrived.

Chrysippus had a tutor who taught him arithmetic and rhetoric, poetry and philosophy and music, and everything else he needed to learn. Laius, who had a talent for managing horses and driving chariots, became Chrysippus's instructor in these arts and the two spent a huge amount of time together. Chrysippus was a beautiful, charming and clever child and Laius became particularly attached to him.

We leap forward now to when Laius was a young man and still residing at the court in Pisa. By this time he had twice attended the Nemean Games – these happened every two years – but Chrysippus, still a youth, had never been. Laius believed he loved Chrysippus. He also believed that if he got him to the games, where they would be alone together and far from the court, he would be able to make Chrysippus his lover.

Laius went to Pelops. It was surely time, he said, for Chrysippus to attend the Nemean games and participate in both types of chariot race, those with two and those with four horses. There was a good chance, Laius continued, the youth would win the wreath of wild celery presented to victors, and to return to Pisa with such a wreath would be a marvellous thing, would it not? Might he take Chrysippus?

'Why not?' said Pelops. 'Take the youth.'

In Thebes, meanwhile, Amphion and Zethus died simultaneously and word was sent north to Pelops's court. Laius should return to his place of birth and assume his throne. Laius was exhilerated and desolated in equal measure by the summons. He was of Cadmus's line. The Theban throne was his by right. He would have it and he would enjoy it. He was overjoyed by the news. The sun at home always warms better than the sun abroad. But to return to Thebes, now, before he had possessed Chrysippus, which he was convinced he would manage once he had the youth at the Nemean Games – this appalled him.

King Pelops, who had also heard the news from Thebes, summoned Laius.

'You will want to return to Thebes immediately,' he said. Laius could skip the games, he added, for he was under no obligation, and leave for his birthplace at once.

'No, no,' Laius said. He intended, he explained, to make good on the undertaking he had made. He would take Chrysippus to the Nemean Games and then, and only then, would he go back to Thebes.

'As you wish,' said King Pelops, who knew nothing of Laius's hidden motive.

Laius took Chrysippus to the games. Chrysippus failed to secure a wild celery wreath in any category but he was incredibly popular and was mobbed by competitors and visitors alike who believed that one day he would be a champion. The continuous presence of these admirers made it impossible for Laius to put his plan into effect.

When the games ended, Laius left with his pupil in a chariot. As far as Chrysippus understood, he was being taken back to Pisa and then Laius would go on to Thebes.

Somewhere along the way, Laius stopped for the night. He built a fire. He plied Chrysippus with wine until he fell asleep. Then he undressed the youth, placed him face down on the chariot floor and began to sodomise him. Chrysippus woke up and cried out in hurt and shame but Laius plunged on.

When he was finished Laius pulled out his penis and saw that his foreskin was covered with the youth's brown, gritty and oily excrement. He washed himself and dressed. Then he returned Chrysippus his clothes, kissed him gently, whispered he loved him and advised the youth that he was taking him home to Thebes as his catamite.

Laius entered Thebes and went to the palace where he quietly revealed his identity to the doorkeeper. He airily introduced Chrysippus as his servant to one or two officials he encountered on the way and immediately closeted the youth in the apartment that had been prepared for him. Chrysippus's presence barely registered.

In the city, word spread. Cadmus's descendant and the rightful king was back. Thebans were universally delighted and joyful. Laius's rule would be wondrous and just; their city would flourish and every person would prosper. On the first night of Laius's return, to welcome both their king and their marvellous future, the whole of the city (except for the slaves) flooded onto the streets to sing and dance and drink.

Chrysippus spent the night in Laius's bed. While Laius slept next to him, he lay awake listening to Thebans singing and shouting in the streets outside. When the noise stopped he slipped from the bed and left the palace. Who hesitates, regrets, as he knew.

Outside, in the dark and empty streets, there were puddles of wine, pee and vomit; there were broken sandals, torn tunics, dropped earrings and lost bracelets; and there were Thebans lying insensible in doorways, against walls, and under water troughs

Chrysippus picked his way to the gate that opened onto the Mount Phicium road. The gate was closed and the gatekeeper was lying on a mat on the ground. He was a heavy man with a large head. Chrysippus jogged his shoulder. Two eyelids rose and two dark eyes looked up at Chrysippus.

'What?' said the gatekeeper.

'Open the gate,' said Chrysippus.

'Come back later. I'm tired.' The gatekeeper was drunk.

'No, now.'

The gatekeeper got onto his hands and knees and breathed slowly in and out. Then he struggled to his feet, stared at Chrysippus and blinked.

'What are you doing up this early?' said the gatekeeper. 'It's still dark. You should be in bed, sleeping off last night.'

'I have a journey to make.'

'It had better be worth it.'

The gatekeeper pulled back the wooden bars that held the two gates closed and opened one gate back half an arm's length. The space was just big enough for Chrysippus to slip through.

'Name?' he said.

'What do you want it for?'

'When anyone comes in or out at night, I get their name. It's night still, so I want your name.'

'Chrysippus.'

'I should remember that. Even a drunk man should remember that.' The gatekeeper inclined his head at the space. Chrysippus was free to leave.

The youth sidled through sideways. As soon as he was through, the gate slammed behind and he heard the wooden bars in their keepers being shot back into place.

Chrysippus walked away. A collection of ramshackle huts. A barking dog. Further on, an olive grove, the grey trees almost silver in the strange pre-dawn dark. The rasping, wheezy cry of a donkey. A field of sheep, grouped together, most sitting or lying, very quiet. A bleat here, a bleat there. A tail wagging. A terrace with a vineyard, and young green grapes showing. Two doves on a stone wall. When he drew closer they flew away, as if they were frightened of him.

The road began to climb towards his destination, the cliffs of Mount Phicium. He had never been but he knew their reputation. Even in Pisa, at his father's court, everyone knew about the cliffs of Mount Phicium. Everyone knew what they could do for those who wished to end their suffering. The cliffs would aid him now. He simply had to step off the top. It would be quick, simple and final and once he was gone all the shame would be wiped away.

The road grew steeper. The going was hard. The higher Chrysippus went the farther he saw into the distance. Then the gradient vanished and the road was level and he was, he judged, at the top. There was the cliff's edge and beyond the edge, far below, he saw the plain that spread as far as his eye could see. It was dotted with tiny houses, fields, walls, trees, rocks, terraces and animals. It was not yet dawn and there was no sign of the sun, yet there was light around and everything in that light had a faint, silvery hue.

He got onto his hands and knees, crawled to the cliff's edge, and peered over. He saw a bird flying below, skimming along the cliff's face and he saw the foot of the cliff far below, all uneven ground, strewn with rocks, bushes and a few small trees. It was a long way to the bottom. He felt strange and light-headed, staring down. It was dangerous, too. If he lingered, doubts might follow and he would lose heart. He couldn't be doing with that. This must be done and done now.

Chrysippus retreated backwards on his hands and knees and then got to his feet and took a few more paces away from the edge. He took off his cloak, folded it, placed it on the ground and put a stone on top so it wouldn't blow away. A passing traveller would find it later. The traveller would assumed someone who had jumped had left it for someone else to have. The traveller would take it and use it.

Chrysippus straightened up and closed his eyes. It was time. He took a breath and started running as fast as he could run ...

As Chrysippus dropped he cried and his cry echoed off the cliffs. A peasant heard the cry. He was out early, looking for mushrooms. He thought it was a bird and then he decided it couldn't be a bird. Only a man, a falling man, made that sort of a noise. Another sound followed, which the peasant thought might be the sound of a body hitting the ground but he couldn't be sure.

The peasant went to the bottom of the Mount Phicium cliffs and searched. He found Chrysippus. The youth was on his back. There was blood flowing from his ears and his nose. His eyes were open and he looked terrified.

The peasant stared at the body. If he was an important person he would sling the body over his donkey and carry him to Thebes where he might find relatives who would pay him a fee. But the dead youth, he decided, was too ordinary looking. He wasn't worth taking to Thebes.

The cliff face had numerous little caves along the bottom. The peasant found an empty one. He dragged the body in and left it face down on the floor. He blocked the entrance with stones and scrub so wild animals could not get in and eat the remains. It was not the first time the peasant had performed this service and it would not be the last.

After he walked away the peasant felt gratified. He had shown respect and done the right thing. He went back to his mushroom hunt and got a good haul.

In Thebes, Laius woke alone. He asked one or two

attendants if they had seen Chrysippus. Nobody reported seeing him. Laius also, of course, knew of Mount Phicium. Had Chrysippus taken himself there? There was only one way to find out. He went alone to the Mount Phicium gate and found the gatekeeper who had been on duty all night. He was sitting on the ground holding his head. He had a terrible hangover. The gates were open.

'Did a Chrysippus go out early this morning?' Laius asked.

The gatekeeper confirmed that he had. Laius realised what had happened. Chrysippus had gone to the cliffs and jumped. His body was now lying at the foot of the cliffs. If he'd wanted to walk home he'd have used a different gate and taken a different road.

Laius was disappointed to lose Chrysippus but these feelings were far outweighed by the anxiety that someone should find out what had happened. Laius made the gate-keeper promise to forget that anyone called Chrysippus had ever left Thebes by the Mount Phicium gate and, to ensure that he did, Laius gave him a sum of money. He returned to the palace then and said nothing to the attendants.

Laius didn't know what the peasant had done so his next assumption, which was wrong, was that the body would be found by lions or foxes and devoured. And once a few days had passed and no word had come of a youth found at the foot of the Mount Phicium cliffs, he felt better. And then, as more time passed and the palace attendants said nothing and the gatekeeper said nothing, he felt better still. And then, after many days had passed, he decided he'd got away with it. He'd had Chrysippus in Thebes for one night, which no one knew about, and then Chrysippus had vanished and no one knew about that either. He began to hope that because he had not been found out, there would be no penalty.

He was wrong. With what you handle you are soiled. The thread is cut where it is thinnest. Man has nothing so much to fear as the loss of happiness.

BOOK FOUR

Now he was king, Laius determined he must have a queen-consort, though only a descendant of one of the Sown Men would do. Inquiries were made. Among others, Jocasta was selected for consideration. She had many virtues: she was short and dark. She had black eyes and black hair and small neat hands. Her earlobes were not attached to her neck, which was something Laius loathed. Her knees shone. So, did her elbows. Her feet were trim. Her family were noble. She was without taint.

Laius decided Jocasta was the most suitable. Menoeceus was informed that the king intended to marry his daughter. Menoeceus, in turn, informed his daughter of Laius's intention. Jocasta said nothing. The decision was made and she had no choice in this matter But since she was going away to the palace, Jocasta thought there was one thing she would ask for. In her new position as queen-consort, she would have many beautiful dresses and shifts, even more than she currently owned. Who could she trust to maintain the lustre of her apparel? She knew of only one person. Someone who she had known all her life, who she trusted, who she liked as far as someone freeborn could like someone who was born a slave. Someone who had laundered everything she had ever used or worn.

'I have a request,' said Jocasta, 'which I hope you will grant.'

'Tell me,' said her father.

'I want to take Callidice with me,' Jocasta said.

Menoeceus agreed. Jocasta could take Callidice and furthermore, he said, the laundress's son Antimedes could go too. The lad was already working as a shepherd for Menoeceus and could transfer to the king's flock when his mother and Jocasta moved to the palace. Menoeceus did not make this offer because he cared about Callidice, the laundress, or her son Antimedes, the shepherd. He made it because he thought Laius would be impressed to acquire a laundress and a young shepherd along with his bride. Callidice and her son were not consulted about their move. The small people never are. They are simply instructed.

For her marriage ceremony Jocasta wore her heaviest necklace, her loveliest earrings, her brightest rings, her shapeliest dress and her finest slippers. The night of their nuptials, Laius and Jocasta, now his queen, lay together between the purple sheets that were traditional when a marriage was consummated. The next morning, after they were woken by dogs barking in the city, the sheets, which bore a small bloodstain, were taken by Callidice and washed. The following night, Laius and the new queen lay on them again. They lay together the next night and the next until she began to bleed. After the bleeding stopped they lay together until she bled again and after that ended they lay together again.

On and on it went like this, and Jocasta, who expected to conceive, could not understand why she didn't. Laius did not understand either and was puzzled. He began to ask why it hadn't happened.

'Oh, but it will. Don't worry, it will,' she assured him the first time he asked, and every time thereafter she gave him the same answer.

He believed her and she believed as well. But in her mind lurked the fugitive thought that she could be wrong: perhaps she would never conceive. Every time the thought came near she hurled a stone at it and it slunk off yelping, like a dog driven away from the fire and back out into the dark.

From the lesser god to my father to me, Antigone, flowed the pillow talk of my mother, the new queen, and her first husband, Laius, the king. Should we know what is said in the dark by a husband and wife who never thought their words would be known? Should we know what they think? Should others be told? If we are to understand them they must be told.

These words and thoughts of Laius and his queen, Jocasta, came long before my father's birth and, just as Europa, Cadmus and Chrysippus, shaped the life he lived without his knowing, so too did the pillow talk of the royal couple. All our lives are shaped by unknowns. The stone dropped into the deep well may not sound till long after, by which point whoever dropped the stone has forgotten they did, but sound it does. Every action has a consequence. This is the story of the world.

It was the middle of the night and Jocasta and Laius were in bed, awake.

Out in the city, as usual, there were dogs barking. Every bark sounded like a response to the bark before. It felt like a conversation.

'What are they saying out there?' said Jocasta.

'I don't know,' said Laius. 'I don't speak dog.'

'They're not barking to pass the time,' said Jocasta. 'They must be saying something.'

'People must have something to say,' said Laius, 'and dogs something to bark at.'

Around their dark room night lights smouldered. The oil smelt like fish bones. Jocasta felt they were the only two people awake in the city. If ever there was an occasion to talk, this was it.

'Laius,' she said, 'we lie together night after night, but because it does not happen, everyone is whispering. And you know what they're saying in the streets of Thebes? "The queen is barren. She must have done wrong. She must have offended the gods. They've cursed her. That's why she can't have a child." That's what they are saying and Laius, I want them stopped. You are king. I want you to make it a crime, punishable by flogging, or worse, to speak about me in the way that they do. They cannot say that I am barren. They cannot say that I have offended the gods.'

Laius lay still. He said nothing. He'd heard the same himself. The people of Thebes were worried he would not produce an heir and then that he would die and there would be chaos. He understood. A city needed an orderly succession in place to ensure it always had a ruler. At the same time, Laius was vexed by the lack of faith that the people of Thebes were showing. Did they think he was just going to die and leave a mess for whoever followed to sort out? No, he wasn't. Someone would be found in the event that he was without an heir. Jocasta's brother, Creon, for instance – he could be regent. And if not him, someone else could be found. He, Laius, would see to it. But for now he was saying nothing on the subject of his succession in public. Nothing.

When he decided the time was right he would make the necessary arrangements and in the meantime his subjects should just stop whingeing. It was none of their business. His wife, on the other hand, he would have to handle differently. Silence wouldn't work with her. She'd need words. But what words? He did not quite know which ones yet and, until he did, he would stay quiet and say nothing.

Jocasta watched her husband's profile in the dark. Why didn't he speak? Didn't he realise what it was like to be queen-consort and to have to endure the kind of comments she was having to put up with?

Then another thought crossed her mind. He was acting. He was just saying nothing in order to give her the impression that he was carefully considering the subject under discussion, rotating it in his mind much as one might rotate something in one's hands, looking at it this way, now that way. That's what he was doing, trying to make her think he was pondering deeply. But it was just a ploy. He didn't care about her suffering.

'Well,' she said, 'are you going to?'

'What?'

'Forbid anyone to talk about me.'

'No. I won't do it.'

She felt something sink in her. 'Why not?'

'You think the subjects will accept it, just like that? You think they'll all say, "We should never have chattered about the queen in the first place and the king is quite right to put a stop to it"? No, I make the order, the subjects will say, "Why's he so desperate to stop us talking?" Then they'll ponder the question and answer it. "Hang on," they'll say. "We *are* on to something. She *is* barren. That's why he doesn't want us to talk. Well, we won't shut up. And what's more, since he hasn't an heir, he's got to name a successor and he's got to name him now." That's what'll happen if I make the order you want me to.'

'But you're king,' she said, 'you don't have to agree to anything. They want you to name a successor, you say, no, not until you are ready.'

'That won't work,' he said. 'Once they start clamouring for a successor, it'll be impossible to refuse. I will have to give a name and once I have, this will happen:

'We still have no children. I name my successor. In the beginning the person is very happy to be picked. Then time passes and the successor starts to get impatient. Then one day he says, "It could be years before I become king. So what can I do? I know, I'll do what Amphion and Zethus did. I'll go to a sympathetic king. I'll plead for help. He'll give me an army. I'll come back with the army and I'll storm Thebes. I'll throw Laius out. In fact, I'll kill him. And what about the queen? No, I can't have her lingering in Thebes. She'll have to go as well. Yes, good plan. Leave Thebes, get an army, come back, smash through the gates, storm up to the palace, kill the royal couple."'

'So, you're not going to do anything,' said Jocasta.

'I didn't say that. I will do something, but it will be gentle and persuasive.'

'You, coaxing?' scoffed Jocasta.

'Instead of an order,' said Laius, 'I will just drop a word here and there. I will let it be known that we are displeased. We have heard how Thebans have spoken about their queen and we don't like it. It's disrespectful and we want it to stop.'

'And you think your subjects will comply?'

'Yes.'

'Why?'

'When the king speaks,' said Laius, 'even informally, Thebes pays attention.'

'People only change for a reason. You putting a word out here and there isn't going to give them a reason to change.'

'Yes, it is. It'll spread through the city. Everyone will know we know what they've been saying and once they know we know, anxiety will spread. "They've been listening to us," they'll say. "They know what we're saying. We'd better be careful." That's what'll happen, and once it does, there'll be no more talk.'

'So you're telling me, if you issue an edict it'll lead to demands for a successor to be named and all kinds of trouble, whereas if you just have a quiet word here and there, and let our displeasure be known, the slanders will stop?'

'Yes,' he said.

'Humph,' she said. At this moment Jocasta knew two things: one was that she wasn't content and the other was that she'd have to pretend she was content, though she couldn't seem to have been persuaded too quickly. She'd have to start equivocal and build to full-throated approval. When necessary, Jocasta could dissemble as well as anyone.

'I suppose,' she began, 'that might be the way to do it. No fuss, no hectoring, just you pouring words into the ears of a select few, who in turn will pour words into the ears of a greater number, who in turn will pour words into the ears of an even greater number until, at last, your words have been poured into every Theban ear and everyone will say, "They've heard. They're watching us. We must stop." Yes, I didn't understand at first, but now I see this will work. Clever Laius!'

The king laughed. He was acting too. He needed her to think he was happy and content because she had agreed. But he wasn't. He was far from happy and content because in his head a worrying name and worrying thoughts that came with the name were scurrying about.

The name was Chrysippus.

Previously he'd felt secure that his secret was safe but now he wasn't so sure any more. Did Jocasta know what he had done? No, impossible. Only he knew he had sodomised him. But did she know, or had she heard that he had brought Chrysippus with him when he returned from exile? Perhaps. And knowing just that, did she wonder if he had committed some crime, which had alienated the gods, which had led to his being cursed, which meant they could not have a child, as that was the punishment?

He pondered the question and back came the answer he had given himself many times.

Chrysippus's time in Thebes had been short. One night only. And Laius had kept him secluded. He had only met one or two palace attendants. Might these officials have said anything? Unlikely. Besides, they'd barely had sight of Chrysippus.

There was also the gatekeeper. As far as Laius knew, he was the last person in Thebes to see Chrysippus alive. Might his story – that he had let Chrysippus out of the Mount Phicium gate, since when Chrysippus was never been heard of again – have got back to her? He didn't think so either. He had paid the gatekeeper off at the time and later he'd heard the gatekeeper had been run over by a cart and killed. So nothing had leaked from him either. In which case, if nothing had been said by the doorkeeper to whom Laius first revealed himself when he returned from exile, or by the palace officials who saw Chrysippus during the few hours he was in the palace, or by the gatekeeper who let Chrysippus out the Mount Phicium gate, surely Chrysippus's presence in Thebes had gone undetected? At least by Jocasta and by Thebes.

But there were other forces in play. The gods knew. He'd discounted that previously but now he had lain with Jocasta without conceiving, he'd begun to think otherwise. The gods had seen Chrysippus face down on the floor of his chariot. They had seen Chrysippus at Laius's side when he returned from exile and entered the palace. They had seen Chrysippus lying in Laius's bed. They had seen Chrysippus slip from Laius's bed, climb in the pre-dawn to the Mount Phicium cliff top, and throw himself over the edge. And having seen all this, had the gods decided to punish him by preventing Jocasta from conceiving? They might.

As king what he needed more than anything else was an heir. To deprive him of that would ruin his reign and make the city unstable and make his queen miserable. From this one simple prohibition much trouble would flow. So yes, he thought, this inability to produce a child might be his punishment. The gods might be punishing him.

At some point he heard Jocasta's breathing had changed. She'd fallen asleep. He was alone and somehow, because of that feeling of being absolutely on his own, he could allow himself to think the unthinkable. He had to stop this. And to stop it he had to know one way or the other. He would have to go to the Oracle of Delphi and seek an answer. He would have to ask the Pythia the dreadful question: am I the cause of our childlessness? The Pythia would tell him if he was or if there was some other reason. And then once he knew he could work out what to do. He could act. And the sooner he did this the better.

Whatever is good to know is difficult to learn but Laius felt better as soon as he had committed himself to his course of action. He felt something settling. He grew still and calm. Finally, he fell sleep.

We do not live, we wear ourselves out one against the other. I now know this was how it was for my mother and her first husband. The knowledge of what she suffered makes something tremble in my chest. I feel sorry for Jocasta. I even feel something for Laius. Hard-hearted and vicious though he was, he had his troubles and he felt things deeply too. When you know so much about a person, no matter the wrongs they've done, you can't just hate them. Understanding unravels hatred; and the more you understand, the more it unravels. This is why tyrants always profess that either they would rather not know or they already know so they need look no further. Harm is easiest done when it springs from ignorance.

The following morning a royal attendant came to the queen while she was working at her loom. The man had high cheekbones and a strange, fluting laugh. He was unpopular in the palace.

'I have a message from the king,' he said. Earlier that morning, the royal attendant continued, Laius had left by carriage with Polyphontes, his driver, and was on his way to Delphi. Jocasta was perplexed by this. Laius hadn't mentioned going to Delphi. How strange he should have just upped and left and told her nothing, not even said goodbye. She didn't like that.

'Is that all he said?' said Jocasta. 'He's gone and that's it?'

The royal attendant nodded. He retreated, bowing. She looked at the floor. Her husband had gone to Delphi to consult the Pythia. It was obvious why: they had no child. What would the Pythia say? What if the Pythia said she was to blame? Where worrying leads, misery follows.

She felt her face go hot. No, she mustn't think about this. She must banish these thoughts. She must forget her pre-occupations and turn to the world.

Someone was sweeping nearby. She heard the sound of bristles on the floor, gathering dust and dirt and pushing them along. Jocasta looked round and saw it was Callidice wielding the brush. When she wasn't in the laundry, Callidice swept and washed Jocasta's apartment and mended her clothes and sometimes she even undressed and bathed her and then dressed her again afterwards. As she watched the small, round-shouldered slave woman, a fleeting rush of unbidden ideas flooded Jocasta.

Someone like Callidice – what actually went on in her mind? Jocasta considered for a moment and then decided, probably very little. What would she have to worry about? She had a good life, a kind mistress and her son Antimedes was at hand. She knew exactly where she sat in the world and she was never assailed by the unexpected. Yes, she decided, having no freedom gave Callidice a level of contentment denied to those, like her, who were free.

Her thoughts rolled on. What did the wives of Thebes make of her? They weren't that different, so this wasn't a completely improper comparison. Did they covet her wealth, her position, her power? Would they like to be her?

The obvious answer seemed to be yes but when she thought about it further she decided that no, they wouldn't want to be like her, given her current situation. If their husbands went off without any explanation, like Laius had, they could treat their husbands accordingly on their return. They could be cool. They could berate them. They could refuse them love. She could do none of that. The fact was, she was the queen and she must behave like a queen.

She had always felt she was the one Laius wanted, but Laius had been going at her for months and nothing had happened. She had failed him, that was the brutal truth. Laius was impatient. She could be sure he wouldn't want to put up with this situation any longer. Laius was also practical. If his wife couldn't give him a child he'd find someone else who would. He'd found a concubine, hadn't he? And this morning he hadn't really gone to Delphi. That was just a cover. He'd gone to her. Perhaps he was already with her, ploughing away, hoping she cropped.

And what then? Laius's concubine would conceive. Later, she would give birth. Then Laius would take the newborn from the concubine's grasp and carry the infant to Thebes. He would give the baby to her to raise as their own. Kings were always bringing home their children by other women for their queens to raise. It was traditional but that didn't mean she either liked or wanted it. The very idea made her tremble. The failure was shameful.

For an instant everything stopped and her mind went blank. When her thoughts came back, she was calm again. She would be far better off confirming the truth. The first step, surely, was to find out if Laius had actually gone to Delphi. She'd send someone there and depending on what her spy turned up, she'd know. If he wasn't there, then the chances were that he had another life. And if she knew that he had, well – at least she could plan accordingly. On the other hand, he might have gone to Delphi. It was not impossible. But nothing could be decided till she knew one way or the other. So the first thing was to find out, one way or the other. When the path is before you, do not look for the road.

Jocasta dispatched Callidice to find a particular royal herald. This man had worked for the palace all his life. During the reign of Laius's father, when on royal business, he had been attacked on the Mount Phicium road by robbers. They had beaten him with their heavy staffs and left him for dead. He had been found and returned to Thebes, where his broken bones had been reset. He recovered physically but his speech was impaired. Now he could only manage a few words at a time if he made a tremendous effort and, unless one was used to him, his few words were difficult to make out. It was because of his incapacity that Jocasta had picked him for the task she had in mind. He wouldn't tell anyone her business. He wouldn't be able to get the words out. And even if he did no one would understand him.

A little later, footsteps on the stairs, and then the door opened and there was the herald.

'Here,' Jocasta called, waving the herald over. She was still at her loom.

The herald came up, bobbed and nodded.

'Go,' Jocasta shouted at Callidice. 'Out and close the door behind you.'

Callidice left. Jocasta looked at the herald. He was a stringy fellow with black eyes, long hands and big knuckles that reminded her of walnuts. He had no hair and the skin on his skull was criss-crossed by long scars, the wounds caused by the cudgelling he had received, which had then been sewn up.

'My husband left earlier,' she said. 'For Delphi, I was told. I want you to go after him but he mustn't know you're behind. He never sees you, he never lays eyes on you. Understand?'

'Yes,' said the herald very slowly and with great difficulty.

'Once you get to Delphi, I want you to search him out. Make sure he doesn't see you. And having found him, I want you to ensure he goes in to the Oracle. Then you leave and get back here and tell me what you saw before he comes home.'

The herald nodded his head, which was long and brown while his scars were white and looked like threads.

'But if he's not in Delphi, if you don't see him there, at all, you come back and tell me that.'

The herald nodded and sloped off. Callidice slipped silently back into the queen's room. Jocasta moved the shuttle on the loom up, down, up, down, and as she did she listened to the sound the wood made as it bound the threads and she saw the filaments stretched tight in front of her merging to make a woollen square. Swish, swish, the shuttle went. Now she had only to wait for the herald to return. Either Laius had gone to the Oracle or he hadn't. It was hard to say which was worse. As she thought about it now, Jocasta was inclined to think the first option was the worst. After all, what the Pythia said might be much worse than what a concubine did. The Pythia had the god in her after all, and the concubine did not.

BOOK FIVE

Laius sat in the forecourt in front of the temple at Delphi, surrounded by supplicants, talk and movement. His seat was hard and cold. He had paid his fees. He had performed his rites. He had been vetted by the priests. He had drawn his lot. Now he was waiting his turn.

Laius closed his eyes and a picture formed in his mind of himself and the Pythia in her dark, sacred space under the temple. He'd been filled with this image many times since he sat down. He kept banishing it but it kept coming back, and now here it was, again. He lacked the strength to turn it away, which meant it would flow on.

'What is your question?' he heard. This was the Pythia. Her voice was grave and solemn, slow and stately. Like any other mortal, what went on in Laius's head was a mix of things he knew and things he made up. So, this voice was based on what he remembered from earlier visits when he had heard the Pythia as well as on how he imagined a Pythia ought to speak.

'Pythia,' Laius imagined himself saying. This was his question, the one he had come to ask. 'Why have we not had a child?'

'Chrysippus,' said the Pythia.

Laius felt his face flush, his heart race, his stomach tightening. He shook his head and rubbed his face with both hands, in order to drive what he was imagining from his mind.

'Laius,' he said, moving his lips, forming the words but speaking them quietly so no one in the noisy forecourt could hear. 'Stop it. Stop jumping to conclusions. Stop tormenting yourself. Let your mind empty out and go still. You don't know the answer and you won't until the Pythia has spoken. And until she does, leave yourself alone.'

Laius felt better. He had to stay quiet and calm. There was no point in giving himself an explanation before the Pythia had answered. And after all, wasn't that the point of coming?

Then, from a different part of his being, came different words. These were not spoken out loud. They were spoken in his head and they came from the same part his dreams came from at night, the part over which he had no control: 'The Pythia is going to tell you what you already know,' the voice said, 'and you are an idiot if you think she is going to say anything else.'

Laius, sensing movement, opened his eyes. It was a nearby supplicant. The priest had come to fetch the fellow. He and the supplicant walked off towards the temple entrance. Laius stood and stretched. His turn was closer. He noticed a heavy man with a big head and a broad face. He was a supplicant too. Maybe I could get the man talking, thought Laius. That would pass the time and would stop me thinking. He went and sat beside the stranger.

'I really don't like this waiting,' said Laius.

The man shrugged.

'I don't mind it,' he said.

'I do,' said Laius, 'having to sit here and wait with your question going around and around in your head and your mind coming back with every conceivable answer.'

'I don't know what you mean,' said the other man. 'I'm just waiting. I'm not thinking. I do that after I've been in. There's no point thinking now.'

'Are you telling me you're not thinking at all?'

'Yes,' said the man. 'Mind's a blank. And give me half a chance and I reckon I could probably go to sleep.'

'Sleep?' said Laius. This he found incredible.

'Not a bother,' said the man.

'Well,' said Laius, 'you're lucky.'

'I certainly am,' said the man, 'and so I remain until I get inside and hear what she has to say, that is.'

He yawned, then put his hand over his mouth.

'I'm just going to close my eyes, if you don't mind,' he said.

The man folded his hands on his lap and let his eyelids drop. Laius glanced along the line. How many supplicants were there ahead of him? He counted five and gave up. This torment was set to last and last.

Laius was hot. His palms were moist. Any moment now the priest would come. His turn, he was sure, was almost upon him. He was aware of movement there on his right, on the edge of his sight. He looked up. It was the priest, gliding towards him. The priest nodded. Laius stood. The priest took him by the hand and led him gently through the throng and towards the steps.

Laius and the priest entered the temple. It was gloomy and dark inside. There was a smell of burnt mutton as well as something sweet and putrid. Laius's thighs felt watery. His mouth was dry. His head hurt. His eyes fizzed. But his body, even as he felt these things, acted as it always acted. His feet moved, taking him forward. His throat swallowed, wetting his mouth. His lungs went on working, drawing his breath in and out. It was wonderful the way the body went on despite everything.

They went down the steps. They were in the dark space at the bottom. There were the drapes and beyond the drapes sat the Pythia. Here the smell of mutton wasn't as strong as it was above but the sweet, putrid odour was stronger. The priest held the drape open and Laius went through to the adytum, the temple's inner sanctum. The priest followed him and he heard the drape fall behind.

Laius's eyes adjusted to the gloom. He saw the Pythia in front of him. She sat on a bowl-shaped seat that balanced on the three legs, an old woman in a young girl's short white dress. She held laurel leaves in one hand and her bowl for divination in the other. The priest bent down and put his mouth to the Pythia's ear.

'Laius, from Thebes, the king,' Laius heard the priest whisper.

The Pythia closed her eyes. Her shoulders moved. Her breath quickened. The god was coming into her. The Pythia opened her eyes and looked at him. The god inside her was staring at him with her eyes.

The priest leant in again and put his mouth to the Pythia's ear and began to whisper. Laius couldn't hear what he was saying. Earlier, when he was vetted, he'd been asked what his question was, as was customary, and he assumed that's what the priest was telling her now.

The priest stopped speaking and stepped back from the Pythia. The Pythia lowered her head and gazed into the water in the bowl, her expression rapt, obedient and transfixed. The god is speaking into her mind, thought Laius. And she is listening to the words of the god. The Pythia looked up and stared at him.

'Go on,' said the priest to Laius. 'Speak.'

He said that he was from Thebes, that he was the king and that his name was Laius.

'She already knows,' said the priest. 'Ask your question.'

'My wife, the queen, and I,' said Laius, 'we have no child. So I have come here to ask, why have we no child?'

The priest stepped up to the Pythia and spoke into her ear. Again, Laius could not hear what was whispered. The priest stepped back. The Pythia dropped her head and stared into her bowl of Kassotis water.

'You consider this a misfortune,' said the Pythia, her face down, 'not to have a child?' It was her voice, a woman's voice, but the god's voice was inside her voice. He could feel the god's force.

'I do,' said Laius.

'Well, you are wrong,' said the Pythia.

Laius registered the word. Wrong. *Wrong*? A royal couple like he and the queen were supposed to have children! The god must know that.

'Childlessness is wrong,' said Laius carefully.

'Not if it's a blessing,' said the Pythia. 'Be grateful for your childlessness. Be grateful that despite all your efforts nothing has happened yet.'

Laius heard buzzing in his head. His legs felt weak. 'I need an heir,' he said, 'a son who will rule when I am gone.'

'I know that.'

'Then can you not help?'

'Oh, I can.'

A son was there, tantalisingly certain, he thought. 'You can give me son?'

'Yes. Only you don't want him.'

'But I do,' said Laius. 'I absolutely do. I must have a son, I must have children.'

The buzzing became a pounding.

'I can give you a son, Laius. I can do that. But if I do, you will die at his hands.' The Pythia looked up from the bowl and stared into Laius's face.

'When Chrysippus failed to return home,' said the Pythia, one careful word at a time, 'his father, King Pelops, consulted the great god and the great god told him, "Laius took Chrysippus. Laius dishonoured Chrysippus. Chrysippus threw himself off Mount Phicium because he was so ashamed of what Laius had done to him."

'The news enraged and desolated King Pelops. "Laius, my guest, violated my trust," he shouted at the great god. "Laius must be punished!"

'Zeus heard the words of the broken-hearted father and he was touched. He issued his ruling.

'"If Laius has a son, the son will kill him," said the great god. This was his determination. Now do you understand why not to have a child is a blessing?'

Laius felt as light as an old dry leaf. He also felt as heavy as a stone and of such a weight he would never be able to move from where he stood. He would die there in front of the Pythia.

'You said a son would kill me,' said Laius, 'but not a daughter. Can I have a girl?'

'No!' said the Pythia.

'But you said it was to be a son who would kill me and a daughter ...'

'Stop. You will not bargain. The bad action remains with him who does it. If you have any child it will be a son. Stay childless and you will live long and die old. But have a child, *it will be a son* and he will kill you.'

The Pythia closed her eyes and shuddered. She opened her eyes again. The god had left her. His force was no longer within her. She was herself again.

'The god has spoken,' said the Pythia. Her slow, strange, stilted prophecy voice was gone and she was in her own voice now. It was soft, fluent and female. It was gentle and kind as well. 'Go,' said the Pythia. 'Go, and don't forget.'

Laius felt his hand being taken and the priest pulling. They passed through the drapes, climbed the stairs, moved through the temple, went out through the door, descended the steps and stopped out in the forecourt.

The priest said something and vanished. Laius closed his eyes. He felt the sun on his face. He was stunned. He had no thoughts, none whatsoever. He had just a pain in his head and a feeling of heavy grief. He had ruined his life.

He stood for a long time, rooted to the spot, absolutely without thought and gripped by misery. All he knew was that the sun was above because he felt it on his face. Then something loosened in his head. Thoughts followed. We will always try to escape. Even an animal, caught in a snare, will chew off its leg if it must. In Laius's case it would not be so drastic.

When he got home, Laius knew he'd have to talk to Jocasta. He'd have to tell her he'd been to Delphi. And Jocasta would want to know what the Pythia said. So what did he tell her? He couldn't tell her about Chrysippus. Or Pelops's appeal for vengeance. Or Zeus's declaration. He'd have to tell her something else. What? He saw something glimmering on the edge of his thoughts. Yes. He had it.

He would say the Pythia said he had to be childless or Thebes would falter and calamity would follow. It was a version of the truth and it sounded like something the Pythia might say. Childless he would have to remain, he would remind his queen, because when the Pythia spoke her word was final and one ignored her at one's peril. Wonder at nothing, as the saying goes.

All this, in an few moments, passed through Laius's mind. He was greatly relieved that he had a plan.

Jocasta sat in her room. Her mood was dark and resentful. Laius had been gone five days. Callidice glided up. 'Your herald,' she said quietly.

'Where? Here?'

Callidice straightened her shoulders and nodded.

'Fetch him in.' Jocasta glanced around to see who else was in the room but there was no one, only Callidice. 'And after you've shown him in, stay outside till I call you back.'

Callidice nodded. She went off, the herald entered, the door closed behind him. He approached, bobbed, nodded.

'So?' said Jocasta.

The herald moved his tongue around in his mouth and after a long pause and a great deal of effort he pushed out a single word, broken in half. 'Lai ... us,' he said. Then he added – and this time the word slipped out easily – 'Delphi.'

'Delphi?' said Jocasta. This wasn't what she expected. 'Laius was at Delphi? Are you sure?'

The herald nodded.

'And he didn't see you?'

The herald shook his head.

'You can go. Tell Callidice outside to come back.'

The herald left. Callidice returned. Instead of being relieved that Laius hadn't been away seeing a woman, angry thoughts about what Laius had done bubbled up. Why had he had not told her he was going to Delphi? A visit to the

Oracle was not a thing a husband should keep secret, especially from his wife. He hadn't said goodbye and only sent word after he'd gone. The meaning was clear. He'd meant to slight her. He'd meant to hurt her.

Her rage frothed for a while then abated and new thoughts, far worse than her angry ones, bore in. When she sent the herald off, she suspected the most likely explanation was that Laius had a concubine and that he had gone to her and that he intended her to have a child and then to bring that child back to Thebes for her to raise, as kings did. But she'd been wrong. Laius really had gone to Delphi and now she knew exactly why he had gone: their childlessness. She didn't yet know what the Pythia had ruled. She'd find out though, and the thought made her tremble. Raising someone else's child might be bad but a ruling by the Pythia would be worse. Where the needle goes the thread must follow.

It was the morning of the sixth day since Laius left. A maid approached Jocasta.

'Queen,' she said.

Jocasta looked at the girl. Her wide, flat face was freckled and her eyes shone like wet pebbles. She had a red scarf tied around her head and wore a long, plain red dress.

'Laius has returned,' said the maid. 'And he's coming here, once he's bathed.'

Jocasta issued instructions for the dress and the ornaments she wished to be wearing when Laius appeared: her necklace of gold, her earrings of gold, her bracelets of gold. The girl undressed her, redressed her, put on her jewellery. Jocasta was ready. She took a seat.

The sound of footsteps in the corridor outside. She straightened her shoulders, composed her face and settled her mind. When Laius appeared, she would hold her tongue. She would let him speak first and then, and only then, would she respond. Her words would be calm and smooth and cool. They must be. He wouldn't be candid otherwise and his candour was what she wanted. He must tell her everything and nothing she did must inhibit that.

The door opened and Laius came in. 'Everyone out now,' he shouted, 'and close the door behind.'

The maid in red and another, who was also present, left quickly, closing the door. The royal couple were alone.

'I went to Delphi,' said Laius. He was standing. He had decided not to sit.

'Yes,' she said. Until this moment she had her plan, which she had agreed with herself. She would say nothing. But now with Laius actually there, her determination melted and before she could stop herself, the words tumbled out.

'And you didn't warn me,' she said. 'You didn't even say goodbye. You just slunk off. Did you think I'd stop you? That I wouldn't want you to go? Well, if you did you're a fool.'

She stopped. The tongue always goes to the aching tooth, she thought. But it can't be helped. And in some distant part of her mind she noted glumly that with her very first utterance she had broken with her plan not to provoke. Well, that couldn't be helped either. While Laius was away her rage had grown and now it must be vented.

'Yes, a fool who knows nothing,' she continued, 'especially about his wife. Well, at least I know that now.'

'I am not required to explain everything I do before I do it,' said the king. 'It is one of privileges of being a king.'

'Oh, very pretty, very masterful,' she said, 'but you're still a fool, who slunk away without telling me where you were going and arranged things so I wouldn't learn you'd gone until after you'd left.'

'I'm warning you,' said Laius quietly – he believed this made his threat sound more effective – 'this not the time for a row. You start one, I'll just turn around and walk out. Do you understand?'

'You went without informing me,' said Jocasta. 'That was wrong. I should have been told. And you should now admit it. You should say, right now, "Yes, I was wrong." I doubt you have the courage to admit it though.'

Laius shook his head. She could not be more wrong. He had slipped away like he had, not denying where he was going but not making a lot of noise about it either, because he didn't want to provoke talk or speculation. There would be plenty of that once everyone found out where he had gone. Surely she saw that?

'If I had announced my departure and left with a lot of noise and ceremony,' he said, 'all Thebes would have got excited and worried. So instead I did something much cleverer. I was like the guest who leaves the dinner without announcing his departure, and who the other guests don't notice is gone till they themselves are leaving. I just slipped off. Nobody noticed and everything carried on. Now that I've returned, of course, there will be talk, but because I am here I will face it down.'

As soon as Laius said the word 'talk' and spoke of facing it down, Jocasta knew there was something awful coming. She felt a scratch in her throat – as she always did before she wept – but she did not want tears to come or for Laius to see them. If she couldn't be calm as she had intended, then she would be implacable, stony and determined. She squeezed her stomach. She swallowed a couple of times. She would not cry.

'Enough Laius, enough,' Jocasta shouted. 'What did you find out? I assume it's terrible. Speak to me. Something is wrong. Why have we no children? That's what you went to ask about, isn't it? I know you did. It shows in your expression. You went to ask about us, our childlessness, and our future as parents.'

'I did,' said the king.

'And if the news had been good, you'd have come straight out with it at the start. Good news always gets hurled about quickly. Bad news, on the other hand, gets held back. So, what is the bad news? We will never have a child together? If that's it, tell me now.'

Laius walked backwards and forwards, rolling his shoulders as he went.

'I'm right, aren't I?' said Jocasta. 'We'll never have a child, will we?'

'No, we can have one,' Laius said, 'a boy even, should we want one. The Pythia said, if asked, she can give us a son. But she also said that our not having children is a blessing.'

Jocasta stood and walked across the room. She came back and looked at Laius. She looked right into his dark eyes. 'That doesn't make sense,' she said. 'A child is a gift who guarantees the future. How is it a blessing not to have a child?'

In the forecourt at Delphi with the sun on his face, a notion of how he would explain what the Pythia had said had come to Laius. Throughout the journey home he'd brooded on this, polishing and refining and perfecting it. Now it only remained that he delivered it.

'If a child is the end of the future,' said Laius, 'then obviously it's not a blessing.'

'That doesn't make sense.'

'The Pythia said,' continued Laius, taking Jocasta by her shoulders, 'that the only way this city will flourish will be if I forego children.'

'The Pythia said that?'

'She did.'

'No children?'

'No.'

'So, we will never have a child, boy or girl?'

'No.'

'What sort of a life is that for a queen to lead? I was supposed to have children and one of these, a son, would follow after us and rule here in Thebes.'

'Did you not hear?' he said. 'Thebes will only thrive if I stay childless. If I have a child, it will fail. That's it. So, we will not have children. And this conversation is now over.'

Laius felt tired. Their talk had worn him out. He flopped down on a polished bench. He shook his head. He had nothing else to say. He was spent.

Jocasta's first response to the Pythia's counsel was to wonder if Laius misheard. She questioned Laius again. He repeated what he had already said.

Jocasta's second response to the Pythia's counsel was to rage. She was the queen. It was her duty to bring children into the world and to raise them. It was the natural order. And now she had been told she was to have no child. She had never heard of the like. 'It is not fair,' she said, 'that I forego children to ensure this city flourishes. I want them. I want a son.'

Laius repeated what he had said. The city would only flourish if he remained childless.

Jocasta's third response to the Pythia's counsel was to attack its injunction as illogical. It simply made no sense, she said, that a city could only thrive if its king had no child, by which she meant, of course, no son. Children added lustre to a city because they ensured the city's future, whereas childlessness tarnished a city, for without children there was no heir and without an heir strife and conflict were guaranteed.

Laius rebuffed her arguments. If he had no child but nominated a successor, Thebes prospered. But if he had a child the city failed, and that guaranteed strife.

Jocasta's fourth response to the Pythia's counsel was despair. Their marriage was over. Her life henceforward would be the life of a widow, except she wasn't a widow. Laius wasn't dead, he was alive. And being alive he could give her a child, only he wasn't going to. How would this seem to Thebes? Thebes would see a wife who had failed to do her duty. Thebes would call her barren and worse. Thebes would say the gods had determined childlessness as *her* punishment. Childlessness was always the punishment meted out by the gods to women who'd done wrong.

Of course, as she knew, as Laius knew, she'd done no wrong. She was blameless. But this didn't matter. As far as Thebes went, she would be the one at fault. All she had to look forward to now was a life of hostility and hatred, lived with the certain knowledge that when she did eventually die, her death would be met with universal joy by Thebes. Thebes would not mourn her passing. Her death would make a space for a new queen, and a new queen who would give the city an heir.

Jocasta's fifth response to the Pythia's counsel was to realise she'd missed something crucial because her own childlessness was all she could take in at first. She and Laius could turn their backs on one another in their bed and in that way ensure they did not make a child. But what if Laius met another woman who inveigled him into her bed? Jocasta could imagine, Laius being celibate, that would be easy. And once this other woman had Laius in her bed, Jocasta could predict the rest. When the arrow is on the string it must go. And then, if that woman had a child, Thebes would fail. It was not only with her that Laius must not have a child. It was with any woman. He must never stray. The really happy man must stay at home, went the proverb, and Laius must be that man. But how to make him that man? What exactly was she supposed to do?

Jocasta sat at the window. She looked out and up at a long, fat cloud in the sky. It was flat along the bottom, but then above it was a huge and swollen confusion of white and grey, thick in places, thin in other parts. The top of the cloud was rounded but ragged, and out of it rose long trails, like smoke rising from a fire.

She heard a noise behind her. Footsteps. She glanced back. It was Callidice. She carried a basket with laundry piled in it. She set the basket down and opened a chest and then transferred the clothes in the basket to the chest, one garment at a time. Each dress she lifted with reverence and then set in its place with care.

When she was finished Callidice lowered the top of the chest and picked up the basket. She nodded at the queen.

'Are you cold by the window?' Callidice asked. 'I could get a blanket.'

'No,' said Jocasta. 'You never married, did you?'

'I wouldn't have been able to,' Callidice said. 'Not allowed.'

'But supposing you had, would you have been able to manage a husband? Would you have been able to ...' She stopped. 'You know ... when you wanted to have a child or when you didn't want to have a child would you have been able to ...'

'Which?' said Callidice. 'Having or not having?'

'Not having,' said Jocasta.

Callidice laughed. 'That's an easy problem. How do you imagine I've managed? And if I was married, I'd manage the same way. I'm sure you know all about it. You hardly need to ask me.'

'Well, let's see,' said Jocasta. 'Maybe you can teach me something I don't know.'

'Maybe,' said Callidice. She didn't sound convinced.

'Go on,' said Jocasta. 'I won't be offended. Tell me everything.'

Callidice put her mouth to the queen's ear and spoke. Jocasta listened carefully, gazing up at the cloud.

BOOK SIX

Jocasta was in her dressing room with Callidice. Laius was already in the royal bed.

'Leave the jewellery,' said Jocasta. 'I'm keeping that on.'

Callidice reached down. She found the hem of Jocasta's shift and began to lift. The hem travelled up until Jocasta's face was covered by the shift and she couldn't see. Behind the cloth Jocasta waited. This was the tricky part. Callidice had to get the neck up and over her head and away from the heavy necklace around her neck and the long earrings hanging from her ears.

Jocasta felt Callidice pull and then she felt something catch, near her left ear. Her earring. She wriggled her head, thinking to work the earring free, but the snagging remained. She felt Callidice's nimble fingers near her left ear. There was small, mysterious noise and then Callidice pulled the shift higher and got it away from her head and lifted it away. Jocasta felt the night air on her skin and the sense of not being dressed on her belly and on her breasts. She liked the feeling of being bare. She threw her shoulders back and moved her head. She touched her earrings and her necklace. Her fingers told her that everything was just so.

She turned her back on Callidice, standing with her shift and watching. She opened the door and went through to the king and queen's bedroom and closed the door behind. There were night lights dotted about. Their burning tapers produced a pale, trembling light.

Jocasta went up to the bed and stopped. She stared at the dark form stretched in front of her. Laius was on his back. There was just enough light for her to see his eyes were open. He was staring up into the dark. What was he thinking about? she wondered. Was it of her? He must have heard her feet moving on the floor and he must sense how close to him she was standing. He couldn't not know she was in the room with him. Only he wasn't acknowledging that truth. On the contrary, he was acting as if he was on his own and she was nowhere near him.

It was painful as well as strange to be invisible like this. Previously, at this point, in their life as husband and wife, he would always turn and look at her. Then, sometimes he'd smile, sometimes he'd extend a hand for her to take and pull her down, and sometimes he'd move his head so she would understand she was to cross round to his side and stand where he could stare at her. But whatever he did there was never any doubt that he saw her just as she saw him. But now, though she was standing so very close to him, he did not see her. How vexing. How dare he. She was there and he would see her. She would make him.

She bent down and breathed her warm breath onto his face. In and out, in and out. And he felt her warm breath. She knew he did. Yet no reaction to her warm breath playing on his cheeks came from him. In that case she would speak to him and she very much doubted he would be able to lie still as a stone and pretend she was not there when she did.

'My skin is golden in the dark,' she said. 'The night makes it glow.'

'Yes,' said Laius slowly.

'How would you know if you haven't looked?' she said.

'I just do.'

Jocasta took his right hand and lifted it across and put it on her left hip.

'There I am,' she said. 'Can you feel my skin and the bone below?'

Laius said nothing. Infuriating man. She laid his hand back on the bed. She returned to her side, picked up the sheet and got in beside Laius. Then she folded herself against him so the whole front of her body was touching the whole side of his body.

'Are you just going to lie there all night pretending I'm not here?' she said. 'Will you not turn to me?'

Laius stayed stock still, staring upwards, saying nothing.

'I smell of gold.' Jocasta touched his shoulder. 'You like it when I smell of gold.'

He still didn't reply. She would have to do something else. She would speak her thoughts, her actual thoughts. That would get his attention.

'Why doesn't he turn to me?' said Jocasta out loud. 'Why is he acting as if I'm not here? Why is he pretending I don't exist?'

'I'm just lying here quietly,' he said, 'minding my own thoughts.' She heard him swallow. 'A king is allowed to lie in his bed and think. Or didn't you know that?'

'If you don't reply occasionally, how will I know you've heard me, or that I exist?'

'Oh, from now on, every time you say anything, no matter how meaningless, am I supposed to say, "Oh yes, I hear you." Is that it? I tell you this; you carry on with the whee-dling, it will only end one way. I will stop sleeping in the room with you. I will take myself off to another room and you will never see me.'

She felt fluttering deep down, her legs quivering and a hot, tender feeling in the back of her throat; the signs that she might cry. Since Laius's return from the Pythia, they had had no life as man and woman, as husband and wife. And now he was threat-ening to withdraw entirely from their bed. She would not even have his body to warm herself against in the night.

'I asked you a question earlier and you didn't answer.' She swept her hair back from her forehead. 'I'm going to ask it again. Are you just going to lie there all night on your back pretending I'm not here? Will you not turn to me?'

'I mustn't turn,' said Laius.

This time he wasn't bristling. His voice was quiet. He even sounded a little downcast. She swallowed to soothe her hurting throat and as she did her thoughts floated in. He was such an inflexible man. She must make him understand: they could have something, which was better than nothing, providing they were careful.

'Listen,' she said. 'We can be husband and wife while avoiding what you dread. You know that.'

'Oh,' he said.

One word, but it was sign. She knew his ability to resist could be overthrown if she persisted. And now was the moment.

She reached across and stroked first his shoulder and then the palm of his hand. He liked to be stroked there. She heard his breathing change.

'Every creature does according to its nature,' she said. 'You can no more stop yourself, than you can order the waves back. You are what you are. And here am I and I can't stop being what I am, either.' She moved her hand across his chest and down to his stomach. 'We can still be one, we can still be together and yet avoid a child.'

She kissed his shoulder and moved her hand down and began to fondle Laius between his legs. 'Pull back at the end,' she said. 'This way we have everything and nothing.'

They began to make love …

'Yes,' she whispered. 'Go on, go on.' She tilted her pelvis towards him. His hands came down and took hold of her behind her hips. It was coming, the end was coming.

'Go on, go on.' she called. Everything faster and faster.

Laius pulled out of her just before he finished and his seed spilled onto her thighs and the mouth of her sex. It was warm and thick.

Laius took himself off her and lay on his side facing her. Jocasta did not stir but stayed lying on her back. She heard Laius's breathing slowing as he drifted towards sleep. She felt Laius's seed cooling. As it cooled it dried and as it dried it pulled her skin taut.

Tonight was a victory, she thought. This way she would keep him in their bed. And whatever happened she must keep him there.

Her thoughts rolled on. She would have to practise other kinds of pleasure. She would take him in her mouth. He would take her like a boy. A little goose fat and it was easy. By these ploys she would keep Laius close and they would avoid a child. But what if? There was always a chance, wasn't there? If that happened, she would go to the old midwife. The wise woman would give her laserwort. Laserwort would save them.

*

In the royal bedroom night lights flickered. The royal pair were in the royal bed. Laius was on Jocasta, drilling into her. She felt him heaving up and down, and smelt the smell of his wine breath. He had had a lot of wine earlier. She heard his breath too. His breath went faster and faster and faster. He must stop. He must pull out. She pushed her hips down to make him come out but at the very same instant she did this, she heard the little cry he always made on completion.

Laius rolled off her, turned his back towards her and before long, as Jocasta could tell from the quiet, even way of his breathing, he was fast asleep.

Jocasta lay still, looking up into the dark. She should have been feeling Laius's seed cooling and as it cooled, she should have felt it drying, and as it dried she should have felt her skin going taut. This was what had happened on those nights since Callidice whispered to her what she must do. But Jocasta wasn't feeling his seed drying and tightening now. She was feeling a small milky tear coming out and running down her thigh. Oh, she realised, Laius, in his drunken state, had spilled his seed inside her. She felt her heart heaving and pushing against her ribs. Here was everything she wanted and dreaded in one moment. Had what had never happened before happened this time? How could she know? She'd have to wait before she could be sure.

In the morning, when the king woke, he looked at her and asked, 'What happened last night?'

'Nothing,' Jocasta said.

'Nothing?'

'Nothing.'

'Are we safe?'

'Yes.' Jocasta didn't think he believed her but he didn't say anything else.

Laius got up and went about his day. He didn't believe what Jocasta said. She was right. But he decided he would say nothing, not yet. He would bide his time. He would watch and wait.

Jocasta knew herself well. She knew when she should bleed.

She counted down the days until the day came. Nothing.

She waited another day. Nothing.

She waited a third. Still nothing.

She bathed and dressed and took herself to the midwife. She found the old woman sitting on a stool outside her door, dozing. All she need do now, Jocasta told herself, was walk up to her, wake her and ask for the bitter draught. But instead of doing this she stopped several paces short of the midwife. Once she'd glibly thought she'd take the draught, if or when she had to, and that would be that; but now, when she was a spear's length or so from the dozing midwife, she understood she'd been wrong. She might have thought she could swallow the bitter draught without any difficulty but now that she carried a life she knew she couldn't. It would be a crime for which she would be punished.

Her mind moved on. She would keep the child. But if she kept the child, what then? The answer came to her then in quick hot thrusts, as she stood a spear's length from the dozing midwife.

Her problem, she realised, was she had forgotten that everything has two handles and she was holding the wrong one. All she had to do was grab hold of the other one and all would be well. Had the Pythia said anything about her having to be childless? No. The Pythia had said not one word about her. It was Laius who must be childless in order for Thebes to thrive, not her. That's what the Pythia had said.

And he would be childless. It could be contrived. She would bear the child and, immediately after it was born, she would send it away. Far away. To foster parents in a distant land. The foster parents would swear an oath never to reveal whose child they had and always to maintain the child was theirs. She might visit from time to time but she would not let on to the child who she was because she too would have taken an oath never to reveal the truth. To everyone, including the child, the foster parents would be *the* parents. Laius, meanwhile, would appear childless because his child would never claim him as the father. A father was only a father because he was known as the father by his child. If he wasn't known as the father, he wasn't a father and therefore he was a childless man. And if Laius was childless then Thebes must prosper like the Pythia promised. This was what Jocasta decided.

And having thought all this, Jocasta immediately felt lighter, relieved, buoyed up, even hopeful. And these lovely feelings reinforced her belief that her thinking must be right. And, how wonderful to know she could have the child and occasionally see the child, yet ensure Laius appeared childless and thereby guarantee Thebes flourished. She could have it all. Jocasta had always thought of herself as a fox who knew many things but now it occurred to her that actually she was a hedgehog who only knew one great thing.

Jocasta turned from the midwife, still sleeping and oblivious that she had been so near, and began to retrace her steps towards her rooms, her thoughts humming. Now she knew where she wanted to go, she needed to work out how to get there. But with a scorpion sleeping under every stone, she would need to exercise extreme care.

Her immediate task was to keep her secret a secret. When Laius had asked, 'Are we safe?' the morning after and she had said 'Yes,' he hadn't really believed her. And Laius was a sly man. He would know better than to ask her again. He could find out by going to Callidice, for instance. He could put a simple question and Callidice's answer would tell him. Jocasta would have to talk to the laundress – mentioning Antimedes in the process would do no harm – and bind her to silence until such time as she informed Laius, which wouldn't be any time soon. Certainly not. On that point she'd wait till she began to show, by which time, it would be too late for the midwife's draught. There would be arguments then, of course there would but at that stage it would be too late to abort. You can't unscramble eggs, she would say to Laius, before explaining what she planned to do with the child after it was born.

Jocasta reached the steps that led to her rooms and began to climb, quickly, lightly, brightly.

Do I blame Jocasta for allowing herself to believe her scheme would work? Not for an instant. Hers is a common error. We all deceive ourselves. It's what we excel at. There are never any faults in the things we want badly.

It was morning. The water had been carried to her room in jars. Jocasta was due to bathe.

'I want Callidice, not you,' she said to the maid with the flat, freckled face and the eyes like wet pebbles who was due to wash and dress her. 'Go on, fetch her.'

Callidice was brought up from the laundry room. She

smelt of potash. Her face was red. Her dress was damp and stuck to her in places.

'Antimedes goes out to Mount Cithaeron, doesn't he?' said Jocasta when she and Callidice were alone.

'Yes,' said Callidice. Mount Cithaeron was where the royal flocks grazed, so all the shepherds, including her son, went there.

'I have been told he is a hard worker,' said Jocasta.

Callidice knew this was one of those standard compliments that the powerful liked to trot out and to which the powerless, to whom the compliment was usually paid, could only respond in one way. They must smile and show gratitude.

'Thank you,' said Callidice. Her tone was meek and sweet. She smiled to indicate gratitude that Jocasta should speak about her son as she had but deep inside Callidice felt a tremble of anxiety. Why was the queen interested in Antimedes? She couldn't remember Jocasta ever asking about him before. Indeed, Callidice doubted Jocasta would even recognise Antimedes if she passed him. Yet here she was asking her questions about him.

'Well, it's hardly surprising he's such a hard worker, is it?'

Callidice waited, unsure where this was going or how to react. Jocasta saw her uncertainty and pointed at her.

'Obviously he gets it from you – you are a very hard worker,' said Jocasta.

This second compliment coming on top of the first could only mean one thing. Jocasta was preparing to ask her something and Callidice already knew this would be something she wouldn't want to do.

'I …' Callidice closed her mouth. Jocasta stared at her. Callidice lowered her eyes. She must show gratitude but with a thread of modesty added for balance. It didn't do to have too high an estimate of one's achievements, particularly when talking to a queen.

'I don't know,' said Callidice. She waited. What was the queen going to say?

'I'm ready,' she heard Jocasta say.

Callidice looked up and saw Jocasta had put her arms up in the air. Callidice knew what was required. She took the hem of her dress and lifted it away. She saw all of Jocasta, her smooth skin, the dark, wiry hair between her legs.

Jocasta stepped over the narrow lip and into the shallow wooden bath and sat down. Callidice poured one jug of water after another over different parts of the queen. Then she stood and Callidice patted every part of her body dry, from top to the bottom.

Next, Callidice fetched the oil bowl and the oiler. The oiler was a flat stone with a skin wrapped around it. The cloth was gathered at the back and tied with animal gut into a handle.

Callidice dipped the oiler in the oil and began to rub oil onto Jocasta's neck and shoulders. The oil was brown but once applied it did not change the colour of Jocasta's skin. It just made her skin glisten and shine. And it made her look more solid, like she was made of stone.

Callidice went lower, rubbing Jocasta's breasts, her ribs and then began to oil her belly. Jocasta put her hand out and stopped Callidice's hand.

'Do you see anything?' Jocasta asked. There was only one reason she would ask that question.

'No,' said Callidice.

Jocasta peeled one of Callidice's hands from the oiler and put it on her belly. 'Do you feel anything now?'

'No,' said Callidice.

She pressed Callidice's hand down. 'You don't feel anything at all?' Callidice felt cords of muscle under the skin. Otherwise she felt nothing.

'No.'

'You will.'

Now Callidice understood.

'I won't be bleeding for the next while,' said Jocasta. 'But if Laius asks, you tell him I do and every month you wash my things. You understand?'

Callidice nodded.

'I am glad you understand,' said Jocasta. 'Do not let me down.'

Callidice nodded again to show she wouldn't let her down and that she had understood.

'You can go on oiling me,' said Jocasta.

When the oiling was over Jocasta asked for a particular purple dress. As Callidice padded over the smooth floor towards the chest where the dress was kept, her stomach pulsed. Jocasta had asked her to lie to the king. And if she were brought before Laius and interrogated, what would she do? Should she tell the truth? Or should she lie?

If she told the truth Jocasta would punish her for breaking her promise. Something horrible would happen, though she wasn't certain what. She would certainly be sold. If she lied, Laius might initially believe her but once Jocasta began to show he'd know Callidice had lied to him. He'd have her whipped, the customary punishment for slaves who were caught out lying.

She was in trouble, whatever she did, and on top of that it wasn't just her. Antimedes was in trouble as well. Why else had Jocasta asked after him if it wasn't to remind his mother that if she fell, Antimedes would be pulled down too?

Callidice's legs quivered. She wanted to sit down. That was impossible. She had been sent to fetch Jocasta's dress and fetch it she would. She located the dress. She carried it back. She dressed Jocasta. Then she brushed and platted and arranged the queen's hair and put on all her jewellery. Then she left the royal room and went into the corridor. Here she began to shake badly. She put her hand against the corridor wall to steady herself.

'What's wrong?' It was the maid with the freckled face.

Callidice shook her head. 'Give me today and take tomorrow,' she said.

The maid screwed up her face. 'What do you mean?' she asked. 'Are you sick?'

'I'm not myself,' said Callidice. 'Ignore what I said.' Callidice pushed herself from the wall and staggered away.

BOOK SEVEN

Jocasta and Laius lay in bed, side by side. Jocasta turned her head sideways and glanced at the king. His lips were closed and he was utterly still. She looked up into the black above. She listened to her breath and to his breath. They were breathing slowly, in and out and in parallel yet separate at the same time.

As she lay there, Jocasta's mind began to turn and thoughts came. In the end, the truth must emerge and it would happen in one of two ways. Laius might somehow find out. She didn't like this idea and it made her shiver. Or, she might tell him. She liked that idea better. Of course, she wouldn't tell Laius straight out. She'd have to introduce him to the facts in a slow and careful way. And she'd probably have to do it at night, when they were in bed, like they were now.

She pictured the scene: the two of them lying here, side by side, just like they were this night. Then, in her mind, she heard herself speaking.

'You are thoughtful this evening,' she would say in her lowest, quietest, most alluring voice. 'What is it you are thinking about? I will help you bear the load of whatever it is you are carrying.'

She imagined the effect of her words. Laius would be soothed by them. He would be charmed. He would speak back in a smooth, calm voice. He would say, 'What I am thinking about is you. What have you on your mind, will you tell me?'

'Ah well, what I have to tell you,' she would reply, 'is something rather huge, and shocking. The truth is, I'm going to have a child. But listen to me. I have a plan. The moment it is born it will go straightaway to foster parents. It's all arranged, they live far away, and they will bring it up as their own, and you and I will have no contact with the child whatsoever, though I might visit it from time to time. I will never let the child know who we are, either, because as far as that child is concerned the foster parents are its parents. It will never know who you are or where you are. It will never come and harm you ...'

When she came to the end of her speech Jocasta imagined Laius smiling and murmuring 'Yes, yes,' to signal he agreed with her and then taking her hand and squeezing it.

Meanwhile, and at the very same moment that Jocasta was imagining their conversation, Laius was thinking about the same subject, though his thoughts were very different to hers.

Though she'd said nothing, Laius felt sure that the night she denied it happened they'd slipped up and it had, and now Jocasta was carrying. But if he asked her, straight out, she wasn't going to tell him, was she? So, what did he do. He had to know.

Then it came, quick and bright and hard. Callidice, he thought. The laundress could tell him. In fact, now he came to think about it, Jocasta had probably anticipated this. She was clever and cunning, after all. She'd surely talked to Callidice and made her promise not to tell him, if he questioned her, that she wasn't washing Jocasta's scraps and rags. In which case, he'd have to talk to Callidice in such a way that she would forget what she'd promised Jocasta and tell him everything.

Then he had another thought. Callidice had a son, didn't she? He was one of his shepherds. What was his name?

Antimedes? That was it. He was a quick, reasonable, hardworking fellow, Laius remembered, and he was much attached to his mother and she much attached to him. His worst might not necessarily make the mother buckle but if he dragged in the son she would be sure to yield up her secrets. Oh yes, if Callidice thought Antimedes might suffer, she'd definitely talk.

His thoughts ran on. As far as squeezing the facts out of Callidice he'd do it in two stages. To start things going he'd send a royal attendant to see Callidice. He knew exactly who, the unpopular one with the high cheekbones and the fluting voice. This attendant would be rough and he'd mention Antimedes because Laius would tell him to. Callidice would be scared by her encounter. She'd sense she was in danger, as was her son. Laius would let her stew for a few days. Then Laius would call her in. He would make the laundress confirm what Jocasta had made her swear not to divulge, which, the more he thought about it, the more certain he was Jocasta had done. But just to be sure, he had to hear it from Callidice and then, once he'd heard it, he could turn to Jocasta and she would be in no position then to deny it.

The next morning Laius woke early and remembered what he had planned the night before. He slipped out of bed without waking the queen and went to set things in motion.

Callidice was sitting outside the laundry on a stool, back and head to the wall, feet and legs side by side. She wore a short work dress, an apron over her dress and a headscarf. Her eyes were closed and her face tilted at the sky. She felt the heat of the sun on her eyelids. She was not awake and she was not asleep. She was somewhere between the two.

'You. Wake up!'

She felt a hard bang on the side of her knee. It hurt. She let out a cry. She opened her eyes and saw, standing in front of her, a royal attendant. It was the one with the high cheekbones and the fluting voice. He carried a polished wooden staff and she guessed this was what he'd just hit her with. 'Why did you hit me?' she said.

'How else was I to wake you?' he laughed. 'Are you Jocasta's laundress?'

'Yes,' said Callidice. 'I have that honour.' What did this man want? Why had he sought her out?

'Just her laundress?' asked the royal attendant. 'Do you do anything else?'

'Sometimes I help her to bathe. I help her to dress. I comb her hair. And I sweep her rooms. I clean them.'

'Aren't we doing well,' said the royal attendant.

Callidice said nothing. A wolf is accused, whether he is guilty or not guilty. The royal attendant could sneer and she had to take it. That's how it was.

'You've a son?' said the royal attendant.

Callidice nodded.

'Antimedes,' he said.

'A shepherd,' she said. 'Just a youth.'

The royal attendant turned on his heel and left. Callidice felt something inside her body shrink while at the same time her heart began to pound. She got up and began to walk back towards the laundry. Her leg hurt. The attendant had really hit her hard. And then he'd said all those strange things. She knew something was about to happen and she knew it wouldn't be good.

*

It is peculiarly painful to know something awful is slithering towards one, while at the same time also knowing there is nothing one can do to get away. Small, powerless people are familiar with this misery.

When she got up the following morning Callidice looked at her left leg and saw a black bruise running from her calf over the side of her knee and up her thigh. One or two other women in the laundry noticed the bruise as well, later in the day.

'What happened to your leg?' one of these women asked.

'I got a kick,' said Callidice. 'From a donkey.'

'I hope you thrashed the beast back,' said the woman.

'I did,' said Callidice, but she knew her listeners didn't believe her.

Jocasta was alone in her room. She felt her waist, all the way round as far as she could reach. Then she prodded up and down her front. Had she started to thicken? She didn't think so. Thus far there was nothing Laius could notice.

Hermes told my father he admired the manner in which Jocasta let nothing slip for as long as she did. That showed her mettle, he said.

Callidice was in the laundry pounding garments with a paddle.

'You.' It was the royal attendant with the high cheek-bones, the one who'd hit her.

'Yes?' said Callidice,

'Follow me,' said the royal attendant. She followed him out of the laundry and across the courtyard outside. Callidice limped as she went. Her leg still hurt where he had hit her.

'You're dragging,' said the royal attendant. 'What happened? Hurt your leg?'

He raised his staff to stop her. Then, with the tip of his staff, he lifted her hem to reveal the bruise. It was yellow in places, the colour of old earwax.

'Nasty,' he said. 'Nasty.'

The royal attendant herded her into the palace, then drove her along a succession of corridors. She sensed the very thing she had been dreading since Jocasta issued her injunction – an interview with the king – was coming. The thought made her fizz and pop and boil inside. Jocasta had instructed her to lie. Could she? As she hobbled along she wished the earth would open and swallow her. She remembered animals she had seen being led away by crowds of worshippers to be sacrificed. She'd always suspected the animals had known the worst was coming. She sensed, like those beasts she remembered, she too was being dragged to her doom.

Callidice and the royal attendant arrived at a closed door in a part of the palace she had never been in before. The attendant knocked on the wood. The door opened. A man came out.

'In,' said the royal attendant.

The royal attendant shoved her forward. She found herself in a dark room. The king was in front of her, standing in the middle of the room. Deep in her middle she felt a bubbling sensation. The bubbles were small, like the ones in a pan of water threading up towards the surface as the water warms.

'Leave your staff and wait outside,' said the king to the royal attendant.

The royal attendant set his staff against the wall, went out and closed the door behind.

'You do Jocasta's laundry, don't you?'

'Yes.' The bubbles grew bigger.

'Has she bled recently?'

The water murmured as it began to boil and bubbles burst the surface. 'Yes,' said Callidice.

The king crossed the room, took the staff, then swung it really hard. He caught Callidice on the back of her thighs. She screamed in surprise and pain and fell to the floor like a sack.

'Really?' said Laius. 'Think again. Yes or no?'

He whacked Callidice's shoulder. She screeched and slid sideways. Laius followed, jabbing at her as he did. 'Yes or no?' he shouted. 'Yes or no?'

'No,' said Callidice. The word flew out before she could stop it.

Laius put his foot on Callidice's ankle to stop her wriggling away and stabbed with the staff at her thighs, hips, belly. He stabbed hard. He intended to hurt.

'Did Jocasta tell you to lie about this?'

'No,' shouted Callidice.

'Yes or no, yes or no?' shouted Laius.

He pressed his foot down, crushing her ankle.

'Yes,' Callidice shouted. 'Yes.'

He prodded her again, savagely. 'She told you to lie about it?'

'Yes.'

'So, she's carrying a child and she didn't want me to know and she told you to keep me ignorant?'

'Yes.'

'You've a son, a shepherd, haven't you?' said Laius.

'Yes,' said Callidice. 'Antimedes.'

She felt feverish. Jocasta had asked about him and the royal attendant had mentioned him and now the king was asking about him. This couldn't be good.

'You say a word to the queen about today and what you have told me,' he said, 'I will have him taken to Mount Phicium and thrown off. Do you understand?'

Laius took his foot off Callidice's ankle. 'Get up,' he said.

He lifted her by her shoulders and stood her on her feet. He looked into her eyes. Her body throbbed. Her brain was locked. The violence had stopped all thinking.

'You never saw me today,' said Laius. 'We never spoke. You will not mention this conversation to your queen. Or anyone. Nor will you tell anyone the queen is carrying. Understand?'

'Yes.'

He handed her the staff. It was thick, heavy, polished, lethal. 'Give the attendant his staff, will you?' said Laius. 'He's standing outside.'

Callidice hobbled across the room. The small of her back, her hips and her legs were where she felt sorest. She opened the door and went out. The royal attendant was in the corridor.

'Enjoy that?' he said and smirked.

'Your staff,' said Callidice. She felt her voice trembling. She proffered the royal attendant his staff.

'Well,' said the attendant, taking it and winking at her, 'thank you very much. That's very kind of you. Very kind indeed.'

The attendant went back in to the king and Callidice went away along the corridor. In the room, physical pain had stopped her thinking. Now she was out of the room, her thoughts started again though they were slow and sluggish. Jocasta had asked her to lie and she'd failed to lie. The king had beaten the truth out of her. Then the king had told her to lie. And somehow, mixed up in it all, though she didn't understand why, was her son.

She stopped. Her insides were trembling and fluttering. She put her hand to her face. She was sweating. Her face was wet with tears. She was crying and she hadn't even noticed. She wiped her face with her apron. Nobody must know anything was amiss. She must go back to the laundry. She must smile. She must keep everything hidden.

She dropped her apron and smoothed her front. She started to walk. Her whole body ached and vibrated with pain. But she managed to keep walking on and nobody she passed appeared to notice how ungainly her movements were or that anything was wrong with her.

In the room where Laius had just wrung the terrible truth from Callidice, the royal attendant stood, awaiting his instructions, while the king sat, his eyes closed, his head resting on his hands. So, there it was, Laius thought. His wife was carrying. As he'd suspected. What to do? Laserwort? No, it was too late for that. She'd have to have it and then, once it was born the problem would have to be dealt with. He began to work things out.

First, he needed a birth-house. That was easy. He'd use a secluded royal dwelling near Mount Cithaeron's foothills, a lodge where he sometimes stayed when he was hunting. Of course, he'd need a pretext to send Jocasta there, but that could be arranged. He would give out in Thebes that the queen was unwell. Then he'd send her there until after the birth and while she was there no one in the city would know anything. Now, while she was away she would have to have a small hand-picked group with her. Who would he send? Laius pondered on.

There were the twin sisters, both mutes who worked about the palace – old, hardworking women, who only communicated in a private language of their own. They'd be ideal. They could do the fires and the cooking and draw the water and all the domestic work.

Then there was the boy with the split lip who slept in the kitchen and who spoke mostly in single words, expressed with enormous difficulty in a strange, flat tone that listeners found unnerving. Laius would send him along too. The boy with the split lip could carry messages and do the mutes' bidding.

To attend to Jocasta, to wash her, to oil her, to dress her, there was only one candidate, the only person he believed, apart from himself and Jocasta, who knew the queen was carrying: Callidice. Until all this was over it was imperative the wretched laundress was far away and unable to talk to anyone from Thebes, so she would have to go to.

To get the queen and her party to the birth-house, two carriages would be sufficient. That meant two drivers. Polyphontes would be one and the other, a silent, taciturn fellow, wouldn't talk either. There'd have to be a herald of course. He'd use the one who hadn't been able to speak much since he'd been cudgelled. On Jocasta's orders, as Laius had subsequently discovered, this herald had followed him to Delphi: this man had even watched Laius as he sat waiting to go into the Pythia – and Laius hadn't known he was there. He was good. Later, when the birth itself was about to happen, Laius would send the midwife who'd brought him into the world and who'd carried him to the court of King Pelops. She was trustworthy too.

And finally, the last figure in his scheme was Antimedes. He would be nearby, on Cithaeron and after the birth he would do what had to be done, and if he baulked his mother would be there to persuade him. The young shepherd would take the newborn to the slopes he knew so well. He'd find some little nook or crevice nobody went to. He would lie the newborn down there. He would leave. And that would be that. Starvation or wild animals would do the rest.

Once everything had been taken care of, he'd send the same drivers and the same herald back to the birth-house. The queen and her party would be carried back to Thebes and Antimedes would go back to the slopes unless, of course, … well, perhaps he might have to promote the shepherd, but that was the work of another day.

And that would be that, Laius thought. No one in Thebes would know what had happened to the queen while she was away and the newborn would be gone. There would be no taint on his or Jocasta's head. Everything would continue as before. He would be childless and Thebes would thrive, as the Pythia predicted. That was Laius's plan.

Callidice was with the queen. She had washed her and now she was oiling her. 'Do you notice anything,' Jocasta asked when Callidice ran the oiler over her belly.

'No,' said Callidice.

'Has my husband said anything to you?'

'No,' said Callidice.

'Are you sure?'

'No,' said Callidice again, holding herself very tight and hoping her bruises didn't show. After the queen was oiled, Callidice went off and got a dress from the chest and came back.

'You're limping,' said Jocasta.

'It's nothing,' said Callidice.

'Let me see.'

'It's nothing,' said Callidice again.

'I order you,' said Jocasta. 'Show me.'

Callidice put down the dress and lifted her hem a little.

'Higher,' said Jocasta, 'higher.'

Callidice crept the hem up and showed the bruise from the time the royal attendant beat her as well as the bruises from the beating Laius had administered. The bruises were mauve, yellow and green, colours that were never seen except on a damaged body.

'What happened?' asked Jocasta.

'I fell over.'

'You want to look where you're going.'

Callidice dropped the hem. 'I feel different,' said Jocasta. She cupped her breasts. She pointed at her middle. 'Are you sure I'm not showing?'

'No,' said Callidice. Her stomach trembled. The more she heard from the queen, the worse she felt. She wished she could always be in the laundry and never leave it and never have anything to do with the queen and the king and whatever was happening between them ever again.

The next time he saw his mother, Antimedes noticed she was moving stiffly. 'What's wrong?' he asked. 'Did you fall?'

She wouldn't tell him at first but, in the end, she told him first she was struck by an attendant and then that Laius had beaten her with a staff.

'Why?' he asked.

'I can't tell you,' she said, and though he pressed she wouldn't.
'I'll tell you one day,' she said. 'I just can't tell you now.'

Jocasta woke with Laius's hands on her stomach. He was pressing down in one place after another with his fingertips as if he were feeling for something.

'What are you doing?' she said.

'You're looking heavier,' he said. 'I was seeing if it was true.'

'No, I'm not,' said Jocasta. 'Nothing has changed about me.'
He lay back.

'I'm the same as always,' said Jocasta, though this was not true. In the mornings she was sometimes sick. She felt tired all the time. She fell asleep in the day. She was thicker, somehow. She couldn't see it but she felt she was. Deep in her breasts she felt tingling. Of course, she was careful to stop any anxiety showing. She was always vigilant, always calm, always seemingly unruffled. But still, it was happening; she was changing even if nothing showed yet.

'Truth and morning always become light with time,' said Laius.

The stick falls on the sore, always. During this period my mother felt threads of anxiety darting through her all the time. It was agony and she longed for this secrecy to end but she also dreaded what would happen when it did and so she put it off until she couldn't put it off any more ...

Night lights guttered in the royal bedroom. The darkness around the points of light had a mobile, shifty, unstable feel. Outside, the only sound was a cat, making a noise like tiles being smashed.

Laius was already in bed, on his back, quietly considering the scheme he'd devised since he beat the truth out of Callidice. The more he thought about it, the more certain he became it would work. It was as if he were a traveller who had climbed the first hill of a long journey he had to make and had seen all that lay ahead in one sweep, and now it only remained that he put one foot in front of the other and go forward, all the way to the end.

Jocasta entered and padded across the floor towards her side. She was naked. As she drew closer, Laius turned sideways to face her. Then he propped his head up on his forearm. It was too dark to see his eyes but she knew what he was doing now. He was staring at her belly. Since the morning she had woken to find his hands on her middle, probing, pressing, exploring, she had often noticed him staring intently at her like this. But there was nothing to see. In time, yes, but not yet.

She took the sheet, lifted it and slipped under. Laius flopped onto his back. She glanced sideways. He had closed his eyes. He had put his hands together and laid them on his chest.

Jocasta turned and stared up at the ceiling. Laius was impossible to grasp this evening. He was just a blank, an unreadable blank. Was it possible he did not know? Or did he know but was keeping his knowledge hidden?

Sometimes she thought he did know but had decided to hide his knowledge by being silent and aloof. And sometimes she thought he was silent and aloof simply because he was moody. In and of themselves his behaviours confirmed nothing. Not definitely.

And then if he did know, how did he know? Her secret was still a secret, wasn't it? But she couldn't be sure.

One moment she thought he didn't know, the next she thought he might, the third she was back to thinking he didn't, and so on.

But his knowing or not knowing was also an irrelevance. Once the moon was full, it must begin to wane; once the waters were high, they must overflow. At some point he would realise, if he hadn't already. At some point, she would show. Should she really do nothing and wait for that moment to arrive? That seemed wrong. No, she must do something. She must take the initiative. Obviously, she couldn't just blurt it out. If he was to agree to her plan, which was to let the child come and then give it away to foster parents who lived far from Thebes who would bring it up as their own, her words must emerge slowly, quietly and without causing rancour. Not only must they not provoke him – they must carry him, persuade him.

So how might she create the right atmosphere that would allow her to speak of what she ached to speak of, which in turn would be followed by Laius agreeing to what she proposed? After love, she thought. That was the only way. First there must be love and then she would tell him.

And why wait any longer? Why not do this now? The thought came with considerable force. She would reach out to him and then, afterwards, she would whisper the words she had ready and waiting to be spoken.

Jocasta stretched forward and touched Laius's hip. She scooted closer and lower, positioning herself for the next part. Her intention was obvious. But before she could go on, Laius's hand dropped onto hers and gripped it. He wasn't holding her so hard that it hurt, but there was no mistaking the fact that his hold was forceful and not amorous. He knew exactly what she was about to do and this was not what he wanted.

She felt Laius lift her hand up and put it down in the middle of her belly. He was sending a message, she thought. He knew. She felt a hot flush of despair. What a fool she was. She thought she was clever, watchful and capable, but she'd gone about this in completely the wrong way. She'd gone about everything in completely the wrong way.

'When I returned from the Oracle of Delphi,' said Laius, 'do you remember what I told you?'

Now she knew for sure. 'Yes,' she said, taking care to sound neutral.

'And what did I tell you?'

'You must be childless.'

'And you propose to ignore that?'

Where her hand rested, his hand on top of it, her skin boiled. She wriggled in the bed to displace the weight. Laius took his hand from hers and she lifted her hand away. She threw off the sheet. Her belly, exposed to the air, was damp and sweating.

'You're not answering,' said Laius.

'What is there to say?'

'"I'm carrying a child," is what.'

So, it was out, at last, and undeniable. For a moment she wondered how he had found out but she quickly decided that no longer mattered. He knew. That was all that mattered. And now that he knew she no longer needed to be quiet or polite, submissive or ambiguous. She could just speak the truth.

'You took me, you made this. I didn't force you. You had too much wine and you were careless.'

'So, I am to blame?'

This was pointless. She would try a different approach. 'What do we do?' she said.

In Laius's mind, a series of memory shards appeared involuntarily, one after the next, which were sharp, bright, quick and fierce; Chrysippus on the chariot floor crying out as Laius forced himself into him; washing Chrysippus's shit off his penis, and the strange vegetable smell that came off it and that he then realised arose from the roasted tomatoes they'd eaten together the day before; waking in his bed that first morning in Thebes and finding Chrysippus gone; touching the place where Chrysippus had been asleep beside him and finding it was cold; his interview with the gatekeeper who told him Chrysippus had slipped out of the city early; the strange, sweet, putrid odour at Delphi; the Pythia on the tripod in the dark; the Pythia's words spoken in her strange voice; 'I can give you a son, Laius. I can do that. But if I do, you will die at his hands.'

'If I have a child,' he said, 'the Pythia said I will have to pay a penalty.'

'That wasn't what you said before,' said Jocasta. 'You only said Thebes thrives if you're childless. You said nothing about a penalty.'

'Yes, but if I'm not childless,' said Laius, 'then there's a penalty.' He still hoped this version would be sufficient but as he spoke the words he doubted they would be. 'The city fails,' he said, 'that's the penalty. Remember, every fountain goes down to the sea.'

Threads of anxiety ran through Jocasta. Laius's tone, she thought, was bleak. He seemed hollow, defeated. Her proposal would not find favour if this was his mood. She would have to move him to a different place.

'Maybe you're taking this all too seriously,' she began. 'You said that if you have a child the city falters. So, let's imagine that happens. You have a child. The city begins to fail. It won't happen quickly. It'll be gradual. And what will happen as, I don't know, some people get sick, some springs run dry, the harvest is poor? Well, factions will form. One lot of men will think you are to blame, another will think you aren't. But you will still be king and kings have power. You will play this faction off against that one. That's how to manage in bad times.

'And you are not just ingenious. You are a superb helmsman too. You will not let the ship sink. You will bring Thebes through the storm. You will get her safely into harbour. You will prevail!' Jocasta felt quite pleased with the last part. It made sense, she thought.

'Wrong,' said Laius. He would have to tell her, he realised. If he didn't, she would never understand, and if she didn't understand, they'd never get through this.

'The Pythia told me something else,' he began.

'Something else you didn't tell me?'

'She told me the child would kill me,' said Laius. 'That's why childlessness was a blessing.'

'Any child?' asked Jocasta. She already thought she knew the answer. It was only one kind of child, the boy kind, which left another kind of child whom it was safe to have, the girl kind.

'Only a boy child,' he said.

'Why did you not tell me this? Why did you not tell me everything when you came back from Delphi? I should have been told everything.'

'I am not obliged to tell you everything.'

'Yes, you are,' said Jocasta. Her throat hurt. Her eyes were wet. 'I am your wife. You ought to have told me. What you told me, when you returned, was a truth that only went so far. You should not have done that. You should have said exactly what the Pythia said. I needed to know. Everything. Why didn't you? Why did you give me this half-truth, that we cannot have children if Thebes is to flourish. It's untrue! Because, it turns out, we can have a girl.'

'No,' said Laius. 'We can't. We won't. If we have a child it will be a boy. So, for us, no children whatsoever and therefore no risk of a son. That was all you needed to know. And now we are not childless, we need to act. That too, is all you need to know.'

'But what if it is a girl?' said Jocasta. 'We could keep it if it's a girl.'

'It isn't a girl,' he said.

'You don't know that.'

'I do know,' he said. 'Of course it's a boy. Why would the Pythia have warned me if it wasn't a son I was going to have?'

Jocasta knew he was right. Of course it was a boy. Great waves of grief ran through her.

'What are we going to do?' she said. 'Don't tell me what we can't do. Tell me what we are going to do.'

'I will give out,' said Laius, 'that you are unwell and, on the advice of our doctors you must go to the mountains to recover.'

Laius mentioned the hunting lodge in the foothills of Mount Cithaeron, far away from Thebes. Jocasta had heard of the dwelling but had never visited it.

'You will stay there,' he said, 'for the duration. It will be your birth-house.' He took her hand again and squeezed it tenderly. 'Then the newborn will come … and then what must be done will be done.'

Jocasta closed her eyes and wailed.

'Stop it!' Laius shouted.

Jocasta stopped wailing and opened her eyes. Laius, she saw, had sat up.

'Just think about what will happen if we don't act,' he said. 'I am slaughtered in some as yet unknown but vile way. What then? Your child will be a known king-slayer, a regicide. They are always slain. So, having lost me you will then lose the child. And then what? Thebes will have a new king. He'll come to you and say, "How could you have a son who you knew would kill his father?" And all you'll be able to say is, "I did, yes. I'm guilty." And having convicted yourself, the new king will pronounce your doom as the woman who knowingly had the son she knew would kill her husband. If you're lucky it'll be exile. If you're unlucky you'll be taken to Phicium and hurled off the top. And if you're very unlucky you'll be tied to a bull and dragged around like Dirce. Is that what you want? Because it will happen if we disobey.'

'The Pythia never said if you had a child you were to kill it,' said Jocasta.

'No, but she told me what would happen if I had a son,' said Laius. 'She told me the child will kill me. And when the Pythia speaks she isn't just telling you what will happen. She's also telling you what to do. Otherwise, why would she have said what she said? By telling me he would kill me, she meant me to understand that if he came I must strike first, before he does.'

Jocasta felt as if a sword handle was pounding the back of her forehead. She didn't want this dire sequence of calamities Laius had outlined with all its deaths and disasters. But she didn't want to lose her newborn either. Why was she caught between these two impossible alternatives? Why was this her fate?

'I did nothing to deserve this,' she said. 'This is monstrous.'

Laius lay back down. Beside him Jocasta stared upwards, swallowing and blinking. Two roads had appeared ahead of her, she thought. If she went down one she kept the newborn and if she went down the other she did not. It might appear she had a choice but she didn't. She knew which road she would take.

'So, what's it to be?' she heard Laius say. 'Do you want me to die and then endure all that will then flow from that? Or, do you want us to go on as we are? Which is it to be?'

'Won't we be tainted by this?' she said.

'No. Callidice's son, the shepherd …'

'Antimedes?'

'Him, yes. He works on Cithaeron. I'll use him. No one will know or see. We'll be blameless.'

'And afterwards,' Jocasta asked quietly, 'what happens then?'

'You will leave the birth-house and return to Thebes. I will put out that you have been ill but you are better. And we will go on as before, except we will not make this mistake again. We can't afford to.'

Jocasta curled herself into a small tight ball. She was with child. She would have the child. She would lose the child. This truth sat in the middle of her being like a great hot stone burning everything it touched, burning her from the inside out.

While Jocasta lay in turmoil, Laius felt much better. Because of what he had done to Chrysippus he had put himself in the way of certain death, his killer being his own child. But he would put a stop to that. His plans would save him. He would outwit his doom and die in his own bed, a childless old man with white hair and a leathery, wrinkled face. He was safe, or so he believed, and because he believed he was safe, he was happy.

Of course, deep inside Laius knew he could not cheat the pronouncement of the great god, though he'd never have admitted this. He was terrified, and those who are in terror are brilliant at committing themselves to the better future they have dreamt up to replace the awful future they know is coming. So instead of accepting what was certain and behaving accordingly, Laius told himself his idea was so good it *must* triumph. He was a brilliant man, he thought. He had a brilliant proposal. It would succeed brilliantly. He would thrive. He was sure of it.

The gods, seeing, hearing and knowing everything – they knew otherwise. They were amazed as well as baffled. Did he not understand? they asked. The Pythia had told him what would happen, and *it would happen*. And the answer they got back, communicated by all Laius did, was no, Laius did not understand. He believed he could elude his fate. And worse: not only did he not realise his impudence was a catastrophe for himself, he did not realise it was a catastrophe for others. But so it is, with every impudent man. He doesn't care that his schemes, far from being brilliant, are doomed to fail and will humble not just him but many others. He just ploughs on, like Laius did.

BOOK EIGHT

Heralds moved through the city streets and shouted the message they had been told by the palace to put out. On account of her health, they said, the queen was to have a period of seclusion in a royal house far from Thebes. She would be leaving the city shortly but in due course she would return.

It was a plain message delivered in simple language. Thebes received the words without comment. But in private Thebans wondered. Why was the queen *really* going away? Among Thebans there was a general suspicion that the queen's absence and the couple's childlessness were connected. But nobody knew how exactly. Nobody knew what the Pythia had said or that Jocasta was carrying a child. Other than Callidice, Jocasta and Laius, only the gods knew the truth, so for now, it really looked as if Laius would escape his fate and live a different future.

Livestock, poultry, wine, oil, and all the other necessaries were sent ahead to the birth-house. Laius informed the two mute sisters and the boy with the split lip they were going away with the queen. He'd didn't tell them what would happen while they were away – obviously they'd find out in due course and he'd decided there was no need for them to know yet – but he made it clear they were never to discuss with anyone what happened while they were away. They understood.

Laius also spoke to Callidice privately. He explained she was going away with the queen and that, when she required additional help, she was to summon Antimedes from the slopes of Cithaeron; he had told the other shepherds, Laius added, that if Antimedes was called away by his mother they were to do his work without complaining. Callidice was also to tell her son that he would have to perform a task for the king at a later stage and he had better prepare himself to do what he would be asked to do. Finally, Laius made it clear that he expected Callidice and her son to keep everything secret and to mention nothing to anyone at any time. And if either betrayed him, Laius reminded Callidice, he would have her taken to Mount Phicium and hurled off the top and he would send a party of spearmen to the slopes; they would mutilate her son and then dispatch him, and his body would be left where it fell for the wolves to eat.

'Do you understand me completely?' Laius asked when he had been over it all.

'I do,' said Callidice and as she spoke she felt her stomach curdling.

It was the middle of a moonless night when two carriages, four-wheelers made of thin wood and roofed, with swinging doors and open windows on the sides and one bench outside at the front for the driver and two benches inside for the passengers, left the palace and proceeded slowly through the streets of Thebes. The horses wore leather hoof boots, which deadened the noise of their hooves.

The first carriage was driven by Polyphontes and pulled by two brown horses. Beside Polyphontes sat the herald whose hairless head was covered with scars from the cudgelling he had received and who could barely speak. Behind the two men sat the mute twin sisters. The second carriage, driven by a second driver, was pulled by a black horse and a white horse. Beside the driver sat the boy with the split lip. Inside the carriage behind them sat the queen and Callidice.

The carriages reached the Cithaeron gate. The gatekeeper here had been warned to expect them. He opened the gates quietly and the carriages passed out and once the carriages were through, the gatekeeper closed the gates again and that was that. Lucky Laius. It was a smooth departure. No one had seen the queen and her party slip away. Oh, the king knew how to organise these things.

Now they were out of the city the herald got down. For as long as it was dark he would walk ahead checking the road for debris and the carriages would follow. The herald began to walk and immediately behind him, the two brown horses pulling the first carriage gently clip-clopped. The second carriage followed.

Inside the carriage Jocasta and Callidice were both staring out into the black world streaming past. While it was dark neither spoke or even acknowledged the existence of the other. Then dawn came and, as the royal herald got up beside Polyphontes, a greyish pale light floated in through the carriage windows. Callidice thought she'd risk it and glanced sideways at the queen. She saw her face was tight and drawn, angry and grief-stricken. Callidice had encountered the queen's moods before and knew what to do. She must avoid catching her eye altogether.

Callidice closed her eyes and started listening to the wheels rolling, the horses walking, the wood and leather all around her squeaking, and as she listened she felt herself gradually becoming slower and heavier.

After a while she opened her eyes and looked out. While she'd not been watching, a bright day had come with a milky sky of white cloud. She stared greedily out at what was passing: small flowers along the road's edge, vines with twisted, flaking onion-red bodies, olive trees with dark trunks and branches reaching out like hands. Then, jolting her out of her absorption in the world, she heard a voice.

'Prepare to stop,' Polyphontes shouted. Callidice felt their carriage's forward motion slowing and then the carriage stopping.

'Why have we stopped?' These were the first words Jocasta had spoken since leaving the palace.

'I don't know,' said Callidice quietly.

Outside, the horses whinnying, the brittle noise of the their tails swishing, and further off a scampering noise and the rumble of croaking.

'Don't just sit there,' said Jocasta. 'See what's happening.'

Callidice put her head out of the right-hand window. In front of the first carriage she saw a great brown river of frogs coming in from the higher ground and streaming across the road. Callidice moved to the other side of the carriage and looked out the left-hand window and saw that the frogs, having crossed the road, were flowing away like honey across the lower ground. She watched Polyphontes jump down and heard him bellow through the window of the first carriage to the mutes, 'Brushes, clear the road,' while miming the act of sweeping.

The mutes climbed down. They wore long black dresses, aprons and caps, and each carried a stave with light twigs tied in a clump to the end.

They walked towards the frogs, the soles of their sandals slapping on the stony road, and when they reached the edge of the mass they began to sweep, right to left, moving great swathes of the creatures, like tumbles of leaves.

Callidice sat back in her seat. 'Frogs,' she said. 'We've had to stop for frogs.'

Now Jocasta looked out of the window. 'Frogs, yes,' she exclaimed.

Frogs on the move were not uncommon on milky days and, moreover, as both Jocasta and Callidice knew, anyone who harmed or killed the creatures could expect punishment by the gods. That was why they'd stopped. But a torrent of frogs like this – neither had heard of or seen such a thing in their lives.

After a while the queen sighed. 'This is taking such a long time,' she said. 'What is going on? The frogs are surely away by now.'

Callidice put her head out her window again and looked up the road. She saw the mutes had put their brushes aside. One had lifted her apron to make a carrying pouch and the other was picking stragglers up by hand and piling them into the pouch.

'They're picking up the stragglers,' said Callidice.

'By hand?'

'Yes.'

'Well, get out and help,' said Jocasta, 'so we can get on.'

Callidice got out. Her shadow on the road was weak, light and grey. The sun wasn't that strong yet. She walked up and stopped. A frog sat at her feet. It was brown and speckled like the others.

Callidice bent slowly, expecting the creature to hop. But it didn't. It was probably exhausted, Callidice thought, and unable to decide whether to make itself move or not. She took the frog by the neck. Its skin was surprisingly dry. She lifted it up. It paddled its dangling legs feebly. It opened its mouth and attempted to make a noise. Callidice walked to the mute holding her apron out and dropped her catch in. Then she joined the other mute, collecting laggards.

When a bulge was visible from below, the mute with the frogs in her apron walked to the edge of the road, knelt, and carefully tumbled her charges out. Freed, these last frogs hopped off in the direction in which the rest had gone.

Finally, the road was empty. All the frogs were on the lower ground, a dark mass hugging the earth over which they moved. The mutes and Callidice returned to their respective carriages and got in. Polyphontes raised his goad. The carriages moved on. Callidice felt queasy. From deep within she felt the notion rose up. The frogs were a sign. They were there to stop them. They shouldn't have cleared them away so they could go on. They should have turned the carriages round and gone back to Thebes.

Callidice's whole body fluttered and trembled. What good was this insight going to do her? Jocasta's laundress could not put her head out the window and shout at Polyphontes, 'Turn around. Go back to Thebes.' No one would listen to her. They'd still go on to the birth-house as planned. Nor could she as much as even hint at what she thought. That would have been impudence and impudence would be reported back to Laius and she'd be punished for it. The king would have her beaten, or worse. So she sat perfectly still while the carriage moved on, her face inscrutable, no sign at all showing of what she had thought.

Yet the idea couldn't be banished. Inside her head it rattled about like dice being jigged in a cup, noisy and frantic. She didn't enjoy the sensation of this terrible intuition. It made her pulse race and if she had not been holding her body as tight as she was, the thought would have made her visibly tremble, which Jocasta would have seen. And then after that Jocasta would have started asking questions and she wouldn't have given up until she'd wrenched the truth out of Callidice.

The carriages rolled on. Why had she been given this insight? It would have been better if she hadn't, she thought. Ignorance over foresight any day when you were powerless. And following on from that came the question: why had she been allowed to know when she could do nothing? And who had organised this misery? She began to blush. The colouring was hot and fierce and ran from her hairline, down her face, over her chin and all the way to the flat of her chest below her throat. This was not a question to pose, let alone to answer. The very idea of it! She drove away the impudent thought.

The little convoy arrived at its destination. The birth-house was a single-storey building with two courtyards. It was clean and had recently been swept on Laius's orders. Fires were lit. Water was drawn. Beds were made up for Jocasta, Callidice, the mutes and the boy with the split lip, plus Polyphontes and the second driver and the herald, who would return to Thebes the next morning.

The first night, having fallen asleep quickly, Jocasta was woken by something moving around above her. She opened her eyes. There were burning nightlights dotted about the room and though the light they gave was meagre, nonetheless they allowed her to see something was flitting about the blackness above her. It swooped close by at a tremendous speed. There was only one thing that moved around in the dark like that. There was a bat in her room, she thought, and no sooner had she had the thought, hard and forceful and certain, than terror surged through her.

'There's a bat in my room,' she screamed.

She pulled the covers over her head and pulled her knees up to her chest. She was as small as she could make herself and completely wrapped up and unassailable, yet that did not stop her mind. She imagined the creature's bony, furry wings brushing against her face, her bare back, her calves. Then she imagined the creature's little claws getting entangled in her hair and then, struggling to free itself, getting further and further ensnared. Something alive and trapped so close to her scalp, thrashing and struggling, was appalling. What would she do? Reach up in the darkness, grasp its bony, furry body and pull it free? No, that was beyond her. It was intolerable, she thought, to have to lie like this, cowering below her covers. This was not how a queen lived. A queen lived in her palace and did not have to endure such miseries.

'There's a bat,' she shouted again.

Callidice, sleeping next door, was woken by Jocasta's shouting. She jumped out of bed and rushed into the room.

'Queen,' Jocasta heard her say, 'what is it?'

'A bat,' Jocasta cried from under her covers.

A long pause and then she heard Callidice say, 'I don't think so. There might have been but it's gone.'

'Are you sure?'

'Yes.'

Jocasta carefully worked her head free. She saw the outline of Callidice's bare, bony body near her bed.

'Has it gone?'

'I think so.'

Callidice left and went back to her own bed. Jocasta lay for a long while. Could she hear anything? No, nothing. She turned an ear out to the room and stopped breathing. Was anything out there in the dark swooping about? No, nothing she could detect. Eventually, reassured, she drifted away. Then swooping by, over her face, the bat again. She was wide awake in an instant. Her heart racing, she shot under the covers and shouted, 'It's back!' She heard Callidice running in.

'No,' Callidice said. 'There's nothing here.'

Jocasta dropped the cover from her face.

'Maybe it only comes when I'm alone,' said Jocasta. 'Get in beside me,' she said.

Callidice got in on the other side. The women lay side by side on separate sides of the bed, the covers up to their chins. The night lights burnt. The wind murmured in the trees outside. Without warning, the bat swooped in front of their faces. Both the queen and Callidice cried out. The bat was back. Both threw the covers over their faces and made themselves small.

'We'll have to close the house at night,' said Callidice.

'It might live in the house,' said Jocasta. 'Do that and we might be trapped inside with it. At least now it can get out. Close the house and it won't be able to.'

'We'll catch it then.'

'How?'

'Antimedes,' said Callidice. Laius had instructed her to have him come to the birth-house whenever she needed. 'He'll catch it. I'll send the boy with the split lip to Cithaeron for him tomorrow.'

Callidice and Jocasta lay under the covers, breathing quietly. The space grew warm with their breath. Jocasta began to sweat. Callidice went back to sleep but Jocasta did not. She wanted to throw off the covers and cool down but she didn't dare risk it. So she just lay there in the hot space under the covers and let her mind turn.

First the frogs, now this. Perhaps the frogs were nothing to worry about. Great processions of these creatures would be seen moving around once the days lengthened and the heat of the sun grew. But this bat, coming and going, like it did – was it something else? Did its appearance mean she shouldn't embark on the course of action she had planned? Was it telling her to refuse?

But how could she, after what the Pythia had said. It was impossible to return to Thebes and give birth and keep the child. That was proscribed. Should she take herself up Mount Phicium and hurl herself from the top? The idea terrified her – stepping off the top and tumbling and knowing just before death that she was about to split open and then hitting the ground and actually splitting open. She trembled at the thought of it. She couldn't do it. So what else was there to do but to go on as she was going?

Jocasta cried. She cried quietly, for a long time. Later, she stopped crying and lay awake, shocked and hot and miserable.

When she heard a cockerel crowing, she poked her head out from under the covers. The shutters were closed but there was enough light seeping in for her to see the ceiling and the walls and the floor of the room. Now day had arrived, she was no longer terrified and she was able to think.

The house was unoccupied most of the time and that's why the bat had moved in. Then she and her party had arrived. That's why it had come into her room – to signal its outrage. If she'd been the bat, she would have done the same. Jocasta felt much better after this thought. She had nothing to fear. There was no message here, no meaning. It was no omen. Now it only remained to do what always was done when bats came in. It would be found and carried away and the house would be kept closed at night so it would not be able to get back in.

Jocasta nudged Callidice on her shoulder. 'Fetch me a shift,' she said. 'Then tell the mutes to get the fires going and send for your son.'

Polyphontes and the second driver and the herald returned to Thebes and Callidice sent the boy with the split lip to Cithaeron. He returned in the afternoon with Antimedes.

Antimedes was dispatched with a net and a bag to find the bat. He searched the house and found it hanging from the edge of a table in a cold room filled with oil and grain. It was a strange place to find the bat as the door was closed and there was no obvious means of entering or leaving.

He stealthily slipped the bag over the bat from below; then he snapped down, tearing the bat's grip from the table edge, and drew the bag's mouth shut with a string. He had it.

Antimedes heard the bat twittering in the bag as he left the birth-house and set out across country; later, he noticed the animal crying and twisting less and less until eventually there was no sound or movement coming from inside the bag at all. He wondered if the bat was dead but he decided it couldn't have died that quickly. It was just tired and frightened; that's why it had gone so quiet and still.

When he was a good distance from the birth-house Antimedes stopped. He opened the bag and tumbled the animal out onto the ground. It extended its wings and began to pull itself about feebly. Its wingspan was the same as from the end of his middle figure to the crook of his elbow. This was an enormous bat. The creature made a little whimpering noise and tried to lift itself into the air. It was stuck, earthbound. As Antimedes knew well, bats always hung upside down in high places and when they wanted to fly they let go. They couldn't take off from the ground like birds.

He bent down and pinched the animal gently by the neck. It opened its mouth, baring its gums and made a sharp, anguished squeak. He lifted the creature up. It was heavy. Heavier than any bat he'd ever come across before. The wings went in and out. He flung it upwards, very high.

Its body pulsed, its wings moved, and it started to fly. It went, here, there, skittishly changing direction without discernible reason at incredible speed. Antimedes followed the bat's progress through the air. It stayed near to him for some time, then turned, as if intent on striking away. At that same moment, he thought, it altered its nature. He wasn't sure because it was moving so quickly but he thought it had turned into a bird. Or had his eyes deceived him? Maybe he just thought it had become a bird because it was so big? Before he could decide one way or the other it was gone too far for him to see for sure. Then it vanished.

As Antimedes was walking back to the birth-house he met his mother coming the other way, looking for him.

'There's a snake,' she said. 'It's in the kitchen.'

Jocasta and the mutes and the boy with the split lip, she continued, had shut themselves up in a room and they would stay there until Callidice came to tell them the snake was gone.

Mother and son walked side by side along the path. As they went, Callidice told Antimedes about the frogs on the road on the journey from Thebes. She said nothing about her fears that the frogs were an omen.

When they got to the birth-house, Callidice relieved Antimedes of the bag he had used to carry the bat and she handed him a set of tongs she had found somewhere. They were a sturdy item, with brass arms, flat rounded ends the size of coins and a wooden handle.

Antimedes pushed the kitchen door open with the tip of the tongs and peered in. The snake lay on top of the table. It was black, thick-bodied.

He waited, watching for the head to lift, the mouth to open, the tongue to dart in and out between sharp teeth as it readied to strike. But none of this happened. The snake lay without moving, utterly still.

'Do you see it?' Callidice called from behind.

Antimedes flapped a hand at his mother and whispered, 'Be quiet!' He didn't know if the creature was asleep but if it was, he certainly didn't want to wake it. He slipped across the floor quietly until he was close enough to see an open eye. Why wasn't the snake moving?

He opened the tongs and reached forward until he had the ends on either side of the neck. Then he snapped the tongs shut. The snake's curled-up body shot back like a rope straightening, extending the length of the table. The creature was about as long as he was high. Just like the bat had been, this was a big creature.

Antimedes squeezed the tongs harder. The snake whipped its body backwards to try and free itself from the flat ends and he felt its power as it thrashed and squirmed. It couldn't get away, though. Antimedes had it held fast.

'Get back,' he shouted to his mother.

He lifted the snake up. The black body hanging downwards coiled and jerked.

Antimedes went through the door and out into the courtyard heading for the gap in the wall, the tongs in his hands, the ends gripped hard, the snake coiling and agitating. He gripped even harder. Whatever he did, he must not let the creature drop. It could turn and bite him before he could escape. He got through the gap in the wall. Underfoot he now felt bare earth and then the stones of a gravel path. On he went, carefully, one step after the next. Eventually he came to the ditch he had in mind. It was as deep as he was tall. Once he released the tongs the snake would tumble down to the bottom. It would never be able to get back up and at him.

He stretched forward. His arms were well over the lip of the ditch. He opened the tongs. His captive tumbled. He heard the noise its body made as it struck the earth below. A moment when nothing happened. Then the serpent turned and wriggled away. He watched it go. It went slowly. It was not an animal in flight but one going about its business at its customary pace. After it had slithered some distance it changed from black to silver and finally it became a stream of water that soaked into the earth – or so he thought. It happened a long way away and, as with the bat, he couldn't be completely sure he had seen what he thought he had seen.

Callidice had followed and was standing behind. She'd watched her son drop the snake into the ditch but after that she couldn't see what happened.

'Why didn't you kill it?' Callidice said.

'How could I do that?' said Antimedes. 'I'd have had to let it go before I could hit it and it would have bitten me before I could get my blow in. This way it fell too far to come back at me.'

Later, Antimedes was called in to see the queen. She had heard from his mother what he had done.

'Why didn't you kill it?' she asked.

He gave the same explanation he had given Callidice.

'But it could come back,' she said.

'It won't,' he said.

'But you don't know that.'

He wondered if he should mention that he thought it had turned into water and soaked away into the earth. He decided against saying anything, as that was likely to make the queen even more anxious.

'After I let it go,' he said, 'it headed away from the house. It knows better than to come back. I'm sure of it.'

'I hope you're right,' said Jocasta.

'It headed off,' he said, 'and I'm absolutely certain it won't be back.'

She stared at him. Her expression was hurt and sorrowful. She thinks I'm just telling her what she wants to hear, he thought. She knows I'm not telling the truth.

This encounter with the queen unsettled him.

The next morning Antimedes went back to the ditch and began to tread its length, following the direction in which the snake had slithered away. He found the snake curled up on a rock, sunning itself. He had his staff. He might be able to creep closer and then smash his staff down on its head and kill it, he thought.

With his mind's eye he saw the scene unfold ... creeping forward ... raising his staff ... bringing the staff down ...

the snake jerking and writhing ... the snake trying to slither away ... bringing the staff down again and again and again until it wasn't moving anymore ... touching the head with the tip of the staff ... the head flopping sideways, lifeless ... Now he'd got to the end of imagining he wondered how he'd feel. That was simple. He'd be morose, wouldn't he? Bound to be, having killed what hadn't menaced him or caused him harm. Yes, that's exactly how he'd feel and he didn't want to feel like that. In which case it was obvious. He mustn't kill it. He wouldn't kill it. He'd let it live.

As he had this thought, the snake lifted its head and looked at him. Then it shivered and turned into a pool of water and the water spread over the rock. Antimedes was relieved he hadn't struck. He also felt sure that the black snake would never return now. He turned and retraced his steps to the birth-house.

He spent the day splitting logs with a wedge. He carried the wood inside and lit fires in every room. His mother fed him olives and cheese and bread. He slept on a cot in a corridor. The next day he cleaned the fires and re-lit them. He cleaned out the wells. He scrubbed walls and swept rooms at his mother's direction, then he pulled the weeds from the cracks between the stones in the courtyard.

The following day he returned to the slopes. A few days later he was back at the birth-house. So began his pattern. A few days on the slopes with the royal herd. A few days at the birth-house. A few more days on the slopes. And so on. The frogs were never mentioned. The snake and the bat were never mentioned. Instead, the three omens were ignored.

BOOK NINE

When he began his time at the birth-house, Antimedes was informed the queen had been secluded there because of her health. But when she began to show, Callidice told him the queen was carrying a child that no one knew about and no one could know about either. 'Do you understand?' she said. 'You are to say nothing about this.'

She did not mention what Laius had told her he would have his spearmen do to Antimedes if he did tell anyone.

'Not a word about the queen's condition,' Callidice continued, 'to the other shepherds or to anyone else.'

'So you're saying this is a secret,' said Antimedes, as if he didn't take her seriously.

'Yes,' Callidice said again. She didn't understand his humour. 'Not a word to anyone. Only you and I and the two mutes and the boy with the split lip know about the queen. No one else in Thebes does.'

'Apart from Laius, of course,' Antimedes added.

'Don't be impudent,' said Callidice. 'Not one word to anyone, ever.'

Antimedes was on one of his visits to the birth-house. He was carrying a basket of wood across one of the courtyards. The queen was coming the other way. She was walking slowly through the blistering air. She held a fan in one hand, which she was waving in front of her face. Her other hand was pressed against the small of her back. Her huge stomach stuck out through her dress. Her face was pinched. She was in obvious discomfort, even pain. Antimedes stepped to the side to let her pass and set his basket down. Jocasta came closer.

'This heat,' said Jocasta, 'is unbearable.'

Around her head, holding her beautifully plaited hair in place, she wore a wide fillet decorated with distinctive bright red blocks. She stopped and pulled it off and mopped her brow. Then, using just one hand, she roughly pulled it back onto her head but failed to get it on properly. She resumed walking and the headband slipped backwards and landed on the stone flags behind.

'Queen,' Antimedes shouted. Jocasta stopped, turned. 'You dropped something.'

He ran to the fillet, picked it up, and handed it to the queen. Jocasta took it, pulled it on properly, seating it well down her head.

'Thank the gods you are not a woman,' she said.

Jocasta turned and walked on. Antimedes went back to his wood basket. A strange idea came to him. On this boiling day he had laid eyes on a small and inconsequential item of the queen's dress that he knew he would never forget.

A cold morning. Antimedes was up before it was properly light. He milked the goats and lit the fires. Then he came back to the kitchen to break his fast. He had a piece of barley bread, hard and dry. He dipped it in the cup of wine and water in front of him and then lifted it out. The bottom end of the bread was red and soft.

Antimedes put the soft end into his mouth, broke the wet end off with his tongue and then sucked. First the wine came out, dark and bitter and warming, and then the bread itself fell to pieces. The boy with the split lip sat opposite, watching him.

'Here.' Antimedes offered the boy with the split lip his bread. 'Do you want to dip?' Antimedes indicated the wine.

The boy shook his head. Because of his split lip he did not like anyone to see him eating, especially barley bread and wine, which was hard for him to manage.

Antimedes dipped again. Another mouthful of warming, bitter wine. Soft bread dissolving and collapsing over his tongue.

Footsteps. His mother hurried in, her face small and scrunched up. He knew the look. It was her worried look.

'You.' She was speaking to the boy with the split lip. 'Run to the palace. A message for the king. We need the midwife, now. Wear a cloak and a sheep's skin. It's cold.'

This was true. They were over the heat and into the rains and the dark and the wet. The boy with the split lip got up and pulled on a sheep's skin and a cloak. He took his staff, which was standing beside the door, and left.

The next day Antimedes was chopping wood outside the wood store when a carriage rolled up. The boy with the split lip got out, followed by a round old woman.

The midwife, Antimedes thought. He knew her reputation. She had spent her entire life in the palace. She had delivered Laius and put the obol under his mother's tongue when she died. She had carried Laius to King Pelops's court. She was known to hold many secrets and she was known as someone who would never yield them up.

Antimedes put down his axe and went to her. The midwife's cloak was heavy and huge and it covered everything except for her two dark eyes, a long, bent nose and a mouthful of teeth, all surprising white and all incredibly crooked.

'Follow the boy with the split lip,' said Antimedes. 'Once you get to the kitchen ask for Callidice, my mother.'

The midwife nodded to him and padded off after the boy with the split lip.

The first thing the midwife did once she got inside was to pass a message from Laius to Callidice. As soon as she got the message Callidice took a pitcher and went out to find her son.

Antimedes was in the wood store chopping when his mother appeared. She set her pitcher down.

'Antimedes,' said Callidice. From the tone of her voice he could tell she had something important to say. 'The king told the midwife I am to remind you to prepare yourself for a task you will be asked to perform.'

Antimedes set down his axe. 'What will a shepherd be asked, do you think?'

She shrugged.

'You must have some notion.'

'To take the newborn somewhere. A foreign court, I imagine. I don't know. Anyhow, when you're asked, don't be awkward.'

'The time you were beaten and you wouldn't tell me. Was that because you were awkward?'

She shook her head. 'No. It was because I lied about the queen's condition.'

Antimedes looked at his mother.

'I knew she was carrying but I wouldn't let on. I said she wasn't.'

'Why?' asked Antimedes.

'Because the queen had asked me not to say.'

'Is this baby Laius's?'

'Of course,' she said.

'It must be something if they're going to all this trouble,' said Antimedes. 'You'd have to wonder what that is.'

'Don't you worry,' she said. 'You'll find out what's what soon enough.' She hefted the pitcher onto her head and walked away in the direction of the well.

The light began to go. Antimedes went in and lit the lamps and as they burnt the house was filled with the smell of oil. He piled wood on the fires. He carried in more wood. The fires would need to be kept going all night.

Later his mother told him that the queen, after a long bout of crying, had finally gone to sleep.

The next day his mother told Antimedes that the queen needed the women with her permanently so he and the boy with the split lip would now have to do the women's as well as the men's work. For instance, they would have to carry in the water for her bath, she said.

Once Antimedes and the boy with the split lip had fetched the water, Callidice and the midwife washed and then oiled Jocasta's huge body. Outside, meanwhile, Antimedes and the boy with the split lip gathered eggs, milked the goats and attended to the other outdoor chores. At midday they came in and sat at the fire to warm themselves. The two mutes were away with the queen, combing and setting her hair. Antimedes's mother and the midwife were at the table. In front of them was a dish of olives, wet, black and wrinkled. Antimedes watched the midwife take a handful and cram them in her mouth. She chewed, cleaning the flesh off the stones, and swallowed. He expected she would spit the stones out into the designated dish on the table. But she didn't. Instead, she kept the stones in her mouth and moved them around with her tongue, clacking them against her teeth. Then she spat the stones out one after the other. All the flesh was off them and they fell like pebbles.

The next morning Antimedes sat at the table with barley bread and wine and the midwife sat at the fire.

It's the queen's time, he thought. The sounds in the house – or the sounds that weren't in the house – were telling him this. He heard his mother's footsteps. He'd know the sound of her tread anywhere. She hurried in, red-faced and breathless.

'You're wanted,' he heard Callidice say to the midwife.

Antimedes expected the midwife to spring to her feet but she only lifted her head and looked at Callidice.

'She's waiting,' his mother said.

'There's no need for haste,' said the midwife. 'It'll be a while yet.'

Slowly and deliberately the midwife pulled her fingers, one after the other, and each time she tugged a finger a click came out of the joint. It was a sound Antimedes hated.

'She doesn't like to be kept waiting,' he called across.

'Your mother or the queen?' asked the midwife.

She stood and arched her back. Then she rotated her head, first one way and then the other. 'I'm ready,' said the midwife.

She padded to the door, light and almost noiseless though she was old and bulky. Antimedes had noticed that the heavy were often light on their feet. She went out.

Antimedes heard the midwife moving down the corridor towards the queen's quarters. He heard a cry, high-pitched and long. The queen's time had indeed come.

'Find the boy with the split lip,' said Callidice. 'Send him to Thebes. Laius should come.' Antimedes went out to find the boy with the split lip. He was milking a goat.

'Go to Thebes,' said Antimedes. 'Pass the message. The king is to come.' Antimedes took over the milking and the boy with the split lip went off.

The next day the sky was the colour of clay. Antimedes chopped wood and carried the logs into the house. He filled the fire baskets. He lit the fires. He stoked the fires. He drew water from the well. He milked the goats. He fetched wine, cheese and olives from the store. He filled the lamps. In the afternoon he heard the sound of carriage wheels. Laius, he thought.

He went in when it began to get dark. Laius's driver, Polyphontes, was sitting at a table, dipping barley bread in wine. The boy with the split lip, who had come back in the carriage with the king, was asleep in the corner. Antimedes went through the house and lit the lamps. When he was done he returned to the kitchen and sat down opposite Polyphontes. They both understood it was best not to talk about what was happening, so they didn't. And having nothing else to speak about, they both stayed silent.

That night Antimedes slept fitfully on a cot in the corridor. He kept being woken by the queen's cries and the sounds of people moving about.

Very early his mother woke him. The lamps were still going. 'Up,' she said. She held a small bundle.

He got up. By the trembling light he could see blood on the cloth around the bundle. Had the queen's baby died? he wondered. Was his mother holding the newborn's little body?

'Bury what's in here,' his mother said, 'and bring back the cloth.'

He received the bundle. It wasn't the newborn. It was too soft and had no form. His first thought was wrong. It was something else.

Antimedes pulled on a cloak, went out, found a digging tool and set off. It was dawn – walls, trees, paths were all half lit, spectral and insubstantial.

He made his way to the ditch into which he had thrown the snake. He climbed in and followed the direction the snake had gone until he found a stretch of earth beside a rock suitable for digging. He put the bundle down and dug. When he had a big enough hole, he picked up the bundle and tumbled the contents out: a crinkled umbilical cord, which reminded him of a sheep's intestines, and the flat, jelly-like red organ, which he knew was the afterbirth. After he had dropped it he bent down to study it. He touched it, too. It was cold and smooth. Then he brought the finger ends that had touched it to his nose and smelt them. He expected the dark metal smell of blood but it was another smell he got. It was delicate, floral but also faintly salty. Was that the smell of life, he wondered, before it turned into flesh and blood? He filled the hole and, taking the digging tool and the bloody cloth with him, retraced his steps.

When he got back to the courtyard the sun was low in the sky. The light was white and had little warmth. I'll have to stoke the fires, he thought.

*

Antimedes stood outside the queen's room as he had been instructed by his mother to do. On the far side of the door, he heard voices. Laius's voice was calm and reasonable. Jocasta's voice was grief-stricken and desolate. Hearing her made something deep inside him vibrate. He got the same feeling when he heard an animal whimpering in pain or bellowing when it was about to die. When any living thing could not tolerate any further suffering they all made the same sound that produced in him the same effect.

The door opened. It was one of the mutes. Like her twin she had buck teeth but unlike her sister she had a mole on her cheek, a small, brown flat round that looked like a smudge of mud that had been pressed onto her face by a thumb. The mole was how the sisters were distinguished. There was the mute with the mole and the mute without a mole.

Antimedes's gaze flicked from the mute's face to the room behind. He saw little points of lamplight. In the bed, against the far wall, he saw the queen – a dark, pale, bare form with something at her breast. Laius was prowling on the floor at the side. His mother and the mute without a mole were also in the room. He could see their forms but he couldn't see what they were doing. There were three smells coming from the room, he noticed – the iron smell of blood, the salt smell of sweat and the fish smell of burning oil.

The mute who had come out shut the door. She looked at him. Her front upper teeth glowed in the gloom. She pointed into the distance, then moved two fingers of her right hand, the sign of walking.

'I'm going somewhere, yes,' said Antimedes.

She pointed the same way as before. He imagined a straight line running from her finger, through the wall and out into the world.

'Cithaeron?' he said. She was pointing in that direction.

She patted his chest then laid one forearm over the other and made a rocking motion.

Antimedes understood. 'A baby?'

She patted his chest again and then made a shooing motion with the backs of her hands.

Footsteps hurried on the other side of the door. The mute heard them. She shot away in the direction of the kitchen and had put several good strides between herself and himself by the time the door opened and the queen and Laius appeared. In the room behind, Callidice and the other mute stood watching. The queen held a bundle. Inside the bundle something was moving and mewling.

'Take this,' said Jocasta. She put the bundle into Antimedes's arms. 'Go to the slopes where you graze your sheep. Leave him down behind rock where no one will find him. Walk away.' So this was the task he'd been told to prepare for. This was what his mother was told by the midwife to remind him about. He was to take the queen's newborn to the slopes and leave him there.

'Walk away?' he said, baffled.

'Yes,' This was Laius speaking. His voice was one calculated to stiffen resolve. 'You heard. Walk away.'

'But bring the swaddling cloth back with you,' said Jocasta quickly.

'You want me to take it off? Why?' Antimedes thought of the wind.

'I want it back,' said Jocasta.

'But the cold …'

'Take off the swaddling cloth.' This was Laius again. 'Leave him down. Walk away.'

'But if I leave …' Antimedes began.

He got no further because Laius cut him off. 'Take off the swaddling cloth. Put him down. Walk away. Have you got that?'

'Yes,' said Antimedes. 'Take off the swaddling cloth. Walk away.'

'That's right,' said Laius. 'And don't look back. Whatever you hear, ignore it. Walk on and come back here.'

He pointed his thumb at Callidice standing in the room behind. 'You see who I'm pointing at?'

'Yes,' said Antimedes.

'You fail,' said Laius, 'it isn't just you who suffers.'

The king had thrashed his mother before, as she'd told him, and he had no doubt Laius would do so again, or worse.

'Do not fail,' said Laius.

Antimedes hurried up the road with the newborn in his arms. It was early on a winter's morning.

A moon hung above him, a big round of white with dark smudges. The ground underfoot was cold, hard, pale and dry. Wisps of mist flowed over the edges of the terraces and cascaded down the sides like water. He saw bare vines, their ancient trunks knotty and brown and flaking. He saw olive trees, their bark shiny grey but also green and almost greasy in the first light. He saw a field of crows like a crowd of small people in black cloaks, pecking and foraging.

The bundle in his arms was warm, alive. He held it tight to his chest. Strange, unexpected feelings of anxiety rustled through him.

What if he dropped the newborn? And what if he did not do what he had been told to do? That, of course, would all depend on whether or not Phorbas was there. It wasn't quite the end of the season and there were still one or two shepherds on the slopes, one or two herds still taking the very last of the grass that remained, and Phorbas always lingered longest before he returned home to Corinth with King Polybus's animals. Perhaps … if there was still some grass then he might be there, still …

'No more thinking,' Antimedes said aloud. 'Just walk. Get to Cithaeron. That's all you can do. Phorbas will be there. He will help. You know he will.'

Antimedes believed what he had just said. He knew Phorbas would be there. This meant he could stop thinking and just walk. And that's what he did. He simply followed his feet, one after the other. After a bit he noticed warmth under the arms. His ears were hurting. He hunched his shoulders, dropped his head forwards and pulled up the hood of his cloak.

For a while he moved quickly. The road he trod unfolded itself in front of him and rolled itself back up after he had passed, while all the time the light gradually increased. As the sun began to show, its edge appearing above the top of the distant hills, he felt a wriggle in the bundle. Then he heard a murmur. Finally, he heard a screech. He made baby sounds to soothe the newborn. It was pointless. The screeching grew harder and louder. And as it did, he felt the familiar tremor deep inside, exactly the same as he felt when he heard the cry of a beast as its throat was slashed or its skull was split. The sound of another's suffering always had this effect on him.

He saw a woman ahead with a water pitcher balanced on her head, coming his way. Her lower half was small and dainty, but her upper half was heavy and full. She was nursing, he guessed. He would try.

'I have a child here,' he called to her. 'I need someone to nurse him.'

The woman put the pitcher down and he saw water slop out over the lip. They walked forwards and stopped within arm's reach of each other. Under her cap she had red, wiry hair. Her eyes were brown, close set. She had a long face and a sharp nose. There were hoops in her ears. Silver, he thought. She looked at him closely.

'What are you doing out at this time with a child?' she asked. 'It's too cold.'

He hadn't expected such a question. Her voice sounded as if it were coming through her nose.

'His mother died,' Antimedes said. Where had that come from? He noticed one of the woman's hands holding her cloak at the neck. Her fingers were long and thin. No rings, but a bracelet at the wrist. Seeds on a wire. Was she married? He thought so. And nursing? He looked at her front. He hoped so.

'Are you his father?'

The words were already on the edge of his tongue and out before he could think. 'I am, and I'm taking him to my sister. I have a distance to go and he needs a woman.'

'You're lucky to have met me.'

She held out her hands. He passed the bundle. The child was roaring. The noise was awful. She looked around. She nodded at a rock a few feet away. It was high, straight, and could be leant against. It would offer shelter.

'Get the pitcher,' she said, jerking her head back towards it.

She headed to the place of shelter she had picked. He moved down the road. The pitcher was fired clay, a dull red. There was water inside. He swung the pitcher onto his shoulder. He retraced his steps and rejoined the crinkly-haired woman. On her left breast he saw a mouth with her nipple in it. The newborn sucking. He sat and waited. The newborn fed. Then the newborn cried and was sick. Then she fed the newborn from her right breast. Again, it cried and was sick. Then she fed it again from her left breast and instead of crying the newborn fell asleep. She returned the bundle and they went in their separate directions heading away from each other as fast as they were able.

The slopes of Cithaeron rose ahead of him. He saw outcrops of stone, ragged trees and sheets of grass. The grass was pale green, as if its colour had been blown out of it by the wind. This was where he had spent so much of his life, with the royal herd, moving it around on these slopes. He stopped, looked up and scanned. Sheep here, goats there. Not as many as usual. Well, the grass was mostly gone. Most of the shepherds had headed off to overwinter somewhere else. The Thebans were gone, as he'd expected. But not everyone had gone. He could see a shepherd. And yes, there he was. It was Phorbas, with his animals. And now, trembling on the edge of his thoughts, the thought Antimedes had not let himself think before. If Phorbas his friend was there, he could ask him, couldn't he? That way he would not have to do what he'd been tasked to do.

Antimedes grasped the bundle tighter with his left arm and raised his right arm and waved.

'Phorbas,' he shouted. 'Phorbas.'

The other man saw him and waved back. The two moved towards each other. Phorbas's pace was leisurely. Antimedes's was fast. He needed to talk to Phorbas. He didn't want the taint of murder, the murder of a newborn.

Antimedes stopped and looked up. Phorbas was gliding down towards him, passing sheep, big and fat and woolly, and some wiry goats who were stepping carefully by lifting their spindly legs very high. Phorbas's cloak billowed behind and he walked with the help of a staff.

A new and startling idea hit Antimedes. This began as an unlucky day, but his luck was changing. First, the crinkly-haired woman had fed the newborn. That was the first sign of the change. Now Phorbas was on Cithaeron. That was the next sign. His idea might work, he thought. His request would be granted and he would then be released from his terrible task. That would be the third piece of luck, the biggest and most important.

Phorbas strode up. Below his cloak he wore a long tunic and a heavy sheepskin.

'What have you there?' Phorbas asked. He had a thick, wide face, huge ears and glossy, cracked lips.

'A newborn ... a boy,' said Antimedes.

'You know, when I was up there,' Phorbas gestured behind, 'and I first saw you. You know what I thought?'

'No,' said Antimedes.

'I thought, he's brought a newborn up here. Then I thought, no, that can't be right. No one would bring a newborn up here. But I was right. It's funny how we can be right but we won't let ourselves believe.'

The newborn wailed, his cries carried off by the wind. Phorbas leant in to stare at the bundle. He snorted. 'So, what are you doing here with him?'

'Something terrible,' said Antimedes.

Phorbas narrowed his eyes. 'I was never very good at riddles,' he added.

Another cry. Antimedes began to rock the bundle from one side to the other. It did no good. 'I'm supposed to leave this newborn on the slopes here,' Antimedes said, 'behind a rock or something. And then walk away.'

'Walk away?' said Phorbas.

'Yes.'

'Leaving him behind?'

'Yes.'

'But if you do that he'll die.'

'Yes.'

'Then don't,' said Phorbas.

'But if I don't do what I've been told to do,' said Antimedes, 'I'll be killed.'

Phorbas was looking at him with an uncertain, strange expression. It wasn't that Phorbas didn't believe; he didn't want to believe, which was something else entirely.

'You believe me, don't you?' said Antimedes.

'I don't know what to think,' said Phorbas, 'but I do know you wouldn't make it up.'

'It would be Laius,' Antimedes said quietly.

'Who'd kill you?'

Antimedes nodded. The newborn cried. He jiggled it, but the action was pointless. The cries went on.

'Take him to Corinth,' said Antimedes, 'rear him as yours. Else he'll be dead in a few hours. Please?' His voice was flat.

'If I wasn't here,' said Phorbas, 'what would you do?'

Antimedes shrugged.

'And if I say no?'

Antimedes shrugged again.

'I don't have a choice, do I?' said Phorbas. 'All right, I will do as you ask. Pass him across.'

'I have to take back the swaddling cloth,' Antimedes said.

'Why?' said Phorbas.

'The queen wants it.'

'I'll fold him into my cloak,' said Phorbas. 'There's easily room for two.'

Antimedes began to unwind the swaddling cloth, stained brown and yellow in places. The newborn bawled but the wind was louder. When he got the swaddling cloth off entirely, he dropped it and trapped it with a foot to stop it blowing away. The newborn's feet, he saw, were lashed together with the queen's fillet, the one with the red pattern, the one she'd dropped on that boiling day, the one he'd retrieved and returned to her. It had been put on, he guessed, to stop the newborn wriggling. It had been put on to ensure as well as to hasten death. And it had been put on very tight. Too tight. He saw that too.

'Hold him,' said Phorbas. 'I'll free his feet.'

Phorbas pulled the fillet off and dropped it on the ground. The newborn's feet were swollen and red. Phorbas seized the feet and began to squeeze them gently but firmly, like he was milking. The wind howled and whipped the fillet away. It hit a bush and caught on thorns.

When the feet felt better to Phorbas, though the newborn still cried and wailed, he lifted his cloak by the hem and made a pouch.

'Fold him in here,' said Phorbas.

Antimedes laid the newborn down and Phorbas closed the cloak around him. Antimedes released the swaddling cloth from under his foot and folded it. The fillet, stuck on the bush, was twisting in the wind. Let it stay, he thought. Let it fray and rot. Let the king and queen assume the newborn's feet remained tightly bound.

'Good luck,' he said.

'I'll need it,' said Phorbas.

He strode off, the newborn in his cloak. As he watched him go, Antimedes heard the newborn's cries over the sound of the wind. They were thin, fretful, needling. He assumed the wind would soon drown them out. He was wrong. They didn't. He could hear them even when Phorbas had gone some way. He supposed a newborn's cries were meant to carry. Then Phorbas got further and of course the cries could no longer be heard. But Phorbas was still in view, only getting smaller and smaller. And then, finally, he disappeared and the mountainside was empty.

Antimedes didn't move. Instead, with his mind's eye, he pictured the hours ahead. He saw himself in the birth-house, in the birth-room, just him and the queen. 'I did it,' he heard himself saying. 'He was sleeping when I left him by a rock.' He wouldn't mention the fillet as that might raise suspicions but if she was asked he would say it was tight around the newborn's feet.

The picture changed. He saw Phorbas walking, his staff in his right hand, the bundle with the newborn tight in his left arm, his flock in front of him as he wound his way homewards to Corinth.

The picture changed again. He saw Phorbas with his bundle walking through a gate and entering the city of Corinth. More shadowy pictures followed. The newborn on a breast, feeding. The newborn in a crib, sleeping. The newborn on all fours, crawling. The newborn, now a boy, running; now a youth, swimming; now a young man, a figure full of force and vigour, singing.

Antimedes, as he imagined this future, had no actual idea what would happen. These were hopes, these were wishes, which he believed as if they were true facts. Nothing was yet certain because nothing had happened yet. But which of us in his position would not have done the same, thought the same? We would all have hoped as he hoped and wished as he wished and dreamt as he dreamt. The desperate eater always clears hope from his plate.

When he got back to the birth-house, Antimedes found Laius had left for Thebes. He wasn't surprised. The king had done what he must do and there was no need for him to stay.

The boy with the split lip and Callidice were in the kitchen. A cauldron full of water was heating on the fire. His mother took the swaddling cloth from him. She boiled the swaddling cloth and then, with Antimedes holding one side and herself holding the other, they held the swaddling cloth over the fire and dried it. Antimedes knew all about monotony but nothing he had ever done compared to holding the swaddling cloth over the fire, watching small wrinkles of steam rising from the material and smelling the wet wool smell it made as it dried. But eventually the task was completed.

'Take it to the queen,' she said. This was a breach in protocol. His mother should be the one to go to the queen. Why was he being asked?

'You will vouch for it,' said Callidice. 'If she asks you can say, yes, it is what the newborn was wrapped in.'

He went to the queen's room and knocked on the door. It was opened by the mute without a mole.

'Let him in,' said the queen. The mute stepped aside. He went to the bed where she sat propped upright.

'Give it to me.'

He held out the swaddling cloth and she snatched it and put a corner to her mouth and started to breathe through the material. After a couple of breaths, she let out a sob but then, after a few more breaths, something in her seemed first to contract and then to settle.

'It has his smell,' she said. She sat up. 'Put it round me.'

This was addressed to the mutes. One went on one side of the bed and one on the other. Each took an end and the swaddling cloth was opened and extended to its full breadth. The swaddling cloth was spread over the queen's brown shoulders and folded over her front. She clutched the ends and sank back.

'I will never be apart from this,' said Jocasta.

That evening Antimedes and his mother sat alone together in the kitchen, with only a single oil lamp on the table, its small flame the only light in the room. Antimedes could only see the outline of Callidice's head, the slope of her shoulders, her forearms tapering to her hands. Her face was dark and her features indistinguishable other than her teeth. He saw them vaguely from time to time, as she spoke. They were pale squares, floating in the black.

'Where did you leave him?' she asked.

'At the top. Very high. Very cold.'

'Was he awake?'

'No, sleeping.'

'The queen was asking. I'll have to tell her.'

'I thought she might ask me,' he said.

'She won't.'

His mother had introduced the subject so now he felt he could ask. 'What was the reason?' he said. 'Why did I have to do it?'

'The Pythia said that little thing was going to grow up and kill his father. Can you believe it?'

'What?' Antimedes found this incredible.

'Yes,' his mother said. 'When I first heard I didn't believe but, in the end, I did.'

'So that was why …'

'… you were sent to the slopes.'

Antimedes looked away into the blackness. He was glad his mother couldn't see his face because, like a stretch of water ruffled and cast about when the wind blows across it, all sorts of things were showing. By failing to abandon the newborn on the slopes and giving him instead to Phorbas to carry away to Corinth, he had thwarted what was intended to stop the Pythia's prediction coming true. This thought made him queasy and anxious until there came the counter-argument. For the Pythia's dire prediction to come true, both parties would need to live together. The newborn would have to have been reared in Thebes. In such a situation, in time, it was not impossible to conceive of the son murdering the father. After all, in royal families disputes and rivalries were not unknown and such an outcome not impossible. But the newborn was gone. He had been taken to Corinth where he would have a new life and acquire a new history. He would never again see his father; he would never again know his father, not as his father at any rate. The newborn would grow up a Corinthian and Laius would merely be, to him, the ruler of a neighbouring city.

This idea consoled Antimedes but following behind came the other argument, from which he could never shake himself free. To have done what he had been instructed to do would have doomed him. He would have been the one responsible for killing an innocent newborn, and that would have been a taint that he could never have washed away. He would have been guilty and the gods would have harried and punished him. But he had escaped all that. He had avoided wrong. His mother didn't know, of course. She believed he'd done as he'd been told. Well, let her, he thought. His lie made her happy and although he knew it was wrong, in this instance his lie was an insignificant offence compared to the much greater crime of killing a newborn.

The livestock and poultry were sent back to Thebes. The two carriages came from the palace. They were driven by Polyphontes and the other driver as before and they carried the same herald as before.

The queen emerged from the birth-house. Her head and her shoulders were covered with the swaddling cloth. Her face under the wrap was pale and drawn, and her walk slow and tentative. Her whole being had shrunk. Antimedes understood why: she had been made smaller by pain. Misery was like a fist, which squeezed whatever was in its palm smaller and smaller. The insight surprised him, for he was not used to thinking like this.

Antimedes watched the queen climb into her carriage and his mother get in after her. The boy with the split lip got up by the driver. The mutes got into the other carriage, which had the driver and the herald on the front seat. The lead carriage set off. The second, with the queen, followed. The carriages turned and left and bumped away down the road that led back to Thebes.

Antimedes watched until they disappeared from sight and then went back inside the birth-house. He swept the rooms. He put on the well covers and weighted them down with stones. He closed the shutters and tied them shut with cords. He closed the doors and blocked them with stones to stop animals getting in. He did everything else that it is necessary to do before a house is left. And once everything was done he went back to Mount Cithaeron.

BOOK TEN

After Phorbas got on the road from Cithaeron to Corinth with his flock and the newborn, the first thing he had to do was find a nursing mother and persuade her to feed the newborn. He did this. Once this woman had finished Phorbas explained his predicament. He had a newborn and he had to get him to Corinth. Did she know another nursing mother a bit further along the way to Corinth? he asked. She did, as it happened. Could she send a message ahead, he asked, warning her to expect him with a newborn that needed to be fed? She would, she said, and she did.

Phorbas went to the second woman and when she was finished, he reprised the conversation he had had with the first woman and she recommended a third woman and sent a message ahead. Phorbas repeated this process many times thereafter and by this expedient he advanced towards Corinth with his flock and the newborn. He went far more slowly than if he'd just been driving his flock, but Phorbas didn't mind. The pace gave him time to think. He particularly wanted to think about what he had promised Antimedes. He had promised to raise the newborn as his own.

But Phorbas had no wife and, as he realised, this infant had needs he couldn't meet. It wasn't just that he had to be fed and housed, though that was important, but he also needed to be raised. Phorbas was a shepherd and he spent half his life on the slopes. He wasn't going to be able to raise him and he didn't have anyone close to him who would do that either. His promise to Antimedes, he came to realise, was a promise that couldn't be kept. He would have to make other arrangements for the newborn. The notion that came to him pleased him greatly. Of course! His master Polybus, Corinth's king, and Polybus's queen, Merope, were childless. This perfect little newborn he had acquired was surely what they had been waiting for all their lives. But he would have to be tactful and discreet about the next part.

Phorbas reached Corinth. He put the newborn under his cloak so no one would see him. He drove the herd to the pens and went straight to the palace door, still keeping the newborn hidden.

'What do you want?' said the attendant at the door.

He explained he needed to speak to the king and queen. He asked for a private audience. The attendant saw he was carrying something under his cloak.

'What have you under there?' he said. 'It's not a dagger, is it?'

'A lamb,' said Phorbas quickly. 'It's a gift for the king and queen.'

The attendant padded off and communicated the message. Phorbas had been a royal herdsman for many years. He was much liked by the king and queen. 'Yes,' the royal couple said. 'We will see Phorbas. We will accept his gift.'

The attendant returned.

'Request granted,' he said.

He led Phorbas back to the royal apartment and opened the door. Phorbas went in. He waited for the door to close behind.

'You have a gift for us?' said Merope.

Merope was a small, neat woman. Her best feature was her mouth but inside her mouth she had too many teeth and an overbite, which embarrassed her. So that her overbite wouldn't be seen she was in the habit of keeping her mouth closed if she wasn't talking and if she was talking, of keeping her face down when she spoke, as she was doing now. 'A lamb, I'm told?'

'Not a lamb,' said Phorbas. 'A baby.'

Merope lifted her face. 'What?'

Phorbas lifted away his cloak.

'Oh my,' said Merope. She held out her arms and opened her mouth and let her teeth show. 'Here,' she said, 'give him to me.' She took the bundle.

'I found him on the slopes of Cithaeron,' Phorbas said, 'and I took him up and carried him here, for you.'

Merope bent down and smelt the newborn's hair and his neck. She pronounced him marvellous. She pulled each finger in turn. They were good. She announced she would check the body. She checked the head and face, looking up the nose and into the mouth and ears. 'Sound,' she said.

She peeled some swaddling cloth off to reveal the shoulders, the torso and the hips. 'Sound,' she said.

She pulled the rest of the swaddling cloth away. The thighs and knees were also sound but the feet, which had been bound with the fillet, were still red and swollen. 'What happened?' Merope asked.

Phorbas explained. He had met another shepherd on Cithaeron. The shepherd was carrying the newborn. The newborn's feet were bound. The other shepherd's task, Phorbas explained, was to leave the newborn with his bound feet down on the ground and walk away.

'He was supposed to die then?' said Merope.

Phorbas agreed that yes, he was.

'Well, we can't be having that,' said Merope. 'This child is perfect and who wouldn't want a perfect child? Well, someone didn't. Their loss. We will have him, won't we?' This last remark was addressed to her husband, who'd been standing watching everything she did but so far had said nothing. 'He will be our son, he will be our heir.'

'What would you call him?' said Polybus.

It struck Phorbas that by asking this question Polybus had just signalled his agreement to his wife's proposal.

'We'll call him, Oedipus – swollen foot,' said Merope. 'That's what.'

'Phorbas,' said Polybus, 'henceforth, I don't want to hear any talk about his parentage.' He indicated the newborn. 'Ever.'

'No,' said Phorbas carefully and quickly, 'you won't.' He already knew where this was going.

'This is our son now,' said Polybus. 'That is all Corinth needs to know. Let's not give them anything to gossip about.'

Phorbas knew exactly what to say next.

'No one saw him when I came through the city just now,' said Phorbas. 'He was under my cloak the whole time. And you can be sure I will never speak of this,' he said. 'Ever. To anybody.'

Merope held the newborn in her arms and rocked him. Polybus gave the shepherd three gifts – a jar of honey, a length of cloth and a small piece of gold. Phorbas protested that he expected nothing, but the king insisted. Phorbas left with the thanks of the royal couple ringing in his ears.

'I want the doctor,' said Merope to her husband. She was gazing at her son. 'We need to care for his feet. We need to make them strong and good again. And we need a girl to nurse him too. I'm sure there's one in the kitchen who'll do.'

The doctor came. Ointments were sourced and applied to Oedipus's feet, and a girl was found to nurse him. Merope moved the girl into her apartment so she would always be on hand and, when Oedipus cried in the night and had to be fed and the girl got up to feed him, Merope always got up to watch him being fed, and then, after the feed was done, she always walked the newborn up and down the room, patting his back to help the milk to go down and singing sweetly into his ear to sooth his fretful spirits, while the girl, who had never known anything like it – a queen walking a newborn up and down in the middle of the night – sat watching in amazement.

Merope had always wanted a child and the arrival of Oedipus made her happy. The only thing that worried her about the newborn, the only thing that made her unhappy, were his feet. But as time passed the redness of Oedipus's feet began to recede until eventually they were as smooth and white as his mother's elbows and knees. Once this happened Merope was finally fully happy. As things turned out, this would only be for a while.

Oedipus crawled normally and then he began to walk. His first steps were tottering as a child's always will be when they first begin to move about on two feet, until they grow bigger and stronger and start to walk and run with poise and confidence. With Oedipus, however, this did not happen. While other children's balance and stride improved, those of the other palace children he played with, for instance, his balance and stride didn't. His footsteps remained small and his movements remained staggering, as if his feet were still bound like they had been when he was given to Antimedes to dispose of, and when he walked or ran he often tripped himself up and fell over. This started Merope worrying and she became unhappy again. She summoned her doctor.

'His feet,' she said. 'Is there anything wrong with them?'

The doctor checked between the toes. He bent the toes. He bent the foot at the ankle. He examined the skin, slowly and carefully, prodding with his thumbs.

'These feet seem perfectly fine to me,' he said.

'So why isn't he walking the same as other children?' asked Merope.

'Perhaps he needs to be shown how to walk,' said the doctor.

Merope set about the task of teaching her son to walk, but he couldn't learn. His steps remained small and uncertain. He was clumsy; he lacked agility; he was ungainly; he frequently had accidents. Merope was in despair. Her son, perfect in every other way, would never move like others moved, so in this one important respect he was not perfect, and she hated that. But Merope had forgotten that we grow. And when we grow, we change. And when we change, what were previously insuperable problems are quite unexpectedly overcome.

Oedipus grew. His shoulders widened, his arms strengthened, his legs thickened. He became stronger and his new strength enabled him to accommodate his imperfection and adjust to his impairment. He still walked with small steps but he began to tumble less and then less again. By the time he was nine he was not tumbling at all and, what's more, it was already clear he was going to become a considerable athlete, a powerful swimmer and a formidable wrestler.

When he turned ten it was time for Oedipus to start his education. Merope took charge. She selected his tutors and the process began. Thereafter, she checked on her son's progress every day. When he lagged, she chivvied. When he excelled, she praised. Oedipus was quick and bright and lively and he learnt well but Merope was always there, pushing him on. She wanted him to excel and he was happy to excel because it pleased her.

The years rolled by. Oedipus turned eleven, twelve, thirteen, fourteen … With every passing year progress was obvious; with every passing year he was nimbler and quicker, more lucid and more knowledgeable; and so with every passing year Merope's delight and joy increased. She even came to adore her son's small steps and strange way of walking.

She was not alone. Later on, his family, his wife, my mother and his children, we also came to adore those small steps. We never thought of how he moved on his feet as an imperfection, or something that needed to be corrected. We thought of it as just one of those things that were part of what he was, like his laughter and his smell. What others saw as prancing, and sometimes described as prancing, we loved and saw as simply him.

But this was in the future in Thebes and the story, for now, is still in Corinth. The end of my father's time in the city was approaching and to understand why he left I must start his story again …

Antimedes took the newborn to Mount Cithaeron, where he found Phorbas. Phorbas took Oedipus to Corinth and in

Corinth, Polybus and Merope took in the newborn. From the moment he arrived, Polybus and Merope treated the newborn as if he were their child, the product of their love. And then, as time passed, belief hardened into fact, that's what he became – their child, and since he was their child, what need had they to tell him about his origins? None. He was theirs and nothing should be said to overthrow that. In the palace and out in Corinth, though without anything ever having to be said, this was understood as well. Oedipus was the son of Polybus and Merope and one day he would be king of Corinth and he would marry and produce a son who would follow him.

Oedipus was now a grown man. It was evening. A number of Corinthians gathered in the palace to dine with Polybus and Merope and their son and heir, Oedipus. There was meat, there was wine. One of the guests, a Corinthian whose name is forgotten, enjoyed himself hugely. He drank and drank and then, in his wine-fogged state, began to look around. He saw blurred and smeary faces. He heard chatter. He saw the wavering lights of the lamps. He saw goblets and jugs. He saw pieces of meat and knives. He saw the slaves who served moving nimbly and quietly. He saw Polybus. He saw Merope. He saw Oedipus who was sitting near them and a good way from where he was and as he did, the Corinthian remembered – Polybus and Merope had been childless once. Then they'd stopped being child-less. They'd acquired a son, just like that. Oedipus had come to them, as if from nowhere. And no one had said any-thing. Everyone pretended Oedipus was their child, their offspring, the product of their love, which he couldn't have been. And now, years later, there he was, the child, now a man, and everyone was still pretending he was theirs, and still he did not know the truth.

This Corinthian drank another mouthful of wine. He shivered with its force. Ignorance, he thought, was never good. Everyone deserved the truth, and now here he was in the palace, and there was Oedipus who didn't know, who was ignorant, and surely this was the perfect occasion to tell him the truth? The more he thought about it the more it seemed to this Corinthian that it was the perfect occasion, for when would he have another chance? He must seize the opportunity now it was within his grasp. He must do it. He must sing the truth.

All this came to the Corinthian with incredible force and clarity. It did not occur to him that the truth was unwanted, unasked for and undesired, or that his truth-telling might have catastrophic consequences. He was drunk. He was also tainted by arrogance. He believed he had a marvellous way with words. No one would do this better than he would, so he would do it.

The Corinthian saw Oedipus stand. He watched as Oedipus moved and stopped and spoke, now to this guest, now to that. Here was his chance, he thought. He could do this quickly, discreetly. He could go to Oedipus and they could have their conversation and that would be his duty done.

He emptied his cup and stood. He steadied himself with a hand on the table. He was filled with wine so he would have to be careful not to collide with anyone. But his brain was clear. He knew what to say. He knew how to say it. He was completely in charge and he was absolutely sure of the correctness of what he was about to do.

The Corinthian moved off slowly, one step after the next. In the distance he saw Oedipus, also moving, his steps characteristically small, his movements slightly tottery. The distance between the Corinthian and Oedipus was narrowing – closer and closer they got until finally the Corinthian was behind Oedipus, who was talking to a man sitting on a bench. No matter, thought the Corinthian. He would wait for their conversation to finish.

As he waited, he put his hand on the table and stared at Oedipus's head and shoulders from behind. Very fine they were, he thought, very noble, very manly. Finally, Oedipus finished talking and straightened and turned and saw the Corinthian, obviously waiting to speak to him.

'Yes,' he said.

'Oedipus,' said the Corinthian, and he pointed away from the table and into the gloom at the edge of the room. At the same time, he nodded and moved away. Oedipus followed him. They got to the wall. The Corinthian leant against it for support. Then he thought better of it. He straightened up. He didn't want to give the impression he couldn't stand up straight because he had had too much wine. Oedipus was looking at him, waiting for him to speak. Well, here it was at last, the moment when the truth would finally come to be told.

'You're not your father's son,' said the Corinthian. That's all he said. He was delighted that he had put it so clearly and so succinctly.

Oedipus looked at the speaker. This didn't make sense. Was something just said to him which, because of the wine he had drunk and noise in the room, he had misheard?

'What did you say?' he said. 'Say it again.'

'You're not your father's son,' repeated the Corinthian.

Oedipus's face whitened. 'You're drunk,' he said.

'I am,' said the Corinthian, 'but whatever I am, you're still not your father's son.'

Oedipus stared at the speaker. What was this sozzled fool talking about? Oedipus could have asked further questions at this point, but he didn't. The reason for this was obvious. He judged the Corinthian as belligerent and raucous. He didn't like him, he didn't trust him and he didn't think he'd get any sense out of him, either. Therefore, he decided, he would not engage. He would speak to Polybus and Merope instead. They would explain the drunk stranger's improbable and mysterious utterance.

Oedipus slept badly. The following morning, he was awake early. He washed and dressed. He found a palace attendant. 'Go to my parents and tell them I must talk to them and ask when I can come.'

The royal attendant went off and returned with an answer. 'You can go now,' he said.

Oedipus went to his parents' apartment and found Polybus and Merope standing waiting. Oedipus's message, communicated by the royal attendant earlier, had alarmed them. What could this be about? they had wondered. What could their son possibly want to talk about?

'Your request troubled us,' said Merope as Oedipus came closer. 'What can be so important you must talk to us so early?'

'Last night,' he began, 'a man told me I'm not your son. Is it true?'

Oedipus addressed the question to Polybus but Merope answered.

'Not true,' Merope said.

'You're my son,' Polybus said.

'You are our son,' Polybus and Merope said together, speaking as one.

As far as they were concerned, it didn't matter that he hadn't been conceived in their bed and nurtured in Merope's womb: what mattered was that he'd been reared by them *wholly and absolutely*. That made him their son; that made them his parents; and that was the end of it.

'You are our son,' Polybus and Merope repeated, speaking as one.

Oedipus listened to his parents and heard what they said. He believed what they said and yet, at the same time, he did not believe and his doubts were not assuaged.

Oedipus left his parents, assuring them his mind was at rest when it wasn't, and went to his rooms where he began to think dark thoughts. Was the Corinthian the only one who did not believe he was Polybus's son? Were there other Corinthians who believed this? And even if there weren't any who believed this *at that moment*, what was to stop the Corinthian from spreading the story and *it being believed*? There was no way of stopping the credulous believing something if they wanted to believe it. And then, if that happened, what would that do to his mother and father? It didn't bear thinking about. How did he stop this? Well, there was one irrefutable authority: the Pythia. And once he had her ruling, if the Corinthian or any other insolent fool dared to suggest he wasn't Polybus's son, he could shut them up with five simple words: 'The Pythia says I am.'

And so, without telling Polybus and Merope what he was doing or why he was doing it, Oedipus quit Corinth and set out on foot for Delphi, his steps small but sure.

BOOK ELEVEN

On the road over Mount Phicium, rain was falling hard. The ground was so wet it had lost its brown-earth colour and turned grey.

Two men walked on the road, bent by the rain. One was Haemon, the son of Jocasta's brother Creon, and the other was his friend Solon. Their broad-brimmed hats, their cloaks and their tunics were totally waterlogged; this made their clothes not only heavy to carry and freezing to the skin but chafing to move in. Their hands were red and raw. Their cheekbones were so cold they ached. In order to see they had to keep blinking to clear the water from their eyes and, as they plashed along, little bits of grit were carried into the spaces between their toes or under the soles of their feet. These stony fragments pressed into their flesh and made every step painful.

The road levelled and to their right the men could see the top lip of Mount Phicium's infamous cliffs and the great fertile plain that stretched below. It was filled with trees, farmsteads, hovels, byres, sheep-pens and fields, though in the rain these were all smeary and blurred and indistinct.

'Can we stop?' said Haemon. 'I've got to do my feet again.'

'Right,' said Solon. He peered ahead. 'What about that rock?'

They splashed towards it. It was huge, square, sand-coloured, with rain stabbing down and flowing off it. They lent their staffs against the rock and sat down. All around, in every direction, came the sound of the pounding rain.

'This is awful,' said Haemon. He untied both his sandals and set them behind him on the rock. 'It's the worst rain I've ever known.'

'That's what you say today,' Solon said. His sandals came off and went behind him too. 'But the next downpour you're caught in, you know what you'll say?'

Both began to carefully clean the grit from between his toes, one foot and then the other.

'This is the worst rain I've ever known,' said Haemon.

'Exactly,' said Solon.

'We forget the terrible,' said Solon, 'in order to keep going. Childbirth is the best example of that. If that was remembered, who'd do it more than once?'

'No one,' said Haemon.

The friends were clearing their soles, sweeping off the gravelly pieces stuck to their skin.

'My feet are stone free again,' Haemon announced.

He stuck his feet out. As the rain sluiced over his toes he wriggled them. Solon did the same.

'Poor old feet,' said Haemon. 'I'm very sorry I've put you through this ordeal.'

Both retrieved their sopping sandals and held them up so any grit would wash away. When they judged their sandals grit free, they dropped them on the ground, put their feet in place and began to fasten the ties around their ankles.

'My sandals are absolutely wet through,' said Haemon.

'Same here,' said Solon grimly.

'We're having an awful day,' Haemon said, 'but we'll be back in the palace soon enough ... and there'll be a fire, there'll be wine and bread and olives, and in an hour or two, we'll be dry and snug and we'll have forgotten this entirely.'

'I hear you,' said Solon. He finished fixing his sandals first, stood and peered into the rain.

'Haemon,' said Solon quietly.

Haemon heard the anxiety in Solon's voice and in response something in him tightened.

'We've got company,' said Solon. He retrieved his staff.

Haemon tied off his second laces, set down his feet, stood quickly and peered in the direction in which Solon was staring. Along the road, coming from the direction of Thebes, something was careering towards them. It was dun-coloured, four-legged and winged, the wings rising from the shoulders and flapping ferociously. They were for speed not flight.

'What is that?' said Haemon. He picked up his staff too.

The visitor came closer and now they could make its form out better. It was bigger than a dog but smaller than a horse. The body was leonine and so were the legs, which ended in pads on which it bounced along; the head and shoulders, however, that were attached to the body were mortal.

'I don't know,' said Solon. 'It's like nothing I've ever seen before.'

'Staffs ready,' said Haemon. Both gripped their staffs and adopted the fighting stance. 'We're two against one,' added Haemon. 'We'll prevail.'

The creature halted, not far away but not too close either. Through the swollen cords of pouring rain they saw that the neck and shoulders were a woman's and that she had breasts that were round and upright.

She dropped her wings and laid them along her back and then, lifting her feet high, shifted daintily this way and that on the flooded, stony road until she found where she wanted to stand. She was their height, but on account of her leonine body her mass and weight were much greater than theirs.

'Who are you?' Haemon spoke loudly so as to be heard over the din of the rain. Their visitor lifted her head and stared back at them

'I am the Sphinx.' Her voice was female too.

'Well,' said Haemon, 'we are Thebans from Thebes and we are on our way home.'

Haemon went to move forward

'Stop there,' said the Sphinx. She swung her tail round, caught Haemon in his middle and pushed him back. Her tail was as long as her body, thick and sturdy, silver below, grey above, a pattern of shrinking green arrowheads running its entire length like on a snake.

'We ask to pass,' said Haemon. He pushed against the tail. It was huge and heavy and it wouldn't budge. 'We are expected in Thebes today,' said Haemon. 'I am warning you not to stop us.'

'Are you?' said the Sphinx.

'We are legitimate travellers going about legitimate business,' said Haemon. 'You may not hinder us but if you do there will be a reckoning.'

'Will there?' said the Sphinx

'I am the queen's nephew,' said Haemon. 'My father, Creon, is her brother. I wouldn't stop us if I were you.'

'Well, you answer my question,' said the Sphinx, 'I'll let you pass.'

'No,' said Haemon, 'we don't have to do anything.'

'Wait,' said Solon. 'Let's see what she wants.' Solon angled himself towards the Sphinx. 'What do you need to know?'

'Excellent,' said the Sphinx, turning her dripping head and gazing into Solon's face. Her eyes were blue, her mouth wide and soft and her teeth, behind the lips, small and neat.

'You've listened,' said the Sphinx, 'unlike him.' She gestured at Haemon. 'What's his name?'

'Haemon.'

'And yours?'

'Solon.'

'Your friend hasn't listened, Solon, because he doesn't think he needs to listen on account of being Creon's son, the queen's nephew. As he will learn shortly, it doesn't matter who you are – you will listen to the Sphinx when she poses her question, and if you answer her right, you pass by.' She waved a paw at the cliff edge. 'And if you answer her wrong, over the top you go.'

'We have done you no harm,' said Haemon, 'you should do us no harm. Step aside. Let us pass.'

'What creature,' began the Sphinx, 'with only one voice, has four feet and then two feet and then three feet and is weakest when it has the most feet and strongest when it has the least feet?'

The rain poured on. It smashed onto the traveller's hats and the Sphinx's shoulders and head.

'That's a ridiculous question,' said Haemon. 'I've no idea. A pomegranate?'

The Sphinx knocked Haemon's staff from his hands. He half turned and made as if to step back. She opened her wings with a crack, reared up and drove her front paws down on his shoulders and knocked him to the ground. He landed hard on his back and cried out. He tried to get onto his front so he could get onto his hands and knees and get up. The

Sphinx flapped her wings, making a noise like little claps of thunder, and leapt across to Haemon. She lowered her head and started to roll him like a log through the rain and the muck towards the cliff's edge. She moved him with great dexterity and terrifying speed.

Solon ran up behind the Sphinx. He raised his staff over his head, intending to smash it down on her head – but before he could, she sliced her tail sideways and caught him on the hips. The blow was vicious. He fell to the ground, losing his staff as he went, and banged his head hard. He opened his eyes and saw shiny, fuzzy improbable things as rain poured onto his face. He heard a shout, long and drawn out and terrible. Haemon falling, he thought. The shiny, fuzzy improbable things vanished. Solon struggled back to his feet. He saw the great black sky boiling above and javelins of rain hurling downwards and the Sphinx peering over the cliff edge. His friend was gone.

The Sphinx backed away from the cliff edge, spun about and sprung at him. Next thing he was down again on the ground and the Sphinx had her paws on his chest and her face was above his face. Her hot breath smelt of straw and dates. The rain was plinking into his eyes and he had to keep blinking in order to see.

'Get off,' Solon shouted. He tried to squirm free but the weight of the Sphinx was too great. He groped for his staff but failed to find it. He wondered if he too would be thrown off the top of the cliff.

'Solon,' said the Sphinx, 'you won't die, not today.' Had she read his thoughts? Impossible to know. 'You will run to Thebes,' the Sphinx continued, 'and tell them I have a riddle.

No one passes unless they answer it right. A wrong answer means death; over the edge you go. And if anyone should ask, you say I am retribution – for what Laius did to Chrysippus.' The paws came off Solon's chest. 'Go.'

He slithered backwards from the Sphinx and stood up. He heard ringing in his ears. There was his staff, lying on the ground. Should he get it? No, he thought, he should forget his staff and run.

Solon pelted off, his feet kicking up water and debris as he did. He was hot with apprehension as he expected the Sphinx to strike from behind. He had gone a good way when he thought he could risk glancing back. There was no sign of the Sphinx. She was gone.

The road began to fall away in front of him. Solon pounded on, letting the descent carry him down, and as he went he saw nothing except the road snaking ahead and the city's walls rising far away and slowly, slowly, as he ran on and got closer and closer, he saw the walls rising higher and higher. He had only one thought. He had to get to the city. He had to get to the palace. He had to report what he had been told.

The Phicium gate appeared ahead. It was open. The gate-keeper was sheltering from the rain under the arch overhead.

'Hey, you,' the gatekeeper shouted at him. 'What's with the hurry?'

'Don't stop me,' Solon shouted ahead. 'Let me through.'

'Is something coming behind?' the gatekeeper shouted back. He stepped out into the rain. 'Do I need to close the gates?'

Twenty paces and Solon would be there, right up to the gatekeeper.

'Nothing behind, nothing,' he shouted.

The gatekeeper took his staff in both hands. Solon saw the gatekeeper would block him. He faltered, stopped.

'Nothing, nothing behind,' he said. 'I have a message. For the king. Let me past.'

Solon registered a change in the gatekeeper's expression. The man lowered his staff and peered through the rain at him. 'What sort of a message?'

Solon's legs were shaky. 'It's for him, not you.'

'What happened to you?' said the gatekeeper. 'You look terrible.'

'I saw something on the road ... death.'

'At the Phicium cliffs?' asked the gatekeeper. 'A suicide?'

'No,' said Solon. 'Not that kind of a death.'

The gatekeeper lowered his staff entirely. 'You'd better go and tell what you have to tell then.'

Solon stepped forward, stopped and turned. 'Come to think of it,' he said, 'I think you should close the gate. And don't let anyone out either. No one should go near the cliffs.'

Solon ran through the gate and into the city. The city's streets were slimy and wet. The channels running alongside were filled with gushing water. Every house, tavern, shop and brothel was closed and shuttered. There were only a few people, cloaked and hooded, hurrying wherever they needed to go. Dogs cowered everywhere, whimpering and soaked, their coats matted. As Solon passed, they wagged their tails, hoping the person pounding by would take them some-where dry and warm. One or two stalwarts even ran after him before giving up and scurrying back to where they'd been sheltering.

Solon ran into the front courtyard of the palace, then sprinted towards the open main door. A doorkeeper sat inside on a chair, staring out at the rain. He had a staff across his lap. When he saw Solon running towards him he stood.

'Hey,' the doorkeeper shouted.

Solon stopped a few steps from the door.

'You must be lost. This is the palace. You're in the wrong place.'

'No, I'm not in the wrong place,' Solon said. 'I have a message. For the king.'

'Oh really,' said the doorkeeper. 'Everyone says that when they come here. All right, what is it?'

'It's not for you.'

'I repeat, that's what everyone says when they come here. Go on, get away.'

From behind the doorkeeper appeared a bearded man. 'What's going on?' he asked.

The doorkeeper straightened up. The bearded man was Antimedes. He was no longer a shepherd. He had been promoted. This was inevitable after what he had done for the king and queen on Cithaeron's slopes. He was Laius's personal servant now.

'This man has a message,' said the doorkeeper quietly. The rain pounded on the roof tiles and surged along the gutters and cascaded down the walls and gushed across the courtyard.

'What sort of a message?' said Antimedes.

'Something important,' said the doorkeeper. 'He has to tell the king, he says.'

Antimedes looked at Solon. He noticed how Solon's cloak clung to his body and how his hair was stuck to his face. 'Do I know you?' said Antimedes. 'I do, don't I. I've seen you, haven't I. You're Haemon's friend.'

Solon peered through ropes of wet at the figure in the doorway. His dash to the city had heated him up but now he had stopped running he was terribly cold in his rain-soaked clothes. He shivered. He felt faint.

'Yes,' said Solon. 'I'm Haemon's friend.'

'Come inside,' said Antimedes.

Solon struggled up the steps and went into the hallway, then followed Antimedes into a room with a fire and a chair.

'Sit,' said Antimedes.

Solon threw off the wet cloak and dropped into the chair. He held out his hands and folded himself forward towards heat. There was rain coming down the chimney, he noticed, and the drops, when they hit the flames, sizzled and fizzled.

'Tell me what the king must know,' said Antimedes, 'and I will pass it on.'

'Haemon and I,' Solon began, 'were trudging up the Mount Phicium road in the rain. We stopped so we could take stones out of our sandal and this lioness – woman, bird creature, the Sphinx, she called herself – bolted up to us. She told us she had a riddle, and she said it must be answered or she wouldn't let us by and from now on every traveller would be asked and everyone who gave the wrong answer would go over the top.'

'What was the riddle?' asked Antimedes.

'What creature, with only one voice, has four feet and then two feet and then three feet and is weakest when it has the most feet and strongest when it has the least feet?'

'Go on ...'

'I didn't answer but Haemon did. He was wrong and she hurled him off the top because that's what happens if you answer wrong. Then she told me to bear the news to Thebes that she was on the Mount Phicium road, and she told me to say it was because of what Laius did to Chrysippus that she had come here.'

Antimedes nodded. He didn't know who Chrysippus was but Laius was his master and he must serve his interests. His task was to stop any of this leaking out.

'The first thing I have to say to you,' he said quietly, 'is you can't mention this to anybody. Not a word.'

'Why would I?' said Solon.

'You can't even tell your mother or your father,' said Antimedes. 'It seems extreme but I have a reason and I'm going to tell you what that is. The Sphinx let you live.'

'So,' said Solon.

'Yet she killed Haemon.'

'Yes.'

'Think about it. This Sphinx stops two friends. She poses a riddle. One dies. The other, who survives, comes back to Thebes and tells the story. But there is an inconsistency. She asks everybody the riddle, you said, so why doesn't she ask you like she asked Haemon? Frankly, when you look at it, your story about the Sphinx having you bear the news to Thebes does look a bit convenient.'

'What do you mean? She didn't ask me to answer the riddle,' Solon shouted, 'that's all that happened.'

'But why didn't she?'

'I don't know, because she needed me to come to Thebes and …'

'But you said everyone has to answer. What was different about you?'

'I don't know!' Solon shouted.

'How about: you pushed Haemon forward, made him answer first, and he got killed. You got him killed, in other words. And then you said, to save your skin, "Let me take a message to Thebes" and the Sphinx, who hadn't thought of this before thought, "Yes, I'll spare just this one and he can go and tell the city about Chrysippus and Laius …"'

'No,' said Solon.

'For unless she had a messenger – you, who had cunningly volunteered himself – how was she going to get the message to Thebes?'

'I never pushed Haemon forward,' said Solon, 'I never thought of saving myself. What happened was what I told you.'

'And you think Thebes will believe you?'

'I didn't sacrifice Haemon,' said Solon. 'I just didn't answer. That's why I was spared.'

'I repeat: you think the people of Thebes will believe you? No. They'll think you sacrificed Haemon, the queen's nephew, so you could live. Now, what do you think the king will do to the man who let his friend die so he could live?'

Solon began to cry. He shook his head.

'Alright,' said Antimedes, 'this is what we'll do. You say nothing about this to anyone. Not a word. Understand? You leave it to me.'

Solon wiped his eyes with the back of his hand and looked at Antimedes.

'Do we have an understanding?'

Solon nodded.

'Can I hear a yes?'

'Yes.'

'I'll take you to the kitchen and get you something,' said Antimedes. 'Once you're settled I'll go to the king and queen and talk to them. You won't be in trouble, don't worry.'

Antimedes took Solon to the kitchen and then he went to the king and queen. He told them everything except for the part about Chrysippus. Antimedes had never heard of Chrysippus but he guessed Laius had and therefore it would be cleaner and simpler if he just left him out.

Despite the rain, Laius sent a search party to the foot of the Mount Phicium cliffs. They found Haemon's body. They found the bodies of other unlucky, hapless travellers who, in the time since Haemon had been killed, had been waylaid by the Sphinx, and having failed to answer her riddle were also heaved over the cliff. The bodies were carted back to the city and identified by their mothers and wives as sons and husbands. Laius issued a decree. All Thebes' gates were to be kept permanently closed and all Thebans were banned from using the Mount Phicium road. Unfortunately, travellers from other cities couldn't know this and so bodies continued to turn up at the foot of the cliffs. And as the bodies continued to mount up, the rains did not stop. They just went on and on and on.

Laius, meantime, lurked in the palace and brooded. Something was wrong, he didn't doubt that, but what was the cause? The only way to find out was to ask the Pythia. He must go to Delphi, he realised, and consult the Oracle and learn what he needed to learn. It would be awful he didn't doubt, but it was better to know, far better to know, than not to know.

*

In the pelting rain, Laius's carriage rolled out of the palace courtyard, the same one that had carried the queen to the birth-house. It was pulled by two horses, both black this time. On the outside seat, in cloaks and hats, sat Laius's driver, Polyphontes, and the herald with the black eyes, the long hands, the big knuckles and the skull criss-crossed by long scars: inside, also in cloaks and hats, sat Laius, Antimedes, and a servant.

The carriage rolled through Thebes' wet streets, unnoticed except by sodden dogs and beggars, and came to the closed gate to the Delphi road. The gatekeeper was in his shelter at the side, keeping dry.

'Open the gate for the king,' Polyphontes shouted.

The gatekeeper emerged, pulled back the wet bars and opened the dripping gates. The carriage sallied out. The gates closed behind. The carriage rumbled on. The rain fell. A thick slick of water covered the road and the carriage wheels sloshed in the water as they turned. Great sheets of water had formed in those fields where the ground was level. Water poured down the edges of the terraces. Every living green thing looked beaten and brutalised. In the carriage nobody spoke. This was the rain. It stopped all talk.

The carriage moved for a whole day and for the whole day it rained. The carriage stopped in the evening under trees. The travellers lit a fire with difficulty. The ground was too wet to lie on and they all slept together in the carriage, Laius, the servant, Antimedes, Polyphontes and the herald.

When the five woke the next morning it was no longer raining and the sun was in the sky. They set off and, as they trundled on, the five watched great clouds of steam rising up from the earth as it dried out. It was a relief that the rain had stopped and the sun had returned. However, as the day wore on, it became clear that this was a much hotter and a much fiercer sun than any sun they had ever known. Had they swapped the misery of endless rain for the equally dire alternative of a merciless sun? When evening came and it was easy to light a fire and the ground was dry enough to sit and sleep on, everyone in the party gave the appearance, at least, of being in good spirits.

At the Oracle, Oedipus had paid his fees and performed his rites. He had been vetted by the priests and drawn his lot. Now he was sitting and waiting his turn under a canopy strung up to provide some shade from the boiling sun. He was surrounded by other waiting supplicants.

'I hate sitting with the question going around and around in my head,' said his neighbour, 'and my mind coming back with every conceivable answer.'

'I'm not thinking now,' said Oedipus. 'I'll do that when I come out.'

'You're a lucky fellow,' said his neighbour.

Oedipus yawned. 'I'm just going to close my eyes,' he said, 'if you don't mind.' He folded his hands on his lap and let his eyelids drop.

Oedipus felt his arm being touched and opened his eyes and looked up and saw a priest with black skin. The priest nodded. Oedipus stood. The priest took him by the hand and led him off. They entered the temple, a relief after the heat outside. Inside was a smell of burnt mutton mixed with a sweet, putrid odour. Oedipus felt strong and certain and sure. He felt his feet moving, taking him forward, one small step after the other. He felt his lungs going up and down as his breath went in and out.

They descended some steps. The space below was even darker than the temple above. The smell of mutton wasn't so strong but the sweet, putrid odour was much stronger.

There were the drapes and the priest had one open and was beckoning him through. Oedipus stepped forward and went in and the priest followed him and he heard the drape fall behind.

He was in an enclosed space lit by brands. There was a smell of burning pitch as well as the other smells. The Pythia was on a bowl-shaped seat with three legs. She was old, and wore a young girl's short white dress. In one hand she held laurel leaves and in the other a bowl with water in it. The priest bent down and put his mouth to her ear. The Pythia closed her eyes and shuddered as the god entered her. Then she opened her eyes and the god looked out through her eyes at Oedipus. The priest nodded to Oedipus. He should begin.

'Am I my father's son?' he asked.

'Yes, of course you are your father's son,' said the god through the Pythia, 'though you would be right to wish you weren't, because you should also know you will kill your father and then you will take your father's place in the marriage bed as your mother's second husband.'

He would what?

Oedipus reeled. Of course, he only got this horrific answer because he'd asked the wrong question. Notwithstanding what the Corinthian had said, he was certain he was Polybus's son and he had come to have that confirmed. He could not conceive that Polybus and Merope were not his parents. Thus, because he believed something that wasn't true, he wrongly interpreted the answer he got. He thought it was to these beloved two he would do the worst, not realising the

Pythia meant two other entirely different people who he'd never met and didn't know.

The priest brought Oedipus back to the light and left him where they'd started, below the canopy and surrounded by supplicants. He was flooded by waves of rage and shame, despair and terror. How could he have lived his life until now and not known what lurked in his breast? How could he have not known what he was capable of? He had always thought he loved Polybus and Merope.

He must save them and he must also save himself. How would he do both? The answer was obvious. He would never go home again. He would forge a new life and once he was settled, wherever that might be, he would send a message back to Polybus and Merope, letting them know he was alive, assuring them of his health and happiness, and informing them he could not return. Obviously, he would not tell them why. That would destroy them.

But what if my father hadn't made this plan? What if instead he'd returned home to Corinth and had another conversation about his origins with Polybus and Merope. This might, in turn, have led him to Phorbas. Or what if instead he'd thought to search out the Corinthian whose name is forgotten and asked him why he said what he had said? Who knows, second time round, how their conversation would have gone?

But in order for the truth to have come out he would have to have known we must take nothing for granted, especially what we most cherish. He would have to have already known and accepted that it was possible he was not Polybus and Merope's son. But he was too young and too frightened and too confused to allow himself to think that such a thing might even be possible and so he did not go home and ask questions. He went the other way.

*

Oedipus retrieved his cloak, his hat and his staff, slipped out of Delphi and set off along the road to Thebes, which went in the opposite direction to Corinth. And as he made his way, one tottering step after another, his mind turned. He had lost his parents. He had lost his home. He had lost his place in the world. He had lost everything. It was not fair. He had done nothing to deserve this. He had been blameless his whole life. But that didn't matter, it seemed. The way he had lived counted for nothing. He might have lived blamelessly but he was being punished as if he had not.

As he walked on, anger rose from deep inside, a hot, scalding vapour. The further he went, the denser the vapour became until eventually he couldn't see anything anymore. He was in a fog of rage.

The sun in the sky was bright and fierce and the shadows on the ground were short and dark. The road on which the wheels of Laius's carriage turned was winding and stony. The ground on either side of the road was littered with rocks and fallen trees and dotted with untidy thickets of scrub. There were no passing places along this stretch.

Inside the carriage Antimedes sat on the forward-facing seat. The window was on his left and Laius was sat to his right. The servant sat opposite, his back to the driver.

Antimedes was silent, stunned by the heat. So were Laius and the servant, he imagined, for they were silent. On the outside seat, much to his amazement, he could hear Polyphontes talking to the herald but he couldn't make out what the herald was saying.

The carriage stopped.

'We've stopped!' said Laius. He tapped Antimedes. 'See what's happening.'

Antimedes stuck his head out the window and looked up the road. He saw they were just short of the place where the road split, with one arm leading away to Daulia and the other to Delphi, and standing between their carriage and the fork stood a young wayfarer. He was hatted and cloaked and he carried a heavy staff.

'Hey!' Antimedes heard Polyphontes shouting from his seat at the wayfarer. 'Get off the road! We need to pass.'

'Why should the man on foot give way to the carriage with wheels?' the wayfarer shouted back. 'Who made this rule?'

'Don't be a blockhead,' Polyphontes shouted back. 'How can we get off the road? Look at the ground on either side.'

The wayfarer set the end of his staff on the ground, leant on it and laughed.

'This carriage bears a king,' Antimedes heard Polyphontes roar. 'You must give way to a king. You should know that.'

'If this king says "Please, may I pass?" – well, I will let you through,' Antimedes heard the wayfarer shouting. 'But it must be him who asks. You won't do. And if he won't ask, well, you may sit there in the sun all day. I shan't get out of your way.'

Antimedes wondered about the wayfarer's strength. He looked sturdy enough. But he was one and they were five. They would prevail, if it came to it. He sat back on his seat.

'We're where the road splits, and it's one way to Daulia and the other to Delphi,' said Antimedes to Laius, 'and we can't get past. There's a wayfarer in the way.'

'This is ridiculous,' Laius said. He stuck his head out the window. 'Who are you?' he shouted down the road.

'Oedipus,' the wayfarer shouted back.

'Oedipus,' shouted Laius, 'make way for your betters. Get off the road.'

'No, king,' the wayfarer shouted back. '*You* get off the road.'

'Herald,' Laius called. 'Get down. Walk ahead. Push him out of the way. Polyphontes, follow behind. If you have to, drive over him.'

The king sat back. His face was red against his silver hair. Antimedes heard a donkey braying in the distance, its cry sawing the air. He felt the carriage dipping slightly as the herald hopped off the carriage. He heard the clack of the reins as Polyphontes shook them and the carriage started to move. Outside the window he saw straggly bushes, piles of rock, scattered trees and patches of green, all lit by the hard, bright, cruel white light of the sun.

There was a thud and a scream.

'The herald's down!' Antimedes heard Polyphontes shout.

The carriage stopped then juddered and Polyphontes leapt down from his seat.

'Out,' Laius shouted. 'Fight!'

The servant and Laius grabbed their staffs and jumped through the doors. Antimedes did not get out. He did not get out because he knew that if he did he would die.

I do not know how Antimedes knew this, but he did.

And my father, out there on the road, what about him? Had he any thoughts? No, none. With him, at this moment, it was just blind rage. And with blind rage, restraint is

*impossible. Rage has no eyes. It's all doing. So, on he went,
doing what a man with a heavy wooden staff does to other
men: smashing, splitting, breaking …*

From his seat in the carriage Antimedes heard the noise of
human flesh when it is pounded, and the sound of human bone
when it is cracked, a sound like pottery in a pillow being stamped
on. He heard shouting and cries and he distinctly heard Laius's
voice. 'I'm hurt,' he heard Laius shouting. 'I'm down.'

Although he had decided he wouldn't look but would
sit and wait, Antimedes couldn't stop himself once he had
heard Laius's voice. He stuck his head out one of the windows and looked up the road. He saw Polyphontes and
the herald and the servant lying in different places and he
saw the king sprawled face down in the dust. It looked to
Antimedes as if Laius was trying to crawl away on his front
like a serpent. The wayfarer was beside him. The wayfarer
raised his staff and brought it down on the back of Laius's
neck. The blow was ferocious and Laius's body went still and
Antimedes knew Laius's life force had left him.

The wayfarer poked Laius's shoulder with the point of
his staff to confirm he was dead. And once the wayfarer
knew Laius was dead, he turned away and started to poke
the other bodies on the ground: Polyphontes, the herald and
the servant. Antimedes did not need to see any more. They
were dead too. He was sure of it.

Antimedes withdrew his head from the window and
sat back on his seat. He had been right not to get out, he
thought. Had he got out, he too would now be laid out on
the road and the wayfarer would be poking his dead body
with the point of his staff. He had been right to stay. He

had been right to keep alive. That meant there was now someone who would bury the corpses. That meant there was now someone who would carry the news of these deaths to Thebes. And he was that someone.

And outside the carriage once again, on the road, as he confirmed he had dealt death out to everyone, what was in my father's mind? He had intended to harm, he had intended to win, but now it was over he saw what he had done, and that was something else. He had taken life four times, and there were the dead lying around him on the burning ground to prove it. I think he was surprised, even though there could have been no other outcome but this one. He was also impatient. He had done what he had done. There was no going back. He must go forward. He must go on.

In his place inside the carriage, Antimedes heard the horses whinnying and treading their hooves. He heard the sound of footsteps, and then he saw the wayfarer bobbing past the window.

'Stay right there,' the wayfarer said, without looking in at Antimedes. 'It wouldn't be worth it.'

Then Antimedes heard the wayfarer's steps as he moved away up the road down which the carriage had just driven, the road to Thebes.

Antimedes judged it was safe. He got out of the carriage. To his right, the dead. The other way, left, the wayfarer, his staff on his shoulder, the hem of his cloak rising and falling as he went, his shadow on the ground following behind. There was something odd about his gait. He bobbed as he went, like a small boat at sea going over a wave and falling and then another wave and falling and so on.

'You could have stepped aside,' Antimedes shouted after him. The wayfarer stopped and turned.

'You were always going to run me over,' he shouted back. 'What else could I do? Now, don't annoy me. I'm walking away. Be happy I've let you live.'

He turned and walked on. Antimedes smelt horse sweat, horse spit, horse dung, and the damp smell of sweat-soaked leather. The tail of the horse closest to him swished and the hairs of the tail brushed him …

Into Antimedes's mind a memory hurried. He was standing on the windswept slopes of Mount Cithaeron watching Phorbas stride away with the newborn. He remembered the kitchen in the birth-house in the evening. He was with his mother. Antimedes could only see the outline of Callidice's head, the slope of her shoulders, her forearms tapering to her hands. Her face was dark and her features indistinguishable other than her teeth. He saw them vaguely from time to time, as she spoke. They were pale squares, which floated in the black.

'The Pythia said that little thing was going to grow up and kill his father,' his mother said. 'Can you believe it?' He had given the little thing to Phorbas. And now, years later …

Yes, this had to be the newborn, now grown, who had just walked past him, carefree, ignorant of his offence. He would kill Laius; the Pythia said so, and he had. When he gave the newborn away Antimedes believed he was changing the future, but now he saw he had been wrong. He hadn't changed the future. It had turned out as it was supposed to turn out and all he had done was help it along. We live forwards, he thought, but understand backwards.

Antimedes looked up the road. The stranger, further on, heading away. A fly, a heavy, black-bodied thing, buzzed about him. He waved his hand and drove it off. He turned the other way. He saw the bodies on the ground. One of the horses lifted a booted hoof and stamped it down, making a hollow clacking sound as it hit a stone. He would tie the horses up. He would bury the bodies.

And what of my father at this moment as he left the carnage he had caused and moved away? Did he remember the Pythia's words? She'd told him he'd take a life, and hadn't he just taken a life? Indeed, many lives. Did he wonder if there was a connection between what he'd been told and what had just happened? The answer is no, he didn't. On and don't look back – these were now his watchwords.

Three days after he left the bodies on the road, Oedipus arrived at the gate in the city of Thebes that served the road to Delphi. The sun was high and white in the sky.

'Gatekeeper,' Oedipus shouted. 'Open the gate.'

The gatekeeper slid back the trap in the middle of the heavy side gate and put his face to the tiny mesh covered opening.

'What do you want?' said the gatekeeper.

'What do you think?' said Oedipus. 'You're a city. I'm a wayfarer. I want to come in.'

'The gate's closed,' said the gatekeeper. 'All the gates are closed. By order of the king.'

'Why do you want to keep travellers out?' said Oedipus.

'Who said anything about keeping travellers out?' said the gatekeeper. 'This to keep people in.'

'Why would you do that?'

'Obvious,' said the gatekeeper. 'To stop them wondering.' He explained there was a creature, the Sphinx, on the

Mount Phicium road, who waylaid every traveller with a question they must answer before passing and when they answered incorrectly, as they all did, she threw them off the cliff top. The only way the city could be rid of her would be if her question were answered correctly.

'And what is the question?' asked Oedipus.

The gatekeeper shook his head. 'I'm just the gatekeeper,' he said. 'I don't know.'

'Right,' said Oedipus, 'so I really don't get in then?'

The gatekeeper shook his head. 'No, sorry,' he said. 'The gates stay closed till the king orders otherwise. Or the Sphinx gets her answer.'

'Well, I'll have to give it to her then,' said Oedipus, 'if that's the only way I'm going to get in.'

'Looks like it,' said the gatekeeper.

'Which is the quickest way to the Mount Phicium road?'

The gatekeeper told him.

'You'd better warn them at the Mount Phicium gate to expect me later,' said Oedipus, 'and when I appear they had better let me in. You can give them my name. Oedipus. Have you got that?'

'Oh, I have, certainly,' said the gatekeeper. 'Oedipus. I'll be sure to let the gatekeeper over there know. He'll be expecting you. Don't you worry.'

Oedipus didn't believe him, not that he cared. But the news he planned to bring back would open every gate. He turned and walked away, following the line of the city's walls. The gate-keeper, having watched him go, then banged the trap shut.

Oedipus climbed the Mount Phicium road and reached the cliffs. The Sphinx lay stretched out across the road in the sun.

She was asleep but hearing his footfalls she woke and lifted her head and stared at him.

'Stop,' she called. Oedipus stopped.

She rose to her feet and arched her back slowly, like a cat. 'You wish to pass, you answer my question,' she began.

'I know, I know,' said Oedipus. 'Get on with it.'

'And if you fail what happens?'

'I go over the cliff,' said Oedipus. 'Now get on with it.'

The Sphinx was surprised. Everyone always wanted to postpone the moment when the question was put and the answer was offered, but this wayfarer didn't. Something in her trembled and she didn't know why. Was this wayfarer's urgency a sign that for the first time ever her question would fail her? No, she thought. No one had ever answered her question correctly. No one would, either. It was unanswerable.

'What creature,' she said, 'with only one voice, has four feet and then two feet and then three feet and is weakest when it has the most feet and strongest when it has the least feet?'

The wayfarer in the hat and the cloak laughed. 'Is that it?' he said. 'Is that your question?'

The Sphinx tried to see more of his face but couldn't. He had his hat pulled down and his features were in shadow.

'The answer is any man and any woman,' said Oedipus. 'First they are born and crawl on all fours. Then they grow older and walk on two legs, which is when they are strongest. And finally, in old age, bent and tired and stooped, they make their way here and there with a stick to help them, which is why they are sometimes said to have three feet.'

The wayfarer took off his hat and bowed deeply. The Sphinx walked to the cliff's edge, folded her wings down and stepped off. There was a long wail and then nothing except for the shrill cry of the cicadas.

It was dark when Oedipus appeared at the Mount Phicium gate.

'Open up,' he shouted.

The trap set into the gate slid back and the gatekeeper's face appeared in the tiny square space. 'Gate's closed,' he said.

'Didn't you get the message?' said Oedipus. 'You were supposed to have the gate open for me. I gave the man at the Delphi gate my name. Oedipus.'

'No,' said the gatekeeper. 'I got no message. Now go away.' He slammed the trap shut.

'The Sphinx is dead,' shouted Oedipus at the wood.

'What?' Oedipus heard from the other side of the gate.

'The Sphinx is dead,' he repeated. The trap shot open again. 'I thought that would get your attention.'

'What happened?' said the gatekeeper.

'She jumped. Open the gate.'

'No,' said the gatekeeper. 'First I will inform the queen.'

Oedipus sat on the ground in the dark in front of the Mount Phicium gate. He was cross-legged and his staff was across his knees. Behind the closed gates he heard the sound of the wooden keepers being slid back. This was followed by the hinges groaning as the two gates were folded backwards into the city. In the space that appeared stood the woman he assumed was the queen, a royal attendant beside her holding a staff.

'Wayfarer,' she called. 'The Sphinx put her question to you?'

'She did.'

'And your answer?' asked the queen.

'Obviously the right one,' said Oedipus, 'otherwise she wouldn't have jumped.'

The queen, the attendant following, stepped out through the open gateway and walked across the dry earth until she stood a staff's length from Oedipus. He stood up.

'We can send a search party to the foot of the cliffs tomorrow,' said Jocasta, 'and they will find out whether you've told the truth or not.'

'The answer to her riddle,' said Oedipus, 'is us. I told her. She heard me and she jumped.'

He heard the queen's breathing quicken. 'We're saved,' said Jocasta. 'The city is saved.'

She leaned in and stared at the wayfarer's face under the hat. She could only make out the eyes, which were dark and wet and bright.

'Take off your hat,' said Jocasta. 'I want to see your face.'

He took off his hat. She saw the shape of his head was very square, like Laius's.

'Come,' she said. 'The king is away. He will be back soon enough. He will be delighted.'

On the morning of the fourth day since the killings, having buried the bodies, Antimedes set off for Thebes. The sun, instead of giving out the violent hurting heat of recent days, was giving out a gentler and kinder warmth, its rage having subsided. Antimedes didn't pay much attention to this change because his mind was very much elsewhere. What was he going to say to the queen? As he drove he tried out various versions of what he might say to her. Eventually he settled on what he thought was the simplest version and he practised it until he could deliver it without stopping or stumbling.

Antimedes drove through the night and all the next day and it was night again by the time he arrived at the gate that served the Delphi road. He had expected to find the gate shut as Laius had ordered but to his surprise it was wide open and there were Thebans milling on the other side of the gate inside the city. Although it was dark, he knew they were drunk. The gatekeeper was sitting on a stool and leaning against the outside wall.

'Gatekeeper,' Antimedes shouted at the man. The gatekeeper stood up and staggered over.

'Why is the gate open?'

'Because if it was closed you wouldn't be able to come in, would you,' said the gatekeeper. He laughed. He clearly thought his quip was hilarious. 'Now it's my turn to ask a question. Who's in the carriage?'

'Nobody,' said Antimedes.

'But this is the king's,' said the gatekeeper. He went to the window and stuck in his head, then took it out again.

'No king.' He burped. 'Did you lose him?' He laughed again. 'We're waiting for the king, you know. We're all waiting for the king. The whole city. We have some very good news. And he's going to be very pleased when he hears what we have to tell him. It's all over. We're saved.'

In the street beyond the gate, shouting, singing, cheering.

'Why is everyone drunk?' Antimedes waved at the Thebans swaggering and staggering in the street beyond.

'That'll be because,' the gatekeeper began, 'a wayfarer came here two days ago and we told him – I mean he was told – about the Sphinx. And do you know what this wayfarer did? Only flew up there, to the cliff top, like an arrow. And doesn't he answer her riddle? It's us, man or woman! She jumped, of course. Down she went. All the way to the bottom. Splat.

'So the queen ordered celebrations tonight. Wine for the whole city, as much as you want. Now all that remains is for the king to come home so we can tell him the good news. Thebes is saved.'

'This stranger – has he a name?'

'Oedipus.'

'Oh,' said Antimedes. His mouth sagged open.

'I'm drunk,' said the gatekeeper, 'but even drunk I know a worried face when I see one.'

'I have my woes.'

Antimedes saw exactly what he needed to say next. He lifted his head and looked straight into the gatekeeper's bleary eyes.

'Can you keep a secret?'

'Oh yes.'

'Swear. Make an oath.'

The gatekeeper swore.

'A party of robbers attacked the king on the road to Delphi. He is buried on the road back there. I am on my way to the queen to break the news.'

He did not imagine the gatekeeper would keep this information to himself. This was good. Every Theban needed to know the king had been murdered by a party of robbers.

Antimedes drove the carriage carefully along the dark streets full of revellers. One or two recognised the king's carriage and called out. The king was home, they thought. Antimedes didn't bother to correct them. They would know the truth soon enough.

Antimedes went to the room where his mother slept, woke her and told her what he was going to tell the queen.

Callidice hurried to the queen's quarters. She entered the dark bedroom and shook the queen's shoulder.

'Antimedes has returned,' she said, 'and he's alone. You had better hear what he has to say.'

Callidice helped the queen to dress. The queen went to her receiving room and took her seat. Callidice lit the lamps. Antimedes was admitted. Callidice left the room. Antimedes took his place in front of the queen. The queen nodded. Antimedes lifted his eyes and looked at the place behind the queen where the top of the wall met the ceiling above.

'On the third day of the journey to Delphi,' Antimedes began, 'the sun was high and bright. We were on a narrow road with rough ground on both sides full of rocks and dead trees. There were no passing places along this stretch. I was on the forward-facing seat. It was hot. The horses were tired. The king was beside me, the servant opposite. Polyphontes and the herald were on the outside seat.

'Through the window I saw faces. There were men outside the carriage. They'd been hiding behind trees and as we passed they jumped out and swarmed around us. I knew they were going to take everything we had.

'I felt the carriage dip – that was the robbers jumping up onto the outside seat. I heard Polyphontes and the herald shouting. The carriage doors were pulled open. A robber at the door closest to me. I went for my staff but before I had it, he grabbed my arms and dragged me out. I landed on the road like a fish in the bottom of a boat. Bang! A blow across my shoulders. Bang! The next blow would be to the head.

'I rolled onto my left shoulder. My attacker struck again and his staff hit the road and snapped. I grabbed the stump and pulled, and down he tumbled onto the road, head first. He rolled away. Before he got up and came back at me I scampered under the carriage. I heard feet kicking and fists punching. I heard the terrible cries and shouts as Laius and Polyphontes and the herald and the servant were beaten. Then the cries and the shouting stopped. I heard the robbers pulling off hats, cloaks and whatever was portable. Then I heard the robbers running away with their booty. I came out then. I saw the bodies. I set about burying them and once that was done, I came back to break the news to you.'

The queen cried hard for a while. Then she cried less hard.

'Did Laius ask for me at the end?' she said. 'Did he say my name?'

'I don't know,' he said. 'He might have, but I didn't hear.'

'Are you sure?' said Jocasta. 'You would have heard, wouldn't you, something like that?'

'Not from under the carriage I wouldn't,' he said.

The queen cried again and then she stopped crying and she invited him to sit. He fetched a stool, carried it back and sat. The lamps had burnt out and between the laths of the shutters, the early morning light began to show.

Jocasta dabbed her eyes with the sleeve of her dress. 'In the birth-house,' she said. Her voice sounded distant but also sullen. 'Do you remember that?'

Antimedes nodded. 'I do.'

'Can you imagine how I feel now, looking back?' said Jocasta.

Antimedes held himself still so nothing would show.

'Bitter,' Jocasta shouted. 'Bitter. The Pythia spoke. My newborn was wrenched away. And now look how it's turned out! Laius was killed by robbers. My newborn needn't have gone to Cithaeron to die. I could have kept him. And if I had – what then? Go on, answer my question.'

Antimedes shrugged. 'I don't know.'

'Thebes would have a new king – and he would be *my* son. I would be the mother of the new king. Can you see why I rage?'

He nodded cautiously.

'This is too confusing, too tumultuous,' Jocasta said. 'I would like to stop and I would like to go to sleep and I would like to stay asleep and I would like never to wake up.'

Jocasta got up and paced around the room and came back and sat down. From outside came the sounds of the city as it woke. The voices of the women on their way to the wells, the cries of the hawkers, the shepherds and their animals with their tinkling bells, the shouting and singing of the drunks left over from the night before.

'Can I ask a favour?' said Antimedes. The queen waved a hand. 'I'd like to leave the palace and go back to the slopes.'

Jocasta looked at him. 'Do you know something you're not telling me?'

'No,' said Antimedes.

'I feel you do,' she said. 'You mean no harm. I know that too. But you're keeping something from me.'

Antimedes shook his head. 'On the slopes I will be quiet and silent, and I will live a blameless life.'

'If that's your wish,' said Jocasta, 'then I grant it. You may leave the palace and go back to the land.'

The next day at dawn Antimedes went to the yard where the sheep were penned. He carried a skin of wine and a pouch with a huge square of crumbly cheese and a loaf of bread and a knife. He drove a flock of sheep out of the city and up onto the slopes of Cithaeron. He passed the spot where he'd handed over the newborn but he didn't stop. That night he slept in a hut on a sheepskin. He slept soundly and happily.

A servant led Oedipus to the queen's apartment, stopped at the door and knocked. Callidice opened the door. The laundress was expecting the visitor. She nodded gravely. She motioned Oedipus to come in. He slid across the threshold. She pointed. The queen sat in a chair by the window, looking out at the sky.

Callidice stepped out and closed the door, leaving the wayfarer and the mourning queen alone together in the room.

'Are you there?' said Jocasta, who still hadn't turned.

'Yes,' said Oedipus. He stared at her neck and at the back of her head.

'My king is gone,' said Jocasta. Oedipus had heard Laius had died on the road but he said nothing.

'It is obvious what must now be done,' she said. Again, Oedipus said nothing.

'You will be king,' she said.

'And you?'

Jocasta turned from the window and looked back over her shoulder. 'I will be your queen, of course.'

'Of course.'

Antimedes was looking up at the clouds. His sheep were dispersed around him, nibbling away. Their bells tinkled occasionally. A man in a sheepskin approached, another shepherd on his way with his flock.

'Did you hear?' the shepherd called.

'What?' Antimedes called back.

'We're to have a new king.'

'Who?'

'This man who rid us of the Sphinx …'

Antimedes felt his stomach tremble.

'He's the son of a king,' said the shepherd.

'He is?' said Antimedes. 'What king?'

'Polybus,' said the shepherd. 'Polybus is Oedipus's father.'

'Polybus.'

'Yes,' said the shepherd, 'the king of Corinth. And this stranger, he's marrying our queen.'

'Is he?'

'Corinth's loss, Thebes's gain.' It sounded like a line he'd repeated many times. 'Last night there was a ceremony at the palace, pre-wedding. There was a sacrifice and then the queen had the priests burn a child's swaddling cloth. For luck, I think.'

The shepherd stopped in front of him. 'You don't look too good,' he said. 'You've gone pale.'

'I don't know, something's come over me.'

'Free wine for every Theban on the wedding day,' said the other. 'You want to make certain you're back in the city for that.'

Antimedes stood up and vomited up the barley bread and wine he'd eaten earlier.

'Would you like some water?' The shepherd offered Antimedes the skin he carried.

'Thank you.'

Antimedes took the skin, drank, rinsed his mouth and spat. He handed the skin back to the shepherd.

'You look terrible,' said the shepherd.

Antimedes shrugged and lay down and hugged his stomach as if he were ill. The shepherd left. After a while

Antimedes sat up again. He could see the shepherd in the distance walking away. He would need to keep quiet and he would need to keep out of sight, Antimedes thought, in the months and years to come. No one could know what he knew and as long as that remained the case and he alone carried the burden, all would be well and there would be no trouble. Could he do this? Could he keep this secret? He believed he could. He had to. He knew what nobody else knew and he must ensure it stayed that way.

BOOK TWELVE

My parents were blessed with four children, two daughters, my sister Ismene and me, and my two brothers, Eteocles and Polynices. When we were young my father loved to play with us and I particularly remember the great labyrinth games he organised. He would run a red cord through the palace, in and out of doors and windows, with little treats left along the way; and we had to follow it, hand over hand, no short cuts, all the way from start to finish, where we would find him waiting with our big treat, smiling. I would say we were happy. And because our royal house was happy, Thebes prospered too.

Meantime, while we grew up, Antimedes worked on the slopes, out of sight and out of mind, while his mother worked in the laundry. The years rolled on. Antimedes became an old man and Callidice became a very old woman.

And then ...

Jocasta lay in bed naked, her front pressed against Oedipus's back. She was warm and sleepy and she could smell something. She sniffed. What was this? She opened her eyes and sniffed again. It smelt like rotting plants and old fish heads.

'Oedipus,' she said. 'What's that smell?'

Oedipus sniffed. 'That's awful,' he said. 'What is it?'

Later that morning the reports began to flow into the palace. The crops in the fields around Thebes, the crops that the people of the city relied on for food, had been struck – overnight, it seemed – by a blight. That was the smell. The crops were rotting. Jocasta's brother, Creon, was dispatched immediately to Delphi to ask what should be done.

Down in the dark space with the sweet putrid smell Creon watched the Pythia. Her eyes were closed. She rolled her shoulders. Something juddered inside her. That would be the god, he thought, entering her. Her eyes opened and the priest touched his wrist.

'A blight has settled on our crops,' said Creon. 'Everything we grow is tainted and dying. Tell me, tell Thebes, what must we do to stop this.'

'Laius's murderer is in your city,' said the Pythia. 'Root him out, and the blight will leave. Let him stay hidden, the blight will stay.'

'And who is he?' Creon said.

Creon felt a hand on his shoulder. It was the priest again. His touch was forceful.

'You asked your question,' he said, 'and you had your answer. You cannot ask another question.'

Making his way back from the Oracle at Delphi, Creon saw great pyres of rotting crops burning in the fields around Thebes.

In a room in the palace, Creon and the king and queen were together in council. The royal attendant was there in one corner, awaiting instructions, while incense burnt in another corner, its thick scent masking the rotting-plant and fish-head smell. The floor, walls and ceiling were lightly dusted with thin grey ash from the pyres. The ash was also under the fingernails and in the hair, ears, eyebrows and armpits of everyone in the room. All the city's inhabitants were the same.

Creon reported to the king and queen what the Pythia had told him; Laius's murderer was in the city and must be identified or the blight would never end. In response Oedipus began firing questions off like an archer shooting one arrow after another and the queen answered just as quickly.

'How did Laius die?' Oedipus asked.

'Robbers.'

'Was he alone?'

'No. He was with one of five.'

'Were they all killed?'

'No, only four were killed,' said Jocasta. 'One lived and he returned and he told us how Laius had died and was buried on the road with the others who had died with him.'

'When was this?'

'Before your time,' said Jocasta. 'When we were having our difficulties with the Sphinx.'

'And this survivor who told you what happened – what sort of a man was he? Was he truthful?'

'Oh yes, utterly truthful,' said Jocasta. 'He's been with us all his life.'

'So, he's alive?'

'Oh yes.'

'Where is he then?'

'On Cithaeron. He's a shepherd.'

'We must have him here,' said Oedipus, 'seeing as he was there with Laius at his end. He can tell us what happened and out of his account something might emerge, something which ...' Oedipus stopped.

'And what,' said Jocasta, 'what do you think will emerge?'

'Something that will help us find Laius's killer,' said Oedipus.

'But we already know what happened,' said Jocasta. 'Laius was killed by robbers. That's all he'll say and it's what we already know.'

'Yes,' said Oedipus, 'but the Pythia has spoken. Laius's killer is here, amongst us. The first thing we do is we get this man here, and we put him across his story and something may show up that was never noticed before.'

'The robbers are not in the city,' said Jocasta.

'They must be. The Pythia said. I believe her,' said Oedipus. 'Don't you? We must believe her.'

'Must we?' said Jocasta. 'Listen to me. After we got married, Laius and I, there was a son, and that newborn, his feet bound to stop him crawling, was taken away and left to die out in the open, on Cithaeron, because the Pythia told Laius this child would kill him. And then who does kill Laius? The newborn? No. Robbers. So much for divination, I say. Now, you want the man who was there, who saw Laius killed, you want him to come here and tell you he was killed by robbers – we can have him here, if that is what you want.'

'Well, it is what I want,' said Oedipus. 'I want this man here.'

'If it's what you want,' said Jocasta quietly, 'you will have what you want but I am sure that the robbers who killed Laius are *not* in the city today.'

The royal attendant, who had been following the conversation, straightened himself up as he believed he was about to receive an order from the queen. But instead, before she could speak, a strange look came over Oedipus's face and he waved his hand at her and stopped her in her tracks.

'You never said where Laius was killed,' said Oedipus.

'On the road,' said Jocasta.

'Yes, but which road?'

'On the road to the Oracle, where it divides, one way to Delphi, the other to Daulia.'

'How many were with him? Big party? Small party?'

'I said already,' said Jocasta, 'party of five. Polyphontes, the driver, a herald, a servant and Antimedes plus the king, five, and they were all in one carriage.'

'Did the king have silver hair?'

'What does that matter?'

'Did he or did he not?'

'He did. But why does his hair matter suddenly?'

'At home in Corinth, before I came here, I was told by a drunk I was not my father's son. I went to the Pythia. She said I would kill my father and make my mother my wife and after hearing that I knew I could never go home. I set off to make my own way in the world and where three roads converged, I met a carriage with five strangers, one with silver hair. The road was narrow. I would not give way to them. They would not give way to me. We fought and I prevailed. What if the silver-haired man I killed was Laius?'

'Laius was killed by robbers!' shouted Creon. This was the first time he had spoken since relaying what the Pythia had said. 'How often do we need to repeat that?'

'Listen to my brother and then listen to me,' said Jocasta. 'The Pythia told Laius his son would kill him. Wrong. Robbers killed Laius. And what she told you, that you would make your mother your wife and kill your father … Wrong again. Wrong, wrong, wrong. Don't you understand?'

'This Antimedes,' said Oedipus, 'who was there with the Laius at the end. He's the shepherd you spoke off?'

'He is. I already told you that.'

'We must have him.'

Jocasta turned to the royal attendant. 'Do you know Antimedes by sight?' The royal attendant nodded. 'Take a couple of boys and go to Cithaeron. Find him, fetch him back. The boys can stay behind and watch his sheep.'

'I will,' he said.

'And be quick about it,' Oedipus added.

The royal attendant took his staff.

'I shall walk out with you,' said Jocasta to the royal attendant. 'I have been in here too long.' She nodded to her brother. 'I'll be back.'

Jocasta and the royal attendant glided along the palace corridors and went out into the courtyard. There was a strong smell of scorch and ash here, stronger than in the palace, but when she looked up she couldn't see the dust of the pyres floating past although she knew it must be there because every surface in the palace was coated with it and it was under her fingernails and in her hair, ears, eyebrows, armpits.

'Excuse me.'

Jocasta saw the voice belonged to an old fellow in a hat and a cloak, with a face dark from the sun.

'Ask him what he wants,' she said to the royal attendant.

'Yes,' said the royal attendant in his fluting voice to the old fellow. 'What do you want?'

The man explained he was a messenger whom Merope, queen of Corinth, had sent to bear a message to her son, Oedipus: his father Polybus was dead.

Jocasta gave a short bitter laugh and shook her head.

'I am not laughing because I'm happy at the news you bear,' she said to the messenger. 'I'm not happy. I'm shocked, and my reaction is the product of my shock and means nothing.'

The messenger looked at the queen and nodded but otherwise showed no expression.

'Go to the stables, get two boys, and hurry to the slopes,' she said to the royal attendant. 'And you, messenger, you follow me. I will bring you to the king.'

The queen ushered the messenger into the dusty room with the incense burning in the corner and closed the door after herself. Creon was gone and Oedipus was alone.

'This man comes from Corinth,' said the queen. She turned to the messenger. 'Unburden yourself,' she said. 'Tell him what you told me.'

'I have news from home for you,' said the messenger. 'It will throw you down and it will raise you up. It will sadden you, actually desolate you, and it will lift you.'

'What can grieve and please at the same time?' said Oedipus.

'Our people now speak of you as king of Thebes *and* Corinth. That should please you.'

'I don't follow,' said Oedipus. 'Corinth has a king.'

'Had,' said the messenger. 'Had.'

'Your father is dead,' said the queen. She turned to the messenger. 'That's what you've come from Corinth to tell us, isn't it?'

'It is. He's dead.'

Jocasta turned to Oedipus. 'Do you hear? Your father – the man you've avoided because you were told you would kill him – he has died, but not by your hand.'

'How did he die?' said Oedipus to the messenger. 'Was it an accident, sickness, foul play? What killed him?'

'Old age,' said the messenger.

'Old age?' said Oedipus. 'I was told I was to kill him and now he is …'

'He is in the grave,' said the messenger.

'Do you see now, Oedipus,' said Jocasta, 'all your anxiety, your fretting, your scruples on account of what you were told, they were nothing. Nothing!'

'When I came into this room,' said the messenger, 'I sensed something dark and pressing and now I sense it again behind the queen's words. Can what is dark and pressing be spoken about to a stranger, because if it can be I might be the stranger to speak to.'

'I was told by the Pythia,' said Oedipus, 'that I would kill my father and make my mother my wife and after I was told that I turned my back on Corinth. That's why I have never been back, since I left.'

The messenger shook his head and smiled. 'You could have come home anytime,' he said. 'Any time at all. And nothing would have happened. Polybus is not your father. He never was.'

'He's not my father?'

'No more than I am,' said the messenger, expansively. 'You are not related.'

'I was his son, that's what I was told … I don't understand. And why are you the one who knows this?'

'Because I gave you to him,' said the messenger.

'You gave me to him?'

'I did.'

'But I always felt I was his son … he loved me as his son … and Merope loved me as her son … but she's not my mother either? Is that right?'

'She isn't.'

'And you're saying you gave me to them?'

'Yes.'

'Did you buy me?'

'I found you.'

'You found me?'

'I did. I found you,' said the messenger. 'In a manner of speaking.'

'Where?' said Oedipus.

'Cithaeron,' said the messenger.

'Cithaeron?'

'Yes.'

'What were you doing up there?'

'Working as a shepherd, looking after one of Polybus's flocks,' said the messenger. 'And, as chance would have it, I was your rescuer. You were brought to the mountain. You were supposed to be left there to die. Your feet were bound together. I acquired you, let us say, and I carried you away to Corinth.'

'Who wanted me to die? Was it my father or my mother?'

'I don't know,' said the messenger. 'You'll have ask the man who had you and who gave you to me.'

'And who was that?'

'Another shepherd.'

'Another shepherd,' said Oedipus. 'And whose shepherd was he?'

'One of Laius's.'

'One of Laius's shepherds?' said Oedipus. He turned to Jocasta. 'Do you know this man, this shepherd of Laius's?'

'What?' She seemed confused as well as annoyed. 'Which man?'

'This shepherd of Laius's,' said Oedipus, 'that this man from Corinth just told us about. Do you know him? Is this man the shepherd you've just sent for? Is he the one I asked to see?'

'I have no idea who this Corinthian is talking about,' said Jocasta. Her face was red. She was flustered, angry. 'Forget what this fellow from Corinth has said,' she said, loudly. 'It's nonsense.'

'Nonsense to you maybe,' Oedipus shouted, 'but not to me. I shall pursue this trail to the bitter end. I will know who I am. And I will know what I sprang from, even if it's a slave. Better to know that than to know nothing.'

'Leave it,' said Jocasta. 'I implore you. Leave it. For my sake. For your sake. Send this man back to Corinth and forget everything you've heard.'

'I won't,' said Oedipus. 'Our friend from Corinth will stay and I will hear this shepherd when he comes and I will know everything.'

'Do that and you're finished,' Jocasta shouted. 'Do you hear me? You want us done for, finished, ruined? Well, that's what you're going to get.'

Jocasta sped to the door, opened it and rushed away down the corridor. Then she went up some stairs and along another corridor. Her intention was to end her life. She would hang herself. A noose fashioned from a bed sheet tied to something high was what she had in mind. But as she pounded along, the queen saw a spear leaning against a wall. It had a smooth shaft and, at the top, a death-dealing point with sharp, cutting edges. Oh, yes, she thought. This was better than the noose. Much better. Cleaner, swifter, surer.

She grasped the spear, carried it to her apartment, went in and closed the door shut with a bang. She was alone in the room. There were no servants. There was no Callidice. Now there was nothing left to do except to prepare herself and then do it and that way escape the shame and the disgrace, which she knew were coming.

It was afternoon. The sky was as smooth as eggshell. The only sounds were the clang of the sheep bells and the rasp of cicadas. Antimedes sat on the ground halfway up Mount Cithaeron, his back to a rock, gazing at faraway Thebes. He could see fires burning all over the countryside and fingers of black smoke drifting skywards from the fires and he could smell ash and scorch and mixed in with the ash and the scorch he could smell rotting plants and old fish heads stinking in the sun, an odour of mould and decay and taint. Something was going on down below but he'd no idea what.

He heard the tramp of feet amongst the pine trees to his right. Then, out of the trees, three figures emerged, a man and two boys. Antimedes recognised the man was the royal attendant with the high cheekbones and the strange fluting laugh, the one who had once struck his mother with a staff. The two boys he recognised from the stables. When the visitors had nearly reached him, he stood up.

'Antimedes,' said the royal attendant. The boys peeled away and headed towards his sheep. 'You're to come with me. You're wanted at court.'

'Is it my mother?' Antimedes asked. 'Is she sick?'

'I've no idea if she's sick,' said the attendant, sounding mildly irritated. 'I don't know your mother.'

Antimedes wondered. Did the attendant connect him to Callidice? Did he remember hitting her? Probably not, he thought. On the other hand, of course, this could just be pure guile. The attendant knew exactly who he was and remembered exactly what he'd done to his mother but in order to ensure there would be no awkwardness on their walk together to Thebes, he had decided to act as if he had no notion who Antimedes's mother was. That seemed most likely, Antimedes thought, and also, now he came to think of it, the most advantageous from his point of view. He needed to get the royal attendant to talk. He needed to know what was afoot. So if the attendant had purposely set any potential cause of friction to the side, that could only be a good thing.

Antimedes gathered his staff, his carrying pouch and his wine skin. They began to walk. They fell into step. Antimedes gestured at the smoke plumes in the distance.

'What are the fires for?'

'Blight,' said the royal attendant. 'The farmers are burning everything rotten.'

Ah, thought Antimedes. The smells of ash and scorch and rotting plants and old fish heads stinking in the sun. Now he understood.

'There's no blight up here,' he said.

'There wouldn't be,' said the royal attendant. 'It's only what's cultivated that's blighted – olive trees, vines, corn. Whatever just grows, trees, grass, anything wild, the blight doesn't touch it.'

They went on in silence for a good while, each lost in his own thoughts until Antimedes judged he might as well try again with the question he needed answered.

'Who wants me at court?'

'The queen sent me,' said the royal attendant. 'But it's the king who wants you.'

'Oh.' He hadn't expected that. 'And was there really nothing said about why? Surely there are more important things to do than speak to an old shepherd in the middle of a blight?'

'You tell me,' said the royal attendant. 'These are mad times. You don't know the half of it.' They left the open ground and passed into the wood. A bird was calling.

'What don't I know the half of?' said Antimedes.

'It appears …' the royal attendant began. 'This is incredible, but the queen and Laius – remember Laius? – they had a child. Who knew? Right at the beginning of their marriage.'

Antimedes felt his stomach twitching and his thighs trembling.

'A child,' he said. He hoped he sounded doubtful and disbelieving

'Yes,' said the royal attendant, 'and Laius got it from the Pythia that this newborn was going to kill him. So what do you think they did, the king and queen, with their newborn?'

Antimedes felt his face burn red. He feared the royal attendant might notice and so that he didn't he pretended to look at something of great interest in the distance between the trees.

'You'll have to tell me,' said Antimedes. 'How would I know?'

'Only tied the newborn's feet together,' said the royal attendant, 'and gave him to some servant to take to Mount Cithaeron to leave on the slopes to die, which the fellow did. Now that's quite something, but it gets even more fevered.'

Creon, continued the royal attendant, who had recently gone to Delphi to consult the Pythia about the blight, had just returned to Thebes. The Pythia's counsel, Creon reported, was that the murderer of Laius, so many years ago, was in the city: his presence was the cause of the blight and until he was rooted out the blight would rage on.

'And that's where you come in,' said the attendant. 'You were there when Laius was slaughtered, weren't you? You're wanted so you can tell that story again.'

The attendant rattled on. The Pythia's old prophecy about Laius being killed by his son would be shown to be wrong when he, Antimedes, re-confirmed it was robbers who had done the deed. And if that prediction was wrong then her new divination must also be wrong. Laius's murderer wasn't in the city. This was Jocasta's thinking, at least.

'These are fevered times,' said Antimedes, speaking low so his voice wouldn't be heard to tremble.

'And it doesn't end there,' the royal attendant said gleefully. 'There's even more.'

More? thought Antimedes. What more could there be? Wasn't this enough?

'Polybus ...'

'Polybus?' said Antimedes.

'Yes, king of Corinth, father of Oedipus ...'

'I know who he is.'

'He died,' said the royal attendant.

'When?'

'The messenger from Corinth arrived as I was leaving to come here. It can only have been very recently.'

Antimedes looked up. Here and there he could see little bits of blue sky showing through the canopy of the trees.

'How has the king taken his father's death?' Antimedes asked. 'The news couldn't have come at a worse time.'

'I don't know.' The royal attendant shrugged. 'I only know how the queen took it. She laughed when she heard, quickly, and then she corrected herself. If you ask me, they're stirred up. She's gone mad. They've both gone mad.'

They reached the edge of the forest and stepped out into the light. Antimedes had to squint momentarily as his eyes adjusted. They were on a stony path. Their footsteps were noisier now. In the distance Antimedes saw the city's walls, brown in the heat, and between him and the city he saw pyres everywhere. The smells of ash, scorch, rotting plants and the old fish heads stinking in the sun were stronger.

There was something strange about the vines ahead at the side of the road, and Antimedes asked if he could take a closer look. The royal attendant waved approval. Antimedes stepped away from the road and bent down to examine the first plant. The grapes, which should have been juicy and green, were shrivelled and brown. The leaves were spotted with black blisters. The twisting, flaking trunk was split and from the cracks a nasty white liquid had dribbled out, run down and puddled on the ground at the foot of the plant. The next vine and the next and the next and every vine to the end of the row were afflicted in the same way.

Antimedes returned to the road and walked on with the royal attendant, both men silent again. Ahead he saw olive trees. There was someone there, a farmer he supposed, shouting and screaming at the trees. The nearer they came the louder the voice became. When they drew level Antimedes saw the olives were shrivelled and brown, the leaves were spotted with black blisters and the trunks were split and leaking the nasty white liquid.

'My trees, look at my trees,' shouted the farmer.

They went on and after a bit they passed their first pyre. In the sunlight its flames seemed abnormally pale. The closer to Thebes they got the more pyres there were. The smell worsened. They covered their mouths with the edges of their cloaks.

Halfway up the back of the door to her apartment, Jocasta noticed a strut that ran crosswise. She lifted the spear and rested the end of the shaft on the strut and held the point to her heart. She was not ready yet but she was getting there and once she was there she would press down hard and the tip would fly in and go through her.

Antimedes and the royal attendant arrived at the palace. They crossed a courtyard and traipsed down a corridor. A door at the end, closed, a servant standing outside. The royal attendant knocked twice.

'Yes,' said someone inside.

The servant pushed the door back to reveal the king, standing in a dusty, dark room.

'Here is the shepherd,' said the royal attendant from the threshold.

Antimedes smelt the smouldering incense.

'Bring him in,' said the king. The first time Antimedes had seen Oedipus was on the road to Delphi: then he had been a young man. Now, years later, he was a big-boned, big-shouldered, red-faced adult.

The royal attendant stepped aside and Antimedes went in. The royal attendant followed him and closed the door behind them, and now Antimedes realised there was another person in the room. It was an old man, as old he was, judging by the way he stood. He was holding his hat in one hand and his staff in the other. The way he stood seemed familiar. Antimedes had seen him a long time ago, hadn't he? Then, quickly came the contradictory thought. It was hardly likely he'd be here in Thebes. He couldn't be.

The figure turned, and Antimedes saw the old man's face. He was older than when he had last seen him but Antimedes knew there was no doubt. Out of everyone who could have come with the news of Polybus's death, it was him.

Antimedes's hands tingled. His knees wavered. He felt exhausted and terrified. He wanted to sit down.

'Do you know who this is?' Oedipus asked the sunburnt old man while pointing at Antimedes.

The old man came up and stared at Antimedes with a tender expression. 'Yes,' he said. 'This is him.'

The voice was unmistakably Phorbas's. Oh yes. It was his friend, from Cithaeron. Antimedes turned his head away and looked down at the floor. Perhaps if he couldn't be seen properly the other wouldn't be so sure and might even take back what he said.

'So, shepherd,' Antimedes heard Oedipus say. He realised the king was speaking to him. 'You worked for Laius?'

Antimedes nodded. 'Yes,' he said, keeping his face down.

'What did you do?'

'Shepherding … mostly.'

'Where?'

'Cithaeron and thereabouts.'

'Do you remember this man?' Oedipus waved at Phorbas.

Antimedes felt his mouth going dry. He swallowed. 'What man?'

'This man,' said Oedipus. 'Look up. Look at him. Have you ever seen him before?'

Antimedes lifted his head as little as he could get away with lifting it. He could just see Phorbas's face.

'I don't know,' he said. 'I can't say.'

'It was a long time ago,' said Phorbas. He addressed this remark to the king. Antimedes took the opportunity to drop his face again. 'But I'll help him remember Cithaeron,' continued Phorbas.

Antimedes felt the other man's touch on his arm. It was gentle but sure. He couldn't pretend he hadn't been touched and he couldn't ignore what the touch meant either. He had to show his face. He had to return Phorbas's gaze. He lifted his face. The face that looked back at him was brown and creased and friendly.

'You can't have forgotten,' said Phorbas. 'We were there together. Spring to autumn, we were up there, and then I'd take my sheep back to Corinth and you'd go back with yours to Thebes.'

Phorbas stared into Antimedes's eyes. 'Don't you remember?' he said.

Antimedes did remember, himself and Phorbas standing or sitting together, talking, eating, their flocks around them.

'It's all a bit shadowy to me,' said Antimedes carefully. 'And it was a long time ago …'

'But you won't have forgotten the newborn you gave me?' he heard Phorbas saying. 'You can't have forgotten that, surely?'

He hadn't, but how could he admit that? Once he admitted that he was ruined.

'What are you saying?' said Antimedes.

Phorbas, at this moment, felt old and weary. Merope had sent him to Thebes to tell Oedipus that his father was dead. He had encountered the queen by chance in the courtyard and he had then been brought to this room where Oedipus was waiting. He had told Oedipus his father was dead and Oedipus had told him that the reason, having left Corinth as a young man, he had never returned was because he had been warned what he would do if he did.

Now, if anyone was in a position to correct Oedipus, Phorbas thought at that moment, he was that man. He had told Oedipus what he knew and it had been a relief to Phorbas that he had spoken the truth and he had expected the king and queen would be happy to hear what he said. But he had thought wrong. The king was full of heat while the queen was full of terror; so much terror she rushed from the room, leaving him and the king waiting until the door opened and in came Antimedes. And then Antimedes refused to acknowledge him, to even look at him, while the king fumed and the atmosphere darkened.

It should not have been so, Phorbas thought. His and his old companion's good deed on the slopes was out in the light. It should be celebrated. But neither his old friend nor the king was happy and Phorbas couldn't understand why. Well, seeing as the truth hadn't worked, he would try praise. Praise never failed.

Phorbas waved his calloused hand at the king. 'Look,' said Phorbas to Antimedes. Two of his fingernails were black. 'Look what that baby of yours grew into.'

Antimedes felt swishing vibrations starting up inside his skull. 'Stop talking!' he shouted.

'Our visitor has spoken,' said Oedipus. 'Now, shepherd, it's your turn to speak. And if you don't tell me everything you know, I'll have it beaten it out of you.'

'This man,' said Antimedes – he indicated Phorbas. 'He's making a mistake.'

'Spearmen,' Oedipus called out to the royal attendant standing at the door. The royal attendant turned and opened the door.

'Spearmen!' he bellowed at the servant standing outside.

The servant ran off, shouting, 'Spearmen, spear-men!' In the distance, an answering voice followed by a trumpet call. The royal attendant turned back, leaving the door open.

'When they get here,' said Oedipus to Antimedes, 'they'll throw you down on the floor and beat you with the shafts of their spears.'

The swishing in Antimedes's skull became a fierce wind.

'Why would you have your spearmen do that to a servant who's always been loyal?' said Antimedes. 'Why would you hurt him?'

In the distance, the sound of spearmen running.

'This newborn, did you give it to him?' Oedipus nodded at Phorbas.

'I did,' said Antimedes.

'You did,' said Oedipus. 'And where did it come from? Was it yours?'

'No.'

At the top of the corridor, four spearmen running, heading for the room, the leather joints of their armour creaking.

'Whose was it, then?'

'Another man's.'

'And who was that man?'

'Someone from this palace in Laius's day.'

'Come on, who was this?'

'I don't want to say.'

The spearmen appeared at the door with their long spears and their great shields. The royal attendant waved them on. They crowded in, filling the room with the smell of sweaty leather, dust, garlic.

'Either you tell me or they will make you. Whose was it?'

'Laius's.'

'Laius's … why should I believe that?'

'Ask the queen. She'll tell you.'

'*She* gave it to you?'

'Yes.'

'Her newborn?'

'Yes.'

'Why?'

'To be killed.'

'Her own child went to you to be destroyed?'

'Yes.'

'Why?'

'This baby was to kill his father and so to stop that I was to kill him.'

'But you didn't?' said Oedipus.

'No.'

'You gave it to this man.' He waved at Phorbas.

'Yes.'

'Why did you give it to this man?'

'Would you want to kill a newborn?' said Antimedes. 'I couldn't. I wouldn't. I went to him.' Antimedes pointed at Phorbas. 'I thought, he'll take it to his country. He'll give it a home. He took it. He took it and he saved its life.'

'I did,' said Phorbas. His tone was proud. 'I brought the baby to Corinth and gave him to the king and queen, who called him Oedipus.' Phorbas smiled. Phorbas swelled. 'And look what he grew up into?' At last he could sing it out. 'That newborn is now king of Thebes *and* Corinth.'

The spearmen were breathing and waiting, their faces shadowed by their face guards, their eyes on the king. Their armour crackled. There was an undercurrent of threat in the room. Oedipus looked at Antimedes.

'There was a time when you weren't a shepherd?'

Antimedes nodded.

'You were Laius's servant, weren't you?'

Here it came. This would be worse.

'You were there in the carriage on the road to Delphi, weren't you?'

'I was,' said Antimedes bleakly.

'You saw me when I walked past the carriage?'

Antimedes nodded.

'You realised then who I was. You knew I was the new-born, now grown.'

'Yes.'

'Yet you said nothing.'

'Would you have believed me?'

'And I came here. I married. You're also here, weren't you? Backwards and forwards from the palace to Cithaeron. You knew who I was, yet you said not a word.'

'It was too late,' said Antimedes.

Oedipus's face scrunched up. He looked both enraged and appalled. He turned to the door. 'Jocasta!' he shouted.

He bolted out and raced away up the corridor. 'Jocasta,' he shouted, 'where is Jocasta?'

'Keep them here,' said the royal attendant to the soldiers. He meant Antimedes and Phorbas. He sprinted up the corridor after the king.

In the queen's apartment, behind the door, the spear rested on the strut, its end jammed hard against the door, while the point was against Jocasta's heart and the weight of the spear behind was supported by her two hands.

Jocasta had been getting herself ready … and now she was ready. She let out a great cry of rage and despair and drove herself as hard as she was able onto the sharp point while at the same time pulling the other way and plunging the spear into her body. The point punctured her dress and punctured her skin. It slipped through her ribs. The lethal edges that followed the point sliced open her heart. Blood sprayed the back of the door. The point went on because her weight was falling forward and pushed it through. The point passed between more ribs. It pierced the skin of her back. It pierced the back of her dress. And it travelled on until a hand's breadth of shaft was showing.

For a moment Jocasta stayed standing. Then she keeled over and her left side hit the floor. The spear's shaft was still against the door only now it was tight against the bottom instead of the middle. Jocasta's blood was flowing out of her. It was red and sticky. It spread in a puddle over the floor and went up to and then under the door.

When he got to the door of the queen's apartment Oedipus saw something had slithered under the space at the bottom that was dark and wet. He went to push the door open but there was something on the other side that was in the way.

'Jocasta,' he shouted. Nothing came back to him.

He put his shoulder to the wood of the door and he pushed and he felt that what had been blocking the door was sliding away behind. Eventually, he had the door pushed back far enough and there was enough space to get in. He wriggled through and found the queen on the floor, with the shaft of the spear coming out of her front and the point showing behind and a puddle of red on the floor. The blood had a bitter smell. Her blue dress was stained red at the front and the back

Oedipus went to turn the queen on to her back but the point wouldn't let him and so she stayed on her left side. There was a brooch pinned to her dress on the right just where her collar bone was. He ripped it off and there was the pin, vicious and sharp.

Just end this and never see, never see, never see again, not this, not anything. This wasn't a thought, more like a flash of sunlight reflected from a polished shield.

With harsh quick stabs he drove the point first into the left and then his right eye until all sense of light was gone and there was only darkness.

Now he heard footsteps in the corridor, fast and furious. Then the people were in the room with him. 'What,' he heard. And, 'Oh no.' It was the fluting voice. Oh yes, the royal attendant with the high cheekbones. Who else? Then a wail. A female.

'My queen,' he heard. 'My king.'

It was Callidice.

'You, laundress,' said the royal attendant. 'You stay. Keep the door closed. Let no one in. I'll get Creon. Understand?'

'Yes,' he heard Callidice say. The royal attendant rushed out. Callidice began to cry.

Antimedes and Phorbas and the spearmen remained in the room where they'd been left. While they waited nobody spoke. After a long time, Creon appeared along with the royal attendant. He announced in a booming voice that Oedipus was no longer king and that he was now Thebes's regent. He would rule, he said, until there was a new king or kings – Oedipus had two sons after all, Eteocles and Polynices, and they might share the throne. Creon thought this likely.

After Creon finished speaking the spearmen banged the shafts of their spears on the floor as a signal of loyalty.

'Enough,' Creon said. The spearmen stopped banging.

'You,' Creon pointed at Phorbas. 'Go. Return to Corinth and tell Merope you have delivered your message but she shall never have sight of Oedipus. He will never return to Corinth and when she knows what he has done, as she will in due course, she will be grateful for that.'

Phorbas sloped away. Creon turned to Antimedes. The queen had slain herself, he said. She'd driven the point of a spear through her heart. The king had found her, dead. He had put his eyes out with the pin of her brooch, which he had ripped from her dress. He was now regent, Creon repeated, and as regent he was the law. He had spoken to Oedipus, the ex-king, and Oedipus, said Creon, had told him what he had learnt from Phorbas and from Antimedes. And now he had come to tell Antimedes that he had broken the law and how he would be punished.

'Antimedes,' said Creon, 'when you were asked to leave a newborn on a mountainside to die and you didn't, you thought you were acting wisely.

'Antimedes,' said Creon, 'when you realised on the road to Delphi that Laius's murderer was the newborn now fully grown and you decided you would not mention this to anyone, you thought that would be another good deed.

'Antimedes,' said Creon, 'the death of the Sphinx, a happy married king and queen, four healthy royal children and years of plenty, prosperity and stability for Thebes, you thought these were worth your silence.

'Antimedes,' said Creon, 'you believe that instead of a dead queen and a broken and blinded king, we would have a living queen and an active king, had you been allowed to stay silent.

'Antimedes,' said Creon, 'you think Thebes and her inhabitants would agree that if nothing had been said nothing would have happened and the city would be in a far better place. But on every count, you were – you are – wrong. To know and not to speak is a crime. Its name is dereliction and it is only ever punished one way.'

Creon turned to the spearmen. 'Mount Phicium for him.'

The four spearmen and the royal attendant marched Antimedes to the door of the dungeon hall below the palace. The attendant banged on the door. The jail-keeper opened it.

'He's for the drop,' the royal attendant told the jail-keeper. 'We'll be back for him tomorrow, early.' By tradition, executions on Mount Phicium were at the moment sunrise started.

The spearmen pushed Antimedes in. The jail-keeper closed the door and drew the bars over to lock it. Antimedes heard the spearmen and the attendant marching away outside. This was like being dropped into a dry well, he thought. If he looked up all he would be able to see was a little circle of sky above. And he would never be able to get out. He was there at the bottom of the well, for ever.

'What did you do?' The speaker was a prisoner who had sidled up to him. The prisoner was big, broad, bearded.

'Nothing,' said Antimedes.

'Oh, come on,' said the beard. 'You're among friends here. What did you do?'

'Nothing.'

'We're all here for some reason,' said the beard. 'I throttled my wife, for instance. She was unfaithful.'

She wasn't, but he'd never be persuaded of that. Hermes told that to my father, who told me.

'Come on,' said the beard, 'what did you do?'

'I told you,' said Antimedes, 'nothing.'

'Nothing,' said the beard. 'What's this "nothing"? I've never heard of "nothing".'

'Nothing is when you say you'll do something and then you don't,' said Antimedes. 'Nothing is when you know who someone is but you don't say you know who they are. But according to Creon, dereliction is the word for that.'

'Dereliction,' said the beard. 'Was that the charge?'

Antimedes nodded.

'I've never heard of dereliction before. Well, you learn something every day and today I've learnt of a brand-new crime I never knew existed.'

The beard sloped off. The jail-keeper touched Antimedes's shoulder.

'Sleep,' said the jail-keeper. 'Tomorrow will come, nothing can stop it, but it'll be over soon enough, it'll be painless and by sunrise you'll be waiting for the ferryman.'

The jail-keeper pointed at a pile of straw. Antimedes lay down. The straw was dry and scratchy and smelt of animal hide and human urine.

He closed his eyes. He fell asleep. His life story came to him as a succession of dream-memories. Some parts he already knew because he had been present. Other parts he only knew about second-hand because he'd been told about them. Now, in sleep, the parts were stitched together to make a single, seamless whole.

Antimedes felt a rough hand jostling his shoulder. He opened his eyes. The hand belonged to the jail-keeper. In his other hand the jail-keeper held a brand. There was a smell of burning pine. The light from the flames was red and mobile and the pitch was spluttering and spitting.

'Get up,' the jail-keeper said. Antimedes saw the shadow of the jail-keeper's head on the ceiling above. 'They're here.'

'Can I have a drink of water?'

The jail-keeper fetched a cup. Antimedes drank. He gave the cup back. He followed the jail-keeper through the dungeon hall past the other prisoners. Some were so still and quiet they could have been dead. Some were snoring. Some were mumbling. Some were tossing and turning, grinding their teeth, crying and shouting words out.

The jail-keeper opened the dungeon-hall door. On the other side stood the same royal attendant and the same four spearmen who had brought him down here.

He went out and heard the jail-keeper drawing the bars across behind. He saw the spearmen wore no helmets or armour and had no shields, though they carried their spears. Clearly, they were not expecting trouble. Antimedes put his hands behind his back. His wrists were loosely bound with rope.

'Let's go,' said the royal attendant.

They climbed stairs. They tramped across the palace courtyard. Antimedes thought briefly of his mother. She would find out what had happened to him when she woke. Someone would tell her. Most people loved to be able to report the worst when it was someone else and not themselves who were affected by it. He'd noticed that.

They went out into Thebes. The streets were still. The houses were silent. They approached the gate that gave onto the road to Mount Phicium. The gatekeeper was awake. He was eating a melon in the dark. As the party approached he cut a thin, pink wet length from a sliver of green rind. He put the fruit into his mouth, threw the rind in a pail and began to separate the seeds from the fruit in his mouth with his tongue. The party came up and stopped. The gatekeeper spat out the seeds and Antimedes heard them land softly in the bottom of the pail. The gatekeeper opened the gate. They sallied out. The gate closed behind.

It had been dark in Thebes but once they were out in the country beyond the city it was even darker. All around, the smell of rot and scorch. Here and there, in the darkness, small puddles of red, all that remained of the pyres that had raged the day before. His escort had no burning brands so they had no light. All around them different shades of black. Stone walls were one kind of black, trees another, fields a third. The road at their feet was the lightest black of all. The sound of their sandals slapping and their breathing were the only noises.

As they walked, Antimedes tried to empty his mind and imagine he knew nothing, but he couldn't. He simply couldn't imagine not knowing. Unable to unknow what he knew, all he could do was turn everything round in his mind as he slogged up the side of Mount Phicium. Finally the road levelled out and they reached their destination.

'Stop,' said the royal attendant.

There was no sun yet but there was enough light to see. Ahead of him Antimedes saw the lip where the land ended and the drop began and above the lip he saw the great, black, blank sky. After Oedipus bested her, this was where the Sphinx jumped to her death. This was where Thebans went to jump. And this was where the city's criminals were hurled to their death, at sunrise.

'I haven't done anything wrong,' said Antimedes.

Nobody said anything.

'I didn't do anything,' Antimedes said again.

'You did,' said the royal attendant. 'We know. We heard.'

'I didn't,' Antimedes said again.

'We all know what you did and didn't do,' said the royal attendant. 'We all heard what Creon said. You should have left the newborn on the mountainside to die. You should have spoken as soon as you realised who Laius's murderer was. You should have realised Thebes was not the better for your actions but the worse. And nothing you can say or do now will change anything. Creon has decreed this end and all Thebes will approve.'

Antimedes looked ahead. He remembered his mother's story of the frogs on the road to the birth-house. He remembered the bat from the birth-house that he had flung into the air and that he thought had turned into a bird. He remembered the snake he had carried out of the birth-house with tongs and dropped in a ditch. It had turned into water and the water had drained into the earth. He found the snake the next day sunbathing on a rock and the same thing happened again. Should he have reported what he had seen? Of course he ought, but as he also knew it would have been ignored. It wouldn't have changed a thing. Everything that was supposed to happen would have happened anyway, regardless of the frogs and the bat and the snake.

Antimedes closed his eyes and with his inner eye, in just a moment, he saw his whole life.

The royal attendant banged his staff, a hard, heavy noise.

Antimedes opened his eyes. Far away, at the place where the earth met the sky, he saw a smudge of pinkish light edging up into view. The sun was coming.

Two spearmen laid their spears down and each took an arm. Their grip was hard. The royal attendant banged his staff twice again. The two spearmen holding his arms began to pull him forward and as they pulled, his legs followed. In a few steps he would be pitched over the grey lip into the great black beyond. At least, right at the end, before he was pitched forward and the dark was rushing headlong towards him, at least he got to hold it all in his head, he thought, his whole life. At least he had that.

At this moment, while I am talking and the scribe is taking down my words, Antimedes is suffering in Hades. 'If only I'd known at the start what I was destined to do,' I imagine him saying, his voice heavy with regret, as he walks round and round with the twittering dead. If I could speak to him I would say, 'Dear Antimedes, don't torment yourself. The horse must graze where it is tethered. There is no way you could have lived any differently from the way you lived.' Would my words comfort him? I would hope so. I would like to think so. Oh Antimedes, I feel such tender-ness for you, and your mother, the end of whose story now comes.

The execution party returned from Mount Phicium to the palace. The royal attendant reported to Creon that Antimedes had been thrown over.

'Go and find his mother now,' said Creon. 'Tell her what we did to her son, then throw her into the street. Tell her she is never to come near the palace again.'

Callidice was put out by the royal attendant with noth-ing but what she was wearing: a pair of earrings, her head covering, her dress, her apron and her sandals.

Without any means of supporting herself, Callidice had to go to a brothel and offer herself as a laundress. She would wash the dresses of the prostitutes and the sheets from their beds, she said, if in return she could have a corner in which to sleep and something to eat every day. The brothel-keeper knew of Callidice by repute and was delighted to get her cheap. She brought the old woman in and immediately put her to work.

Out in the country there were no sightings of new outbreaks of blight. Thebes's ordeal was over.

Epilogue

Creon ordered his sister's burial and issued his instructions. My sister, Ismene, my two brothers, Eteocles and Polynices, and myself, we were permitted to attend, he said. His brother-in-law Oedipus he prohibited from attending. My father begged Creon to relent but he would not bend. Oedipus, Creon said, was a tainted figure, a miscreant, a pollutant, and therefore he was not a fit person to attend such a sacred rite.

After the funeral ceremony was over I went to see my father in his room. I told him what had happened and what I had seen. He said he could not remain under the roof of his brother-in-law who had prohibited him from attending his wife's funeral. Whatever his crimes, he should not have been denied that last contact and that last opportunity to demonstrate fidelity and remorse. I agreed with him. I thought Creon's attitude contemptible. I could not stay either, I said. We agreed we must go, and go far, far from Thebes and that we would leave that very night.

We rose while the palace slept. In the palace kitchen there were embers on the hearthstone. I stirred them into life. They were almost liquid, like a rare, dense mud.

My father and I sat near the fire and drank wine and ate barley bread. My father knew this was the last meal he would ever eat at home. I did not imagine it would be mine. Unless I died, which I did not think would happen, I would probably return to Thebes.

And as things turned out, I did.

When we had finished our bread and wine we pulled on our cloaks. Once my father was a king with a queen and power. Now he was a man with no queen and no power who would soon be tramping the roads of Greece.

We went to the door. My father's staff was there, leaning against the wall. I put it in his hand and opened the door. Once I was a princess with girls to bathe and dress me and to fit my jewellery. Now I was a half-orphan who was about to guide my blind father along the roads of Greece and I would have no girls to bathe and dress me and to fit my jewellery.

My father went out. I followed. I closed the door behind.

'I've an idea,' I said.

I picked up the end of his staff that he wasn't holding.

'I'll hold this end,' I said, 'and you'll keep hold of your end. I'll lead and you'll follow and we'll never be separated.'

'Good thinking,' he said.

We left the palace courtyard and went out into the streets of Thebes. There were stars in the black sky, small shiny points of light. We stopped at Dirce's spring and drank. I sensed many dogs skulking in the darkness, watching us. One or two growled but none approached. We went on. We met two madmen talking loudly and spitting. They ignored us. Everyone else in the city was sleeping. It was a long way from dawn.

The gatekeeper of the gate to the south, to Athens, opened the gate for us. We slipped through. Now we were out of Thebes, our footsteps seemed abnormally loud in the quiet. There was birdsong, bright and rapturous. Later, the light started to come in and the sky above became kindly. Once we were out of the area belonging to Thebes, there was no more blight smell.

The first travellers we met on the road were Theban merchants, returning to the city. They recognised us. He was the old king and I was his daughter, also his half-sister. They knew our miserable history. They pitied us. I saw that on their faces. My father did not see – a benefit of his blindness, I thought.

The next set of travellers, not being Thebans, did not know us. They simply saw a young girl leading a blind man. They assumed we were beggars. When they passed, they scowled. They also sped up, which my father realised. He heard their accelerating footsteps.

'What are they rushing for?' he asked, once they'd gone. 'Are they being chased?'

'No,' I said. 'They were frightened of us asking for food or money.'

'But we weren't going to ask for anything,' he said, which was true.

'They didn't know that,' I said.

'Instead of fearing what won't happen,' he said, 'they should fear what will.'

When the sun was high we met a shepherd moving his flock. His animals had a mutton smell and were moving in a bunch as if they were one enormous single animal, not lots of separate ones. We got speaking. He did not know us and we did not tell him who we were. He took us for poor wayfarers and gave us bread and olives.

Later we met a farmer with bandy legs, whose breath smelt of onions. He gave us his goatskin and took us to a spring with clean, clear, bright water. We filled the skin with water, hung it from the staff and went on, carrying it together. After that we were able to slake our thirst whenever we wanted, because we always had water.

At the end of the first day, we knocked on the door of a small house. The woman who answered was a widow. She only had her front teeth left. All the back ones were gone. When she closed her mouth, her face collapsed and her chin stuck out like an arrow's head, sharp and belligerent. She let us bed down in an empty outhouse and lent us sheepskins for the night. As I lay waiting for sleep I smelt my hands. They smelt of pine, from the staff, which I had been holding all day. Whenever I smell pine now I am back in Thebes, it sends me straight back to that night when I had no idea what would happen.

On our second day on the road more strangers looked at us. Some knew who we were and pitied us. Others glowered unkindly and hurried by. Again, we were given food. Again, each time we passed a spring, we filled our goatskin and carried it away, and then we were able to drink whenever we were thirsty.

The third day was the same. Every day was the same as we sailed into exile.

After many days we came to a little hamlet of small houses, some occupied, some empty. This was Colonus. The people of Colonus were all old and lonely. 'Move into one of the empty houses,' they said, 'and return it to life.' And we did.

When I woke in that house in the morning after my first night I noticed the bitter smell of the earth, the way the light was stained grey green by the leaves of the olive trees, and the singing of the sparrows outside, shrill, loud, jaunty. It sounded like coins being thrown around in a cup. The sheep bells in the distance were a low murmur.

I got up and went outside. The leaves on the olive trees were drab and dry and when the wind blew they made a rustling noise, which made me think of a giant trying to move around without anyone hearing. Great flocks of sparrows lived here, in and under the olive trees. They made a rushing noise in the air when they flitted by in swarms, but when they bathed in the red dust they made a different noise, a chirruping that was light and joyous.

I knew then that we had come safely into harbour, and for as long as we were berthed here we would be safe and contented.

In Thebes my beautiful idiot brothers Eteocles and Polynices were co-kings, taking it in turns to rule.

At the point in the cycle when Eteocles was in the palace and Polynices was not, the arrangement broke down. Eteocles slammed the gates and informed Polynices, who was outside the walls, that he was banished for ever and the garrison would kill him if he ever attempted to enter the city.

Polynices came immediately to Colonus to see his father. Eteocles, he explained, had broken their arrangement when he'd slammed the gates in his face. He, Polynices, was the rightful ruler now and it was his father's duty to tell the city to expel Eteocles and to install him in his place. Polynices was in no doubt Thebes, despite all that had happened, would do exactly what Oedipus told them to do.

The truth, my father said, was neither brother wanted to share with the other. Had Polynices been in power – had they been at that point in the cycle – it would be Eteocles

who would now be paying court to him in Colonus and telling him it was his duty to tell the city to expel Polynices and
to install him in his place. Each brother was as bad as the
other, Oedipus said. He declined Polynices' request.

Polynices left Colonus vowing he would raise his own
army, and settle his dispute with his brother with violence.
He would take the city, put Eteocles out and take power.

One night, in Colonus, I heard my father talking on the
other side of the wall in his sleep.

'You were talking in your sleep,' I said in the morning.

'Oh yes,' he said. He explained it was with Hermes, who
had visited him in his dreams, and that the god would be back.

Hermes returned the next night and the one after that.

On the third morning I asked what he'd discovered from
his talk with the lesser god. All his life, my father said, it
was if he'd worn a mask and could only see what the eye
holes allowed. In their talk the god took away the mask. This
allowed him to see what had shaped his life but of which he
was ignorant and knew nothing until then.

And what would happen to all he'd learnt? I asked.
Knowledge hoarded is of no value, I added.

'Yes,' he said, 'it must be shared if it is to do any good.'

I felt the pleasure throb that comes when I know I am going
to get what I want, which here was to know what he'd been told.

There were two huge stones outside our little house. I draped
them with blankets so the cold of the stone would not chill us
and we sat down on them. I took his hand and he began.

Since the god and my father had talked for three
nights, my father and I talked for three days. That was
how long it took to get it all out of his head and into

mine. When my father finally came to the end on the evening of the third day, he stopped and squeezed my hand. Did I have it? He needed to know.

I closed my eyes and fell into myself. First nothing, just confusion. Then – ah yes. There was Europa, the start and the end of it all; there was her brother, Cadmus, searching for her; there was Laius, hard and great and cruel and foolish; there was Chrysippus, the beautiful youth Laius ruined; there was Jocasta, my mother, more maimed than any other by everything; there was Callidice, Jocasta's slave whose life was threaded through her mistresses' life, and who I knew by sight; there was Antimedes, her son, the simple herdsman, who I knew of; there was Phorbas, who carried my father away to Corinth; there were Polybus and Merope, Corinth's king and queen, who named my father Oedipus on account of his swollen feet; and there were all the others who were in his life. Oh yes, I had them all.

I came out of the deep within and returned to Colonus and the olive trees with their whispering leaves and the chirruping swallows and the bitter-smelling red earth and the faraway clanging sheep bells. I squeezed my father's hand back so that he would know what he had told me was safe in my mind. He smiled. He was free to die now. The next day Hermes came and led him to Hades.

I left Colonus and returned to Thebes. As I approached the city I saw soldiers drilling on the plains in front of the gates, their helmets glinting in the sun, their feet banging on the ground, and I heard their shouting, loud and vicious. These were Eteocles's forces – Eteocles was still king. Polynices was away raising an army and when he had raised his army, as everyone knew, he would come to Thebes with his forces and the two armies would meet and settle the dispute between the brothers once and for all. And either Polynices would destroy the defenders and kill Eteocles and become the sole ruler, or Eteocles would destroy the invaders and kill Polynices and become the sole ruler. If only the idiots had learnt to share.

As soon as I was back in my rooms at the palace I sent a servant to buy every wax tablet and every stylus he could find in the city. These were hauled to my room. Then I summoned the city's most accomplished scribe. He was a stooped fellow, small, dark, blinking, with thick eyebrows. He reminded me of an owl. I put him at a table with a blank tablet in front of him, empty tablets piled within reach and a stylus in his hand and I began: 'I have closed my eyes.'

Having started like that I went on. It was easy. I just spoke and spoke and spoke. The words rose, my breath carried them into the air, the scribe heard them and wrote them down. On the tenth day of my speaking, Polynices appeared with his forces and my two brothers met in single combat below the walls and managed to kill one another at the same moment so that they fell dead into each other's arms. Creon was immediately declared regent once again and he determined to teach Thebes a lesson about the evils of civil war, using my brothers' bodies as his tools of instruction.

Eteocles – the good brother, as my uncle called him, because he was the defender of Thebes – Creon buried with full honours; Polynices – the bad brother, as he called him, because he had attacked Thebes – he left where he had fallen, unburied, an example to all Thebans of the ignominy that befalls insurgents, with instructions he was not to be touched. The punishment for disobeying this direction, my uncle added, would be death.

The city said nothing about Creon's promulgation, but I was appalled. To leave Polynices's body to rot was a crime. He must be buried and I decided I would bury him since no one else would dare. I would, I knew I would. I couldn't not. But first I had to finish this record and so on I went, speaking to the scribe, and all the while Polynices lay out under the sun by day and the moon by night, pecked by birds, mauled by dogs.

Now I am almost there. I am almost finished – but there is still one last thread, which is yet to be followed to its end. Europa.

In the palace where she had lived her whole life, Europa lay on her deathbed. Her eyes were closed, her breath was shallow and slight. She could hardly draw the air in and out. Surely she could not pant on much longer, she thought.

'Queen?' The voice belonged to the old nurse whose job was to give Europa a good death, as far as anyone can give anyone a good death. The old nurse touched Europa's forehead.

'You're hot,' she said. 'I'll cool you before they come.'

It was true, Europa was hot. Little trickles of sweat on her head, on her belly, on her thighs. These thin cords of wet had trussed her up.

Europa heard the old nurse ladling water from the jar in the corner, then felt something heavy settling on the bed. That, she realised, was the bowl the old nurse had filled.

Splash, splash – that was the sponge, plunged in the water.

Pitter-patter – those were water drops splashing onto water as the sponge was squeezed dry. A moment of anticipation and then the glorious sensation, the sponge on her forehead and cold water running over her face.

The sheet came away. In the bed she was on her back, and absolutely bare, her arms at her side, palms up. Although not yet a corpse she had adopted the pose of one. It was almost over. The race was just about run. Only a few more steps and she would fall across the line. She was sure of it.

Splash, splash, pitter-patter, the sponge being prepared again. Another moment of anticipation and then the cold sponge smoothing her belly, stroking her thighs, wiping away every miserable bead of sweat and leaving her skin wet and cool and clean.

The old nurse lifted the sheet back up but this time, instead of Europa's arms being hidden, they were on top of the sheet and in full view. They were brown and thin. Her hands were bony. There were marks on the skin, big brown marks, like patches of lichen.

The old nurse slipped Europa's bracelets over her hands. The silver was cold on her wrists. The old nurse tenderly threaded the carriers through the holes in her earlobes from which her earrings hung. The weight of the silver pulling her skin was strangely pleasurable. The old nurse laid a heavy necklace over her chest, then brought the supporting chain behind her scrawny neck and fastened the clasps with amazing dexterity. The old nurse spread out her hair and began to run a comb through and to untangle the kinks. Europa knew exactly what this was about. She was being prepared for a visit, a last visit.

Europa heard movement in the passage outside and the sound of sandaled feet slapping on the floor. The double doors were opened by a porter and her visitors entered. They were Minos and Rhadamanthys, the two sons made by the great god's violence after he had swum her across the sea on his bull's back and then taken her into the air on his eagle's back, and Asterius, the king, creeping along with the help of his staff, the man she had married after her rape. They had had a long life together, she and Asterius, though they had had no children – not that that had mattered. The king had esteemed Minos and Rhadamanthys as if they were his own and had adopted them, and they, in return, had esteemed him as their father. At least that part of her life had turned out well.

The family gathered around Europa. She felt her arms being stroked. She felt their lips on her forehead. She heard their words in her ear. She couldn't tell what was said. She was slipping away. At some point, she fell asleep. When she woke up, Minos and Rhadamanthys and Asterius were gone and the lamps were lit. She heard the old nurse on her chair. She drifted off again.

During the night a fierce wind started. It circled the palace. The night watchman heard it howling. No cloud and no rain accompanied the wind. While it blew the stars continued to show in the sky. A hot, fierce wind. Very strange.

The old nurse in her chair had fallen asleep in Europa's room. Her chin rested on her chest. She was snoring slightly. She did not hear the wind. Europa was sleeping as well. She was dreaming. In her dream the wind was in her room and swirled about her. Then it slipped, warm and pressing, into her ear and flooded her brain. Here it swirled, gradually assumed a shape and became the lesser god Hermes.

Europa had never seen the god Hermes but she knew who he was when he appeared and she knew what it meant as well. She was about to die.

'You can have one wish,' said Hermes.

A wish. She was being granted a wish. And where did this come from? The offer came from the great god, said Hermes, and the great god had sent Hermes, the lesser god, to tell her. But, of course, there were conditions, Hermes continued. This did not constitute an apology. The great god did not do apologies. The great god only did what the great god did and apologies were never part of that. But the great god wanted her to have something because of what had been done to her. Something that would make her feel better. And something that would add lustre to his reputation. He wasn't just the great god who did what he did. He was the great god who always gave back munificently, lavishly and ungrudgingly to those to whom he did what he did. That's why he was the great god. That's why he was making the offer – she could have a wish while she was still alive.

'Only you can't ask not to die,' said Hermes. 'You can't ask not to die or for anyone else not to die. But you can make a wish.'

'Just one?'

'Before we go, yes.'

The words bubbled up without her needing to think.

'My sons Minos and Rhadamanthys are unstintingly gentle, reasonable, never excessive, patient and fair-minded,' said Europa. 'So out of my harm can at least this good come? My wish is that my sons will be judges and law-givers, here in this world and in the next.'

'Granted,' said Hermes. Both while they live, and after they die, they will be all that you ask.'

In her dream Europa now saw the palace of Hades and Persephone. In front of the palace she saw three roads going in different directions and at the junction where they met she saw her sons Minos and Rhadamanthys sitting on chairs with wands in their hands, a queue of dead souls, some twittering like bats, stretching into the distance.

Europa went closer. Her sons were listening to a dead soul describing his life and she could tell from their expressions, for she knew her sons well, that they were listening carefully, charitably, generously.

The soul who was speaking finished. Her sons directed with their wands which road he was to take. They had made the right judgement. She knew this with the absolute certainty that one knows something in a dream even though one doesn't know how one knows it. The next to be judged stepped forward; they spoke and were directed. Again, she knew it was the right decision that had been made – every judgement her sons would make would be the right one.

This hadn't happened yet. It was what would happen. Europa knew that. Minos and Rhadamanthys at this moment were alive but after they died they would go to Hades and there they would judge, and they did. They judged Chrysippus. They judged Laius. They judged Jocasta. They judged Oedipus. They judged Callidice. They judged Antimedes. They judged Eteocles. They judged Polynices. And in a while, they will judge me.

Hades vanished from before Europa's inner eye and she saw Hermes again.

The god held out his hand for her to take. So here it was, she thought. The end had come. She put her hand in the lesser god's and made ready to step out of life and into death.

According to the palace watchmen, who gave detailed accounts the next day of the strange night they had just experienced, the wind raged for a while and then stopped abruptly. The old nurse, who had slept while the wind raged, woke once it had stopped to a strange silence. She sat up in her chair and looked across at Europa. She saw Europa wasn't moving and she realised she couldn't hear her breathing either.

The old nurse was frightened. She stood, lifted her long skirts and hurried across to the bed. She put the back of her hand against Europa's mouth. She felt no breath. She touched Europa's face. Cold. She took the silver obol, which had been left for this moment on the bed head. She opened Europa's mouth and slipped the coin under her tongue, which was still warm as well as wet. Then the old nurse wrenched open the double doors, waking the porter who was sleeping on the floor outside in the process, and hurried down the corridor, wailing, 'Queen Europa is dead. Queen Europa is dead.'

Now, at last, my speaking is done. These tablets, a permanent account of what would otherwise be erased by time, will be stored in a cave and tonight, under cover of darkness, I will creep out and scrape the earth over Polynices's remains.

What will happen when it is discovered at first light tomorrow what I have done? I will be punished if I am caught. Do I expect that will happen? Oh, it will happen if it is meant to. I know that too. But will it? I can't think of that. I only know I am not free not to bury Polynices, just as my father was not free not to do what he did and to live as he did. It's as simple as that. Some, like Creon, will doubt-less see sophistry here. 'Like father, like daughter,' I hear him jeering. 'She says, "I am not to blame." Nonsense! The guilty are always the loudest deniers.'

Well, let him say what he wants. Let them all say what they want. Let him impugn my motives. Let them all impugn my motives. One day they will understand. We are all Oedipus now.

My course is almost run. I have started to turn salty. The high banks that once bounded my sides have gone and great wet plains stretch away on either side instead, while straight ahead, beckoning me on and running right to the horizon, the never-ending, the everlasting, grey green blue white black silver sea.

Enough. I will stop.

I, Antigone, have opened my eyes. Hear me, Polynices, hear me. I come.

Author's Note

My source for this novel is Sophocles' *The Theban Plays* (transl. E.F. Watling, Penguin Classics, 1973). From this I've taken what served my purposes and jettisoned what didn't. I have similarly taken liberties, where I felt it would benefit the story, with the history and geography of ancient Greece.

I would like to thank Ian Sansom for putting *King Oedipus* on the reading list for the Seven Basic Plots module at Trinity College Dublin; Eve Patten for her prompt; and Gerald Dawe, Mary-Jane Holmes, Kevin Power, Philip St John, Maggie Brooks and Djinn von Noorden for their wise counsel. Any mistakes are my own.

Also by Carlo Gébler

FICTION

The Eleventh Summer
August in July
Work and Play
Malachy and his Family
Life of a Drum
The Cure
W.9. & Other Lives
How To Murder a Man
A Good Day for a Dog
The Dead Eight
The Wing Orderly's Tales
The Innocent of Falkland Road
Folk Tales of Fermanagh (co-authored with Séamas Mac Annaidh)
Aesop's Fables (co-authored with Gavin Weston)
Tales We Tell Ourselves: A Selection from the Decameron

NON-FICTION

Driving through Cuba
The Glass Curtain
Father and I
The Siege of Derry

My Father's Watch (co-authored with Patrick Maguire)
Confessions of a Catastrophist
The Projectionist

CHILDREN'S FICTION
The TV Genie
The Witch That Wasn't
Frozen Out
The Base
Caught on a Train
August '44
The Bull Raid

PLAYS
Dance of Death
Ten Rounds
Henry & Harriet
Charles & Mary
Belfast by Moonlight

Praise For Carlo Gébler

Heart-warming … a subtle portrait of the first glimmers of sexuality on the threshold of adolescence. —*The Irish Times*

A deeply affecting depiction of the uncertainties of childhood and the end of innocence. —Mary Costello

The texture of London life in the mid-sixties is wonderfully evoked as the backdrop for this beautiful coming-of-age tale. In his spare, tender evocation of a year in Ralph's life, Carlo Gébler depicts that delicate moment between childhood and the end of innocence. —Molly McCloskey

Praise for THE WING ORDERLY'S TALES (2016)
This blistering account demonstrates how fiction can sometimes outdo non-fiction when it comes to arguing for the rights of others…. and reminds us that long-term incarceration is a death sentence as lethal as any injection or the electric chair. —*The Sunday Times*

Praise for THE PROJECTIONIST (2015)
When Ernest died, in 1998, Carlo Gébler inherited his father's chaotic archive, and from it he has fashioned a fascinating depiction of Ernest's enigmatic and troubled personality. And because he has such a zest for narrative this is also a rare picture of the social history of 20th-century Ireland…The Projectionist is simply a great read. —*The Irish Times*

It grabbed me from the word go and I found it a wonderful, wonderful read, an extraordinary piece of work'. —Gay Byrne

Praise for THE DEAD EIGHT (2011)
Gébler is an overlooked novelist. The Dead Eight is one of the truest, least flashy, most human novels I have read for a long time. —*The Telegraph*

It's a powerful tale and one well told… The story might span the first half of the 20th century, but it's a tale that's as timely and relevant as tomorrow's headlines. —*Sunday Business Post*